SHAMAN
EXPRESS

First published in 2018 by Beretta Rousseau

ISBN 978-1-911195-78-8

Also available as an ebook
ISBN 978-1-911195-79-5

Typeset by Hybert Design
Cover design by David Drummond
Printed and bound by IngramSpark

ALIVE

PART 1

Remember:
When a wound is tired of crying
It will start to sing.

Amsterdam, 19 June 2015

I woke up sweating, alarmed, and with a painful erection. The electric clock read 4:45 a.m. Enjoy the pleasures this puppet theater has to offer, it said in glowing green lights. What the fuck? I attempted to masturbate, but the need to pee was stronger. I sat on the toilet without being able to pee, acknowledging the tiny attic room of this Amsterdam hotel. Seated, I rested my head against the wooden roof beam and perceived its solidity. I sensed my skin, the fine layer of flesh composing my temple and my skull. Could I really feel my skull against the beam? Yes, I could feel it all right, but what lay inside my skull was a mystery.

As I sat, I peed partly over the toilet seat and also on the white bathmat. I would have to wash it in the shower in the morning. I tried to masturbate again, but I needed to pee some more. I went into the bedroom and opened the window over Kerkstraat. I sat on the window ledge and only wished that I had some pot to smoke. Or a cigarette. Or a lover in bed. The Blue Dolphin Café across the street was closed, as was any other decent coffee shop in town where I could buy pot if I wanted to. I wanted to, but I was not going to. The fact that all coffee shops were closed supported my decision.

I could get some charlie from the guys down Warmoesstraat at this time of the night. I had not visited that network for a long time, and I did not feel like making new friends. And of course, yes, I did not do charlie. Never had. Not never-never, but it had never been my thing. So why the hell was I thinking about snorting charlie? I had been attributing every strange thought I had to the withdrawal effect. Two years, nine months, and one day sober today, if I made it to the night.

I could take a shower and go to a sex party. I was almost sure that it was naked party night at Club Church, which was just across the street. If I leaned out of the window enough, I would see the glow of Club Church's fluorescent front projected onto the cobbles of Kerkstraat.

I felt my skull leaning on the solidity of the window casing, but I could not feel what was inside my skull. Some sticky grey matter, maybe. Was it just my imagination? I masturbated on the window ledge of the attic over Kerkstraat, neither smoking nor snorting nor dancing naked. This was real. All I needed was to pee. I drank some water and went back to bed. Two years, nine months, and one day. I closed my eyes.

What was it that made me wake up sweaty, alarmed, and with a painful erection? Oh yes, that message from my last shamanic journey: *Enjoy the pleasures this puppet theater has to offer; enjoy it while you are still here. It will soon be over. You are on to a new journey.*

Was I dreaming?

I put my clothes in a plastic bag and check the bag with the half-naked guy at the cloakroom in exchange for a plastic token. We cannot talk because the music is too loud, but he gives me that smile. I keep the token inside my runners and we both laugh, but not really.

I am inside a cubicle at Club Church's toilet, trying to get hold of the last half of ecstasy that is crushed inside a small plastic bag hidden in my runners. I fiddle with the laces, the plastic bag, and the plastic token. Too many things simultaneously. And my jaw aches. In what seems to be slow motion, a portion of the half "e" falls from the plastic bag to the toilet seat. The seat is wet, totally wet, as are the walls and damp yellow light bulbs. Someone is vigorously knocking at the door of my cubicle. I have to make a quick decision: I lick. I lick the rim of the toilet seat, attempting to make the minimum possible contact with the seat but at the same time enough contact to catch the entire fraction of "e." This being my last half-pill, the event is significant enough for my brain to factor in the risks and benefits involved and decide to lick the toilet seat in order to retrieve the magical substance.

I come out of the cubicle drenched with sweat and feeling as if I have achieved a most trying somersault. *Enjoy the pleasures. It will soon be over.* Nobody notices my victory, but my face is radiant and my heart is ever expanding. My eyelashes have turned into a rudimentary shamanic eye curtain, those fringes of beads that Siberian shamans use to separate themselves from the ordinary world. With my eyes almost closed, I ask the glowing demigod behind the bar for a *Spa blauw*. I grab a five-euro note from my runners and hand it to him, making a hand gesture for him to keep the change. He smiles and flexes. Transpersonal clubbing collective consciousness: there is no need to talk.

My eyelashes are still almost down when I dive into the 130 beats per minute of progressive house. *While you are still here.* The melody is standing alone, and the song does not start building up until what seems much later. As the beats become velvety and bitter, I begin grinding my teeth. I welcome the much-awaited midsong climax with orgasmic joy. Daft Punk's "Alive" is exploding inside my skull. I can distinctly feel my pituitary gland oozing serotonin. I can push my pituitary gland with my tongue, in exactly the same way that I can push my prostate with a finger up my butt to make me ooze pre-cum. It itches, and it makes me happy. I scratch my scalp with one hand and grab my balls with the other one. *Enjoy the pleasures while you are still here.* We hug and kiss and jump and have the weirdest empathic visions. Alive.

Later, just before the DJ stops playing, I exchange the plastic token for my clothes at the cloakroom. I dress with great effort and come out to the street. I lean against the wall, and a guy offers me a much-needed cigarette. He clumsily tries to light the cigarette with a plastic lighter. We both laugh. "Hi, I'm Omar, from Argentina."

He answers that he is from Thailand, but I do not catch his name. "Oh yes, I would love you to come to my hotel." *Enjoy the pleasures this puppet theater has to offer.*

"I'm wasted, man. I think I'll take a long shower and collapse in bed."

"Cool, let's take a shower together and cuddle. And take some GHB and listen to music, or watch porn. I would love that."

"No, I don't have Viagra. Let's just cuddle. We can fuck tomorrow." *While I am still here.*

We cross the street to my hotel. I fidget with the keys, and we climb the stairs to the attic. My new friend follows me, but he is too tall for the narrow stairs, or too drunk, or both. There is something out of proportion between him and this little crooked house. We reach my room, and I fling the door open. I see myself sitting at the window ledge with my limp dick in one hand and looking at the Blue Dolphin Café downstairs. "I've brought a friend," I hear myself saying. I feel genuinely happy. I look at myself and start laughing. I have missed this so much. My Thai friend starts undressing and falls asleep half-naked on the bed. I walk to the window ledge and sit. A rolling wave of tenderness falls from the roof and embraces the three of us. The Blue Dolphin Café will not open before 10:00 a.m., and the fluorescent lights of Club Church are already off.

A soft pink light dawns over the roofs of all the crooked little houses on Kerkstraat and beyond.

"Do you want a cigarette?"

"Fuck no. Two years, nine months, and one day today."

"Oh shit, don't tell me. We did that?"

"I should start getting ready. I have a plane to catch in a couple of hours. I'm going to meet Benedetta."

"Is that now? Is that today?"

"Now, yes. That was some party you took us to. I can still feel 'Alive' inside my skull."

"Oh fuck. I'm sorry. It was just the most... the music tonight... are you really feeling the inside of your skull?"

"Did I say that?"

"Yeah, man, you did."

"I guess that I need to thank you for this. It feels more real now."

"Hey, were you with me when I licked the toilet seat? Did you get the vibe?"

"Gross. You know I wasn't with you. I was remembering it. Are you here now?"

"I am. But did you feel that? Man, the stench, ugh, and the texture... any regrets?"

"Well, I wish I hadn't. I had nightmares and woke up with a hard-on."

"I felt that."

"Do you know who I am?"

"I'm not sure who I am. Shit, my Thai friend is dead, man."

"His name is Pak. He passed out. Too much GHB. He'll be all right in the morning. I'll tell the guys to wake him up after we leave for the airport."

"Do you know him?"

"I remember him. I'll tell the guys in case they can see him."

"Maybe we can give him a blowjob?"

"He passed out."

"Just for fun, man. For old times' sake."

"The carefree yogin soars like a great Garuda."

"What the fuck?"

"Longchenpa."

"What the fucking fuck?"

"Two years, nine months, and one day today. That is, if we make it to tonight."

"Fuck man. Fuck, fuck, fuck, fuck, fuck."

"Fuck, yes."

"Okay, okay. I'll take the back seat."

"Back seat is good. I may need you. I think that I'm going to die soon, you know."

"Oh, not that shit again. Have you been meditating?"

"It's not meditating. It's journeying, shamanic journeying. No, it isn't that. The withdrawal effect."

"Listen man, I'm naked."

"I can feel it. I'm naked too."

"I miss you."

"I miss you too, sometimes. But now is better. You have to trust me."

"Where are we going again?"

"Pisa. Benedetta."

"Fuck. Yes. Awesome. That is awesome! Do I know Benedetta?"

"You don't, but I do. You can't remember her."

"I know, but I can imagine her."

"Are you here now?"

"I'm with you, always. I love you man. Back seat, promise."

"Good. Now, go to sleep."

A few hours later I had collected myself and was sat at a café in the Schiphol Airport boarding area. I had a strong coffee and a banana muffin as a substitute for the drugs and sex I did not have the previous night. My shamanic drum was on the chair opposite me, together with my small backpack. Michael Harner's *Cave and Cosmos* lay open on my table with my journeying notes. I had kept a diary for many years but I gave it up when I started keeping travel journals. I eventually gave them up as well, for journeying journals. It was my new drug and source of inspiration. I read and reread my notes about the messages that the spirits gave me. All the love that I was looking for in the wrong places, all the time: I could avoid that impulse, one day at a time. I felt loved like I never had.

"What is this?" the security guy asked me.

"A musical instrument."

"Can you open it, please?"

Years of smuggling marijuana, hash, LSD, and GHB in and out of this country, hidden in my luggage. And porn, dildos, leather restraints, leather chaps, handcuffs, rubber briefs – you name it. Never was I asked any questions. But a shamanic drum raises an eyebrow. The security officer inspected it as if it were an explosive. He hesitated a moment before instructing me to put it back in its case. What is invisible is scarce and attracts attention. A part of his consciousness was telling him that the item was an unusual device that opened doors to new forms of perception, a realm beyond his controlling duties, which made him uneasy. No matter how hard he tried, the more rational side of him failed in coming up with an excuse that was legal and binding to enquire more about my drum and possibly requisition it for further investigation.

"Are you a musician?"

"Amateur."

He thanked me with a polite smile and indicated I should proceed to the boarding gates.

Three years ago I was in a very bad place. I had a vampire lover. A classic vampire: the one that sucks your blood. The vampire dumped me, and I had nowhere to go but deeper into the drugs and sex routine. I was longing for a new vampire and also felt suicidal. I hit rock bottom. As is sometimes the case if one is lucky, I entered a twelve-step recovery program for addicts and spent a few weeks sober for the first time in ages.

It took me some time to understand that the twelve-step recovery program I had entered was a spiritual program. I needed to stop the spiral of destruction so badly that I was ready to embrace salvation in whatever form it came and let go of prejudices. I honestly came to believe that a power greater than myself could restore me to sanity, and started connecting regularly with that power. I went back to the meditation techniques that I knew and devoted more time to practicing yoga. I was enthusiastic, yet it was too early to be able to make the sort of powerful spiritual connection that I was looking for.

After a year committed to my recovery and under the guidance of my program sponsor, I was lucid enough to hop on a plane and go to a spiritual community in Scotland. I spent a few months there working in the kitchen and learning the values of communal living. Being a small fish in a large spiritual pond brought me a sense of purpose, and with it came a figment of hope. The introduction to shamanism came as a bonus.

Each time I tell Europeans that my first steps in shamanic practice were taught in an attic in the Scottish Highlands, they seem disappointed. Most of them expect me to be the disciple of a *maestro ayahuasquero* from the Peruvian Amazon, because I was born and raised in South America. Castaneda delivered to perfection the story that the Northwestern Hemisphere was willing to believe. I apologize; I was introduced to shamanism in the Scottish Highlands. After my first drum-induced shamanic journey, I realized that I had tapped into something very powerful that offered an endless supply of healing, forgiveness, and love. The recovery program had awakened a spiritual connection in me that was manifesting itself gracefully. Things just fell into place.

Between 205 and 240 drumbeats per minute are needed to induce a shamanic trance in order to journey to the non-ordinary reality. All those nights dancing to house music, I was nearly there. It fell short a few beats only. I had always believed that the state of trance I achieved dancing was by grace of the chemicals that I was ingesting. Wrong: human beings naturally possess all the needed psychoactive chemicals. Shamanic drumming is aimed at activating this potential. I could identify the effect that shamanic drumbeats have on the brain when I started journeying with them. The chemicals might produce something like the same serotonin boost, but the drumming is the real thing. In hindsight, all those nights clubbing on "e" were the antechamber to the palace of dreams where the drumming takes me.

What was the previous night's reverie about my clubbing days in Amsterdam? Oh yes, Pak. My Thai friend. I met him that night at Club Church several years ago. Athletic and terribly good-looking, the artful Oriental lover. A serious Buddhist, too: he embodied non-attachment. I saw the toughest Western men crumble in tears for him. Fortunes were offered for the coveted monopoly over his negotiable affection, but he danced with all of us. When he danced with me, he made me incredibly happy. We became inseparable buddies, matching tattoos and all. When I told him that I had fallen in love with him, he responded that my attachment to him was a deluded form of perception.

Pak had affluent sponsors on the club scene. Like so many boys and girls in his trade, most of the money he earned went to his rural hometown to support his family. He was providing for his sister's education. *It will soon be over. I'm on to a new journey.* That is what Pak used to say all the time. He would soon return to Thailand to become a monk. "Am I going to die?" I pondered, chewing on the chemical softness of the banana muffin. That night at Club Church, which I had forgotten, had come back crystal clear. I could feel the toilet seat, the velvety beats, and the inside of my skull. Last night could very well be a loop in time, where I met myself at a crossroads of change. Same place, different time.

Maybe it was a flashback. I had been attributing every strange thought I had to the withdrawal effect. Have I said that before? Or was it a lower spirit that adopted the form of a younger me with the intention of provoking my fall? Paramahansa Yogananda explains that the spirits of the recently deceased spend some time among living human beings, dealing with the anxiety of their new non-physical state until they are ready to reincarnate. A spirit that had a strong attachment to our reality may find a portal into a living person and relive situations to which he was attached. For example, a spirit craving the adrenaline rush provided by wild sex, street fighting, or dangerous driving by a precipice may find a portal into a living being in order to carry out any of these activities.

Drugs, sex, power, and anger are the usual portals to a living being for lost spirits. The sex portal I know well. One night at a club in Brazil I met the hottest guy ever. The music was too loud to talk, so he smiled and grabbed me by the belt loops of my jeans and took me to the dance floor. My reptilian brain started working at full tilt. The reptilian, oldest part of the brain only understands images, not words. The image of that smile and his confidence at grabbing me by the jeans set my reptilian ablaze. Mating opportunity! Sex! Genes-spreading time! And obsession, compulsiveness, worship, fear, submission, and greed. All of that expanded and presented in fluorescent lights, courtesy of the one and a quarter of acid I had dropped an hour earlier. Oh, the reptilian brain does not learn from mistakes. My neocortex was taught that bit the hard way.

I paid for two *caipirinhas*, and he produced *maconha*. Sogyal Rinpoche says that the object causing the deluded mind to arise must have some relationship to the karmic imprint.[1] In a previous incarnation I was probably a British opium tycoon lobbying for war against the Chinese in 1840 or a small-time dealer selling smack to schoolchildren. The object: thick, velvety *maconha*. My karmic imprint: opportunity to suffer and cleanse karma. A lower spirit was

---

1   Sogyal Rinpoche, *The Tibetan Book of Living and Dying* (New York: Harper Collins Publishers, 2012)

about to feed on my soul to get the hormones and the chemical high he missed in his present out-of-body state, while at the same time the suffering I would experience would urge my deluded mind to find the right path. The gods should be satisfied; the jerk that I was was about to be given an opportunity to learn a lesson.

But the suffering and spiritual teaching were nowhere in sight. I got high and drunk faster than ever. We had unprotected sex in a dark corner of the club. We fucked against the loudspeaker. The sound waves coming out of it had a fleshy texture that ripped up my bowels, a prototype of what I would much later experience as shamanic dismemberment. He hinted we should go somewhere quieter. I paid for the cheap motel by the hour, and he produced fresh *maconha*. We fucked and smoked until I passed out. I had never felt such high energy in my whole life.

I woke up with the worst hangover. I knew instantly that I had gotten all possible STDs, been ripped off for the little money I had, and that this guy had left with my hotel card-key. Wrong: everything was there. I went down the stairs to a backstreet in the heat of the early afternoon. I did not have a clue where I was or how I had gotten there. Every single cell in my body was aching. The guy at the motel door waved at me and offered me a *cafezinho*. He did not say a word, giving me the time I needed to reconnect some of my neurons and think about the most important question I had to ask. This guy had probably been at the reception desk all night, and there was a security camera.

He confirmed that I had checked in at 5:30 a.m., alone. No one visited me, and I did not make any phone calls. I had a large alcohol ticket to pay though. "People sometimes come alone to this motel to get drunk and watch porn," he suggested. I asked again. "No," he said, "alone." Then he smiled. "Maybe you met an angel? Every now and then an angel brings people here." It was the spirit of Leãozinho, a rent boy who used to work in the clubs and brought his clients to this motel. He had died tragically and had not been able to cross over to the spirit world. "Well, if you slept with Leãozinho, at least it was for free!" He laughed and offered me a second *cafezinho*. "Nothing is for free," he reminded me. *How we live now can cost us our entire future.* Did he actually say that?

He stared at me, and after an awkward minute I thought that he was going to rebuke me. On the contrary, he recommended I should sit at the Nossa Senhora da Paz church nearby and rub holy water on my private parts. Otherwise, Leãozinho would stay with me until I died a stupid death like his. I paid and left the hotel. Just before turning the corner, I stopped, scratched my head, and looked back. This guy was standing under the glaring sun, watching me leave. I gazed at him, and he gestured encouragingly with his hands in the direction of the church. I did as I was told, to the letter.

It is simple to identify when one is used by lower spirits for sex purposes. In spite of that, I had fallen for the trick over and over again. When it happened I was not spiritually present. I was a kind of porn-star zombie that has no room in its brain except to welcome the sex opportunity that is presented on a silver platter. And it felt magical, not satanic. That is why casual sex and drugs are such a spectacular welcome sign for lower spirits to come and feed on us.

The root and sex chakras have the universal dimension of an all-engulfing black hole. The solar plexus chakra implodes: self-esteem, warrior energy, and power of transformation are the last things one wants to be reminded of when joining an orgy. The heart chakra is reduced to the size of an atomic subparticle, only to point out afterward that one behaved like the lowest beast in hell. The throat chakra is gagged by the lower chakras. It suffocates, but the slow crawl of sperm on the seminal vessels, the pounding of the prostate, and the tumescence of tissue on the penis have such an amplified control over the etheric body that one could surrender to eternal damnation only for a few more seconds of carnal pleasure. The eye chakra turns blissfully blind. It is like driving a car at full speed at night with the lights off; the 99% possibility of crashing cannot override the adrenaline boost. The crown chakra becomes a dead lotus. Who wants to commune with the divine when one is experiencing penetration that feels like thunderstorms, and multiple orgasms that are like volcanoes? Naturally, this has completely fucked up my love life. The heart chakra is so closed that the next time I have vanilla sex with a suitable candidate who is loving, caring, and believes in monogamy, I will not be able to sustain an erection.

Lost spirits feed on our awareness and blur it with the mirage of a separated consciousness. Interesting: I perceived Leãozinho as an entity totally separate from me. It took me time to understand the message. I was in shit deep enough for him to take control of my life for one night. If I kept sinking, there would be no more I but only Leãozinho, or the archetype that he represented.

The previous night in that hotel room in Amsterdam, the separation had been less apparent. There was another me present in the room, coming from a real hell I have known, but the separated consciousness was blurred. I could feel what he felt, and he could imagine what I remembered. This was maybe a subtler, more dangerous form of demon. I sent him to sleep. If I kept doing this, one day there would be no more demons. One day at a time. I guess that if I did not die that night at Club Church, or at that motel in Brazil, why would I die now that I am... um, what? A meditation coach? Not a coach, but it might as well be. An author-to-be? I still write "lawyer" on the immigration cards. The muffin tasted so unreal.

I checked my iPhone for messages from Benedetta. "I dreamed of you, brother. Are you okay? This is my new cell, meet u on Line." I smiled. What the fuck? A message from Pak, the first in over a year. Modern monks have cellphones and chat on the Line app. His time as a celebrated masseur-dancer-whore came abruptly to an end a few years ago when his sister disappeared and he became a monk. A tough and pragmatic monk devoted to saving boys and girls from human trafficking cartels. We remained in touch, and he did a lot to rescue me from my own demons. I bow to his feet.

I almost died when I was a lawyer. True. Intentional misuse. Overdose. There, I said it. But at the last minute I did not die. Also true. Overdose is an unlikely cause of death for a control-freak like me. It was more of a cry for help. Or I might just have been bending the borders. I cannot remember. It was not a death-death thing, rather something close to it. A near-death experience, as it is called these days. I nevertheless was utterly bored in those days and quite desperate.

Sogyal Rinpoche says that the deepest reason why we are afraid of death is perhaps that we do not know who we are.[2] I certainly did not know who I was then, buried in my several subpersonalities. It felt very crowded inside me. I do not recollect if I was afraid of dying when I took myself to the brink of death, but I remember that I freaked out when I woke up and understood what I had done. *I'm not ready to die*, I thought. Those exact words. Utterly bored and lost, but more inclined to change my reality and get to know myself better than to give up and die of a messy overdose preceded by seizures, turning blue, and a coma; spending forty-five days of freedom floating in a limbo, to be brutally summoned back into this life of illusion, my spirit sucked into a newborn, forgetting everything and starting a new pilgrimage through this arid life for seventy or eighty years – if I reincarnated in a human being – only to deal with the added karma of suicide, let alone the unfinished business from my previous lives.

I do not think that I was afraid. I was just not ready to go. It was a good wake-up call, though. I will have to go eventually, but I was still running in circles, oblivious of my karma-cleansing duties. Someone allowing himself to die of boredom and despair would probably come back as unicellular algae in the deepest ocean crevasse. Not what I wanted for my next life. That, however, did not prevent me from

---

2   Sogyal Rinpoche, *The Tibetan Book of Living and Dying*

dating vampires. The clean-up process did not happen overnight; it came in stages.

Maybe I thought of dying for a second, because there was a lot of space in my life, and dying seemed easier than filling that space. Take Benedetta, for example. We had met the previous year at a shamanic retreat in Tuscany. I had just arrived from a month of silent meditation at a temple that Pak had found for me in eastern Thailand, a pure product of my life in recovery. The shamanic retreat in Tuscany was not all that I had hoped, but it gave me the opportunity to remain sober for one more week. Most of the things had not actually been all that I had hoped since I stopped the *sex & drug & money & power* thing, I have to admit. But I was alive and learning to love it.

Working on the book project with Benedetta was one of the few real things that had happened to me in the past two years, nine months, and one day. We aimed at writing a book on experiential shamanism, though we were both beginners in shamanic practices. That said a lot about how flimsy reality was for me since I had started my recovery. Benedetta was very enthusiastic about our book from the beginning. She delivered her drafts on time, made elaborate comments on my notes, and was excited about our reunion at Il Casolare, the small intentional community where we planned to attend another shamanic workshop together and kick off our book project. She was maybe just sympathetic and being supportive. Or maybe there was also a lot of space in her life, and writing this book was easier than dying.

But I did not want to die. I had been in the twelve-step recovery program for almost four years, and as a result my conception of life had expanded and become appealing. Earlier that day, I might have said that I did not know who I was. Maybe not knowing who we truly are is the gift of impermanence to those ready to be aware. But in recovery I have found out that I want to learn shamanism, travel, meet interesting friends like Benedetta, write a book, and find true love. There, I said it.

Enjoy the pleasures this puppet theater has to offer. Maybe it is not a death-death omen but a ritual death. Mircea Eliade talked about dying a ritual death as one way to obtain shamanic powers.[3] Achieving a higher level of consciousness. Using my pituitary for more noble causes. Maybe I was enhancing my perception, and that was why I could meet and talk with a past version of myself, or whatever that spirit that appeared in the friendly form of my younger self was. I would like to believe that. Still, it could be the withdrawal effect.

My flight to Pisa was on time, and we boarded through the last gate of the furthest terminal. I grabbed a vegetarian sandwich and a granola bar from the Grab & Fly stall on my way to the gate. Once we were airborne I went back to *Cave and Cosmos* and forgot about the sandwich. I underlined with a pencil: *The suffering of the ill person could evoke pity by a spirit. In this way, a shaman is sometimes created.* I had a headache, my stomach was upset, and I could still feel the stomp of progressive house inside my skull. It felt more like the withdrawal effect than the creation of a shaman.

Out of the airplane window the sky was bright, and the small manicured farming towns we flew over glowed with the heterosexual promise of predictability. I took five drops of Rescue Remedy to dispel my cynicism and wondered if life still had something good in store for me. Thin layers of clouds divided the sky into three distinct areas, each brighter than the previous, and I glimpsed a pale star, although it was a bright morning. I read the message: yes, there were more and more chapters to my life, and they would get better and better. The unexpected would be revealed. I breathed into that. I closed my eyes to focus on a vision of spirit owls protecting the airplane. Surprisingly, I fell asleep.

"I'm having visions!" was the first thing I said when I met Benedetta at Pisa Airport. She had texted me that she had arrived

---

3   Mircea Eliade, *Shamanism: Archaic Techniques of Ecstasy* (Princeton: Princeton University Press, 2004)

safely and was indulging in espresso and *pasticceria* at the airport's bar. She was radiant in her colorful dress, her huge Hollywood-star sunglasses, and a hairdo that looked casual yet expensive. Large suitcases were piled around her. I was so happy to see her.

"That's fantastic, dear! I've just had a conversation with Winston Churchill!"

"Churchill?" She caught me off guard; I had forgotten her very peculiar logic. "I'm talking visions here, like ghosts, not historical characters!"

"What kind of ghosts then?"

"I'm not sure, maybe the spirit of my younger self, something to do with sex and drugs."

"Oh, I love it! Do you want a coffee reading?" Benedetta has a knack for coffee reading. Apparently she once made a little fortune trading in stocks out of her readings of the coffee she offered to senior executives at the company she used to work for. This triggered an investigation into insider trading by the European Union enforcement authority. Her own lawyer advised her to plead guilty. She might have done actual prison time, though she never talked about this.

"That's just what I need! You're so resourceful. I'm so happy I have you to talk to!"

"I can tell you all! Do you prefer the macchiato or the espresso option?"

"Give me the macchiato."

"Okay. That's the soft version then," she warned, slightly disappointed.

. . . .

Brussels, 19 June 2015

I was once again standing alone in the middle of my empty apartment, a prestigious Art Deco address in Brussels that my uncle LouLou had given me for my thirtieth birthday. I was his only niece, possibly the only girl he ever loved. "Dear Benedetta," he told me back then, "I hope that you are terribly happy in this apartment, but if you aren't, you can sell it and spend the rest of your life drinking champagne." Very much his style. I truly missed him. This apartment was famous for its stunning original granites, the flower patterns of which would surprise an attentive observer. Over the past few months I had spent countless soothing hours staring at them and following the imaginary lines formed by the granular structure, as if a mysterious map would be disclosed to me. I imagined that this map would lead to a place to heal my heart, or to a bottle of whiskey. Average whiskey would do.

"A taxi should be here any minute now, ma'am," said the night clerk when I picked up the phone. Lost in memories, I did not know what to answer. I hung up without a word.

I had met Tony in Monte Carlo almost three years before, in November 2012. With his funny moustache, he looked anything but average to me. Appearances can be so deceiving at times. Tony is my ex-husband, a sophisticated upmarket gigolo turned into an unlikely shepherd. I have this kind of impact on people. No kidding.

I was in Monte Carlo doing LouLou a favor, representing him in the selling of a Kandinsky, which had to go through a second-tier auction house in a second-tier venue because it was a fake. An extraordinarily good fake, as a matter of fact. LouLou was an art dealer. The auction house was run by czarist émigrés who, for a generous percentage of the auction price, were willing to take the blow should the truth be unveiled. Their clients were mostly second-generation Russian mafia transitioning to bourgeoisie. My role was strictly limited to interacting with the auction house, and I could not have cared less about who their clients were.

The Kandinsky was sold without a hitch and delivered the same night to a bling yacht that immediately sailed out of the marina – an operation of 7.5 million euros that was being paid from an archipelago of Caribbean tax havens into LouLou's own archipelago of Portuguese, British, and Singaporean havens. I intended to use my commission from the sale to buy authentic period furniture for my apartment, which I dreamed of one day sharing with a husband. Monte Carlo seemed to me a place as likely as any other to meet the man of my dreams. There was no children's room in my apartment. Raising children was of little interest to me then. Too complicated.

Having successfully completed the sale of the Kandinsky, I decided to make a grand entrance at the Monte-Carlo Casino. I was ready to rock the house in my own peculiar way. I was not in good shape: my face and feet were swollen from antidepressants, and my hips wider than usual. But I knew how to camouflage these shortcomings. I slipped into a suggestive black dress and stilettos to die for and made the most of my hair. I have fantastic hair. I topped my dress with spectacular vintage diamond earrings, courtesy of my uncle. I had just lost fifty thousand euros at the English roulette – bollocks! – when Tony spotted me. We locked eyes.

Tony was handsome, soft, and feminine in an erotic way. He was keeping company with an elderly American woman who also had an unquestionable talent for losing large amounts of money at a fast pace. It was evident that he was a ladies' man. The American woman was proud of him, as one is proud of a trophy. I perceived an instant connection. Tony and I were two outcasts trying to mingle in a rotten society that, in spite of being malodorous, lured us in for the lack of an alternative destination. *Be careful what you wish for.* I made a bold move and sent him a bottle of champagne. Krug 1988. Not that I had ever been a seducer, let alone a manizer, but that was my night.

The waiter approached Tony knowingly. He looked at his manicured fingernails while the waiter whispered a few words in his ear and then shifted his gaze to the bottle that was presented to him. My beau took a few seconds to appraise the monetary value of my offer and smiled at the waiter. The message had been conveyed. Incurable romantic as I was, I was, however, not so foolish as to think Tony was falling for me. Or maybe he was, but who cares now. The waiter disappeared with the bottle lest the American woman be offended. Tony chatted with her for some time. He looked at me with an immensely sad look, his melting hurt-child look, and sighed as he accompanied her to another gaming table. He then came to me with the determination of someone suicidal walking towards the cliff. We were meant for each other.

"Madame, follow me please," he said to me, expressing the anguish of lovers meeting for the very last time. He went into the gentlemen's toilet. I followed him with equally strong determination. I was instantly aroused by the smell of fresh flowers and male cologne mixed with a subtle pinch of urine. Tony gave a crisp one-hundred-euro note to the uniformed young toilet attendant. "Five minutes," he commanded. The attendant obediently stood at the door, diverting clients to other toilets.

Tony grabbed me by the wrist and shoved me into a cubicle. I was ready to surrender; it was a rite of passage. He curled his lips as if to say something. His eyes filled with tears, and he came to his knees as if he were about to propose, only to find his way inside my gown. He sighed deeply and buried his face in my pudenda. I screamed with divine delight. I wanted more. "One minute," announced the nervous toilet attendant. My high pitch was compromising him. Tony emerged transfixed. He rubbed his face with toilet paper and handed me his cellphone. Not his phone number, but the actual device. "I will call you," he said, and left urgently without a kiss. I figured he had only given me a sample of his oral prowess because he had sexual duties to fulfill with his American sponsor immediately afterward.

Tony proposed to me shortly thereafter. We were married a few days later, before Christmas. LouLou disapproved of this impromptu union, though he never met my husband. My uncle was found dead in his Marbella villa four days after the wedding. Homicidal strangulation by ligature disguised as a suicidal hanging. A dramatic change of pulse. The case was never solved, but my guess is that the murderer loved tarot. LouLou was wearing a blue shirt, red pants, and yellow slippers when he was found. *Fake it until you make it* was written on his forehead. The time of death was believed to be around midnight. The Hanged Man in full glory, so to speak. Rider-Waite deck. An unhappy client, maybe, and a macabre reconstruction.

My watch read 4:45 a.m. Two years to the day since I checked out of the madhouse, and I could still see Tony making love to me on top of the dining room table. I could still feel his hands too. Perhaps because there never was any secret map in the flower granites. Perhaps because I had had too much whiskey. Tony used to make love to me in odd places – on top of a table, under the kitchen sink, on the balcony, in the car, and in public toilets, including those on airplanes. Never in our bedroom. Remembering our good days made me nostalgic. I collected my bags, turned off the lights, and locked the doors. A taxi was waiting for me in the street to drive me to Brussels Airport. I was on my way to Pisa to meet Omar, an Argentine former hotshot lawyer converted into a Vipassana coach, who had become a friend. He had a knack for Ayurvedic potions and loved cats too. God bless him. It was 19 June 2015.

Omar and I had met nine months before at Il Casolare del Belsedere, a hidden stone house on the edge of Tuscany, home to a community that knew how to celebrate life in a simple manner. Omar was arriving from a meditation retreat. This was, anyway, what he told us. He gently greeted those of us chatting on the terrace with a smile. I immediately liked him. Comfortably installed in the back of the taxi, I stopped thinking about Tony and started to recall the series of events that had made me commit myself to the madhouse.

I was at work lying on the floor, the cold hard floor leading to the fish bowl. Ugliest meeting room in the world: Big Brother is watching you! Four years I had been working as a human resources consultant for a company named Damocles. I have a master's degree in philosophy, which I carry with much pride, although I find it useless at the same time. Anyway, when I met Tony I was leading the schizophrenic life of a successful yet unhappy human resources professional. My heart never was in this career, and my salary was ridiculously low. LouLou was supporting me financially, and everybody at work thought that I was rich, which stirred up jealousy. He wanted me to join his art business on a permanent basis, but I had consistently refused. I only carried out a few operations for him when there was no other option. Juicy Monte Carlo was one of them. I loved my uncle to bits. Professionally speaking, I had always wanted to build an honest career on my own. I was, however, lost as to the possibilities available to me after college, and it just so happened that the first job I was offered belonged to the field of human resources – it could have been anything. I took it on without much thinking or enthusiasm. Damocles came a couple of years later.

As I was lying on the floor, I heard my colleagues moving nervously around me, whispering words the meaning of which I failed to understand. I could feel their breath on my face. I hated them for making me feel miserable and worthless. I hated them for the four endlessly boring years spent by their sides. A self-imposed lobotomy. For what imaginary faults was I trying to atone? I opened my eyes. I have amazing blue eyes. I was swimming half-unconscious in a pond of cold coffee and broken cups under the stupefied gaze of my colleagues. Could I get a bonus if I pretended this was part of a groundbreaking commercial strategy? My manager George reached down to me.

"Benedetta, can you hear me?"

"What?"

"Are you all right?"

"I think I passed out… I hope I haven't ruined the meeting."

"As a matter of fact you have, but it's you we're worried about."

"Me?"

"You've fainted again. The third time in one month. Not even mentioning the coffee cups you're destroying during your fits. You should take a break."

"A break?" I was puzzled.

"A break, indeed." I remained silent. "Are you with me, Benedetta?"

"Yes. Break. How long?"

"As long as will be needed," answered George. The conversation was over. The truth is that I was burned-out and depressed, but I could not accept that reality. Nor could I anticipate the disastrous events that would follow in the next days.

As George was helping me to stand up, I realized that any resistance would be pointless. I would have to take a break. *Atonement process*, I thought. *So be it.* I tried to walk toward my office in an effort to regain composure. I noticed how my dress had turned from bright white to some sort of disillusioned latte macchiato. Exactly how I would also describe my marriage with Tony. Easy, cheesy synchronicity. I was exhausted and sat on the floor. "I have always been a compulsive coffee drinker," I heard myself saying in an extraordinarily high-pitched voice to the paramedics who had just arrived, seeking comfort in the sympathetic smiles of those strangers dressed in red for the special occasion.

Two days after my blackout, I landed in the office of my therapist of the time, Penelope Eagle-Eye, with a bruised face.

"Benedetta, what shall we do for you today?" Penelope Eagle-Eye asked cheerfully. I answered by imitating a young Tom Waits singing "Virginia Avenue." I had too many troubles and nobody to tell them to. What was a poor girl to do?

"I'm sorry. I can't quite follow you," said Penelope Eagle-Eye upon completion of my little show, handing a few coins over to me. Some say that yesterday's great poets have become today's singers. Or they became therapists and psychiatrists. Who knows.

"I'm definitively channeling David Copperfield's spirit in the twilight. I'm being instructed to become an illusionist," I eventually added.

"When is the last time that you had a proper night's sleep?"

"Who needs sleep when the world is so abundant and providing with so many little miracles? Sleep is overrated. Seriously."

"I see…"

"What do you see?"

"Unnecessary to ask you whether you have been taking your medication properly, I suppose. So, what I see," stated Penelope Eagle-Eye with emphasis, "is that you should consider additional psychological support in these challenging times. As your therapist, I recommend that before reaching Columbus Avenue, Las Vegas, or any other destination, you make a stop at Hôpital des Acacias on our own Churchill Avenue. I was told they have an old jukebox in the cafeteria, and I'm sure we can find you some David Copperfield cups and bed sheets."

The madhouse. Really? A bloody good return on investment on the 1,612 hours of therapy and four therapists I had consumed over the past fourteen years. Maybe the psychiatric option should have been considered right from the beginning instead of making me believe that I would be just fine. "I'm sorry, but I won't go to the madhouse. Never. No way." This was the last time I saw Penelope Eagle-Eye. I liked songs better. The next day I showed up triumphantly at work. Attempting to cheer myself up and to convince myself that I could just do it – I had a reputation of being a super-achiever in my own right – I dressed in a short canary-yellow dress, the striking effect of which I enhanced with black stilettos and a thick layer of scarlet lipstick. I was ready to get back into the game, stronger than ever.

"What are you doing here?" George asked coldly as I stepped into his office.

"We have a meeting with our new clients," I answered, full of exaggerated self-assurance.

"We indeed have an important meeting, but it doesn't include you."

"I need to be in this meeting."

"Damocles can manage this meeting without you, Benedetta. You were asked to take a break, weren't you?"

"I took the bloody break. Sixty-five hours, thirty-six minutes, and eleven seconds."

"You still have bruises on your face. Don't make things more complicated than they already are. Just go home."

"I don't want to go home. George, I want to be in this meeting."

"Are you calling me George?"

"George, yes. So what?"

"My name is Jack."

"Really?"

"Yes. Really."

"Are you sure?"

"Benedetta…"

"Always thought you were a George."

"Stop this!" He was turning red.

"George suits you, frankly speaking, better than Jack, and it's the royal connection, you see. Would you consider changing your name?"

"You're fucking mad."

"Are you talking to me?"

"And insane.'

"And you're boring and incompetent."

"Benedetta, the board of directors decided yesterday that you must leave. On a permanent basis. How boring is that?" This information took a few seconds to enter my consciousness.

"What?"

"You're fired. You've pushed your luck way too far."

"I thought that Damocles wanted creative collaborators."

"Indeed. But you're a freak."

"You cannot do this. You cannot fire me."

"Of course we can! And you have given us all the reasons we needed to fire you! Your results can't save you any more. Game over." I was unable to articulate any sensible response. "*Au revoir!* Bye! *Auf Wiedersehen!* Any chance your twisted brain gets it better like that?" Jack was almost shouting.

"But—"

"Please, leave now. Security will escort you."

This was harsh, and I was stunned. Was an ugly person playing a bad joke on me? I had given Damocles four years of my life, growing the sacrosanct *chiffre d'affaires* and obligingly smiling at clients for the sake of business, and I was being sacked? Brutally chucked out like a useless thing by this motherfucker Jack, as a matter of fact. On the verge of implosion in Jack's office, my eyes were absently staring at the cheap rug that he had brought back from his last vacation in "an exquisite all-inclusive resort on the Turkish Riviera." Unpardonable lack of taste. Unpardonable lack of everything.

No matter how pathetic and incompetent he often was, Jack knew how to make his way up the corporate ladder. Unlike me. I was an idealist who never hesitated to bypass instructions. I openly took sides with our clients against my management when I thought it was the right thing to do according to my values. I wanted to change the world and make the business more human and ethical. This was exactly why my supporters loved me, even at Damocles, and why my detractors disliked me so much: I cared about how we actually made money. But I was often impatient, uncompromising, and frustrating. My results were nonetheless good – really good, I mean – which protected me. Until I started to lose my grip.

From the moment Tony entered my life, I had only wished to be with him. One night at the casino, and he had become my entire world. Besides, I was finally considering joining LouLou's art venture after all those years. Come on, one successful sale in Monte Carlo had earned me more than years of hard work at Damocles, which were in my view meaningless and annoying anyway. Damocles' activities, if plainly legal, were far away from the idea of an honest career that I had once cherished. When I came back from Monte Carlo, my interest in consultancy work disintegrated. I started to make mistakes and lost one important contract. Unfortunately, when the board decided to fire me, LouLou was dead and my husband was being unfaithful to me. Jack took his long-awaited revenge on the too-many times I had exposed him; he pulled the rug from under my feet in every possible meaning.

Staff had gathered close to his office, the door of which had remained open. I do not blame them. It was live cinema, and the movie title was *The Spectacular Fall of Benedetta*. I was the star of the day, and my name was bankable. My emotions were running high. Rage was invading my heart and my mind was being unleashed as the darkest devil. Looking like a Greek goddess perched on stilettos, I wanted Jack to bite the dust too. I perceived anguish on the faces of some colleagues. I then saw an angel in a halo of fluorescent green light. He introduced himself as David, coming to save me. Archangel David? Oh no, too elementary, my dear Watson. God was in a joking mood and sending me the one and only David Copperfield for my own pleasure. That was when things really started to go wrong.

An essential part of the training of an illusionist consists of learning to fly. One is expected to develop the ability to create this type of illusion as an art form. LouLou hated illusionists. "Average con artists sold to the shallow business of entertainment," he used to say. Inspired by David's presence and my canary dress, I decided to test my magic skills. To everyone's surprise, including mine, I walked toward the closest window and jumped off with outstretched arms. A street lamp stopped my ascent, the only miscalculation in my flight plan. That and the fact that it was a second floor window, which undermined the credibility of my audacious exit. I was trying to escape from my miserable life, and jumping out a window was an option worth considering.

I woke up in the paramedics' van parked on the side of the road, wrapped up in a silver emergency blanket like an Egyptian princess preparing to be enclosed in a royal sarcophagus. I felt as if a buffalo herd had run over me. My head was hurting from the collision with the pavement, and my right wrist was broken. I was told I had serious bruises to my legs but that I would be just fine. This pissed me off. I tried to articulate my name properly to the paramedic who was checking my vitals. "I'm the fallen Benedetta," I whispered. This made her smile. Most likely because she had green eyes, what was left of me – the inner survivor – took over and added, "Take me to Les Acacias. I believe they have been waiting for me." Having delivered my personal apocalypse show, I committed myself to the madhouse. It was 19 March 2013. I spent three months in that place.

Hôpital des Acacias had an excellent reputation for treating mental disorders in French and in Flemish, which is exceptional enough for a country like Belgium to be mentioned. It delivered on its promises. I learned there to see life in pink again and became more accommodating. I had opted for the let's-get-better package, mainly consisting of antipsychotics, antidepressants, and anxiolytics. No trace of an old jukebox in the cafeteria, though, and the only cup that I was ever offered was an old promotional mug dating from the US presidential elections of 2008. A confident Obama appeared to say a faded *Yes We Can!* when pouring hot water. I nonetheless took this as a personal message emanating from David Copperfield: "You can do it too, Benedetta!" As far as bed sheets were concerned, they were plain white. Penelope Eagle-Eye was a liar.

The intuition that I could do it was confirmed upon meeting with my Les Acacias psychiatrist, Dr Frank N. Stein. When I entered his office for the first time, he was sitting on an old olive chesterfield sofa skimming through an anniversary edition of *National Geographic*. He was attractive in his trendy blue jeans and open-collar shirt. Most likely in his late forties, I thought. His office reeked of cigarettes blended with an invigorating male fragrance. When the good doctor welcomed me with a smile, I instantly knew that he would be my own guarantee on the road to recovery. I confessed to Dr Stein my occasional participation in fraudulent actions in the art market and how I had met my husband. Having pondered this, he proposed a non-verbal treatment based on biweekly sexual intercourse on his comfortable sofa, *because we are all mad here*. It did not escape me that this was technically malpractice, *because we are all felons here*, but his boldness delighted and impressed me. Whatever the cost, I would be brought back to the path of reason. I could live with these terms and accepted his proposal. He would teach me the concept of contemplation over and over again. Never mind Plato.

The only person with whom I had had intimate contact in years had been Tony, and it had been weird. My husband led all our encounters, and my role was to yield to his moves. And to enjoy them, of course, which I did. Following our *coup de foudre* in Monte Carlo, he had always given me pleasure with his able hands and his full mouth, moustache included, but he sometimes behaved like a curious prudish sex beast. He liked public spaces and making me climax, but he never undressed, and we never had sex in a proper bed. I never saw him fully naked, which was really strange. This probably was his way of expressing his power over me and over the world. My husband dumped me one week after my arrival at the madhouse. I had just had my second session with Dr Stein on the olive sofa. On top of being adulterous, I was being abandoned. Jackpot.

A perk of my stay at Les Acacias was that it allowed me to reflect on my life. Over 1,612 hours of therapy, and I was still at the point of jumping out a window. This realization came as a shock to me, much more than my impending divorce. How had I allowed this to happen? What crossroads and signs had I missed? I knew so little about myself. I was feeling immensely tired and old. My marriage with Tony, my former job, my apartment and its period furniture, the vintage diamond earrings: nothing seemed real to me. I was living the life of someone else, a life that seemed nothing but a painful lie and a sad joke to me. I had gone all the way to Les Acacias for this one bitter moment of epiphany.

When I was discharged, I was encouraged to spend some time in a quiet place before going back to city life. I had nowhere to go. I convinced an old friend to invite me to rural Greece, where an intentional community had gathered and was looking at expanding its resident base. This place of nature and beauty was filled with spiritual seekers and inspired wanderers. The community welcomed me. I learned there to breathe again. I made new friends, too, like-minded friends, in a positive way. No one was into shady business or trying to sell me something or taking advantage of me. I stayed with this community for a year, the time required to face my own devastation and my upcoming divorce. Living a genuine collective life put me back on track and gave me strength. Nothing was simple in this place, though. Many of us were lost and looking for a path of salvation. We were hungry for soul and truth. But we were honest.

I had a remarkable experience there. The spirit of a recently departed woman came to me while I was swimming in the Aegean Sea. Gail had decided to visit me on her way to the other side. She was an unusual woman who had traveled the world for the past thirty years in a ceaseless effort to build peace. She was a treasure hunter, treasures of the soul, and an inspiring peace-warrior who acknowledged her right to be saved and her power to save others. Gail believed in love in action. I had met her two months before in Athens, where a friend of the community was setting up a charity hospital. Gail was involved in the project. Over three days and nights after her passing, we had the most meaningful and silly conversations.

Gail told me that fear was useless, because everything had already been taken care of by the universe. Fear would only limit the expression of my true nature. She told me that living and dying were bound to collaborate, being ultimately one and the same, and that life on earth should be enjoyed to the fullest even in the darkest circumstances. She said that I was responsible for my own life and for each of my choices. She asked me to open my heart and to work with the spirits as I was learning to ground myself. Like a tree, growing branches would be useless if my roots did not reach deep enough and were not strongly anchored in the ground. She was also disappointed with the many people who had been trying to channel her since she had passed away, most of them expecting a revelation. This actually made her laugh. My guess is that she was intentionally providing funny messages to some of them. Gail was out of the ordinary, and she needed no one to perform her practice of conscious dying, or *Phowa*. Somehow, everything had already been taken care of.

Conversing with Gail came naturally to me. Since I was a child, I had been creating and connecting with parallel realities. I had done so out of boredom and to escape my loneliness. I do not believe that I had any particular shamanic talent, but I was creative, an artist and journeyer at heart. The issue is that I spent hours a day wandering in imaginary worlds at the expense of being present and living my life on earth. It became an addiction that got worse year after year. Now and again I would invite elements of my life into my fantasies as a way to change or bend them. I was also suffering from night terrors and obsessions, which I kept to myself and which were invisible to anyone else. I was skilled at maintaining my composure and playing the roles that I was taught were expected of me.

From the age of six or seven I struggled with spiders, especially migales, though there are no really dangerous spiders in Belgium. I was certain that migales would come into my bedroom at night and kill me. This was my war. My survival was at stake. As a consequence, I would meticulously search my room every night for one or two hours at least, to make sure there were no spiders. Even in the summer, I would sleep with tight bed sheets covering my entire body and neck and, whenever possible, my face too. I assume this is how I developed a resistance to heat. Human biological adaptability. And there were also the nasty witches in the wardrobes, the thieves on the staircase, the rapist killers trying to break into the house, and God knows what else. Until a few years ago, sleeping at night with an open window was impossible for me. Open doors were equally challenging. I would only ever sleep with one eye open.

These were strong fears and obsessive-compulsive disorders, but I could not ask for help. I had understood years before that I could rely on myself only. The adults I was living with were unable to pay attention to anything else other than their own ferocious emotional needs and dramas. So I created my own survival strategies, and as a result, I survived. I cannot remember having had any suicidal fantasies back then. LouLou came into my life later. My childhood was thus spent living in simultaneous realities, which eventually led to a shamanic initiation. Each battle won against fear actually deepened my initiation. I never thought that I was mad, even as a child. Besides, I was functioning well in the world according to social standards. Appearances can be so misleading. I was finally awakening at the age of thirty-three to something bigger, something that presented a path of salvation. That is what Gail and the Aegean did for me. Resurrection bells were ringing, though neither salvation nor rebirth happened overnight. It has been more like a multilayered process with the qualities of an onion. An onion, not a bottle in the sea.

While still in Greece, Gail and I continued our conversations. Other departing souls would occasionally visit me, but Gail refused to give me guidance on the matter. She was confident that I would find my own way to deal with them. If communicating with the dead was ordinary to me, I realized the danger of engaging more with it without the needed initiation and mastery. A welcome sign that I was not contemplating suicide again, if need be. I cared about my safety and refused to take the risk of losing my mind and track of reality – that is, even more than had been the case already. I was definitely not going back to Les Acacias, in spite of the good doctor. I opened up to a friend from the community about my situation. She urged me to contact a proper shaman and not to jump to any conclusions. Maestra-shaman had a website, a good reputation in Europe, and decades of successful practice. I decided to write to her.

I knew that shamans were, among other things, masters at communicating with the spirits of the dead and that this was meant to be healing for all involved. Like many non-initiated Europeans, I also imagined that shamanism was typically South American and involved being intoxicated and dancing naked around a fire somewhere in the Amazon. Omar, darling, come on, bring it on! "Having been born and raised in South America is no guarantee to shamanic enlightenment," Omar confessed during our first shamanic retreat in Italy. I think that he was pissed off with the cliché. The truth is that there are shamanic traditions all over the world and that using sacred medicine plants is no prerequisite for shamanic healing. I emailed Maestra-shaman, attaching a summary of my experiences. She replied in less than a day and we talked over Skype. Shamans can also be modern.

I quickly came to the conclusion that shamanism was not about fooling around with the dead but about connecting with one's true purpose, something even more mysterious to me. As we were about to end our call, Maestra-shaman admitted laughingly that she hadn't known what to think when she received my email but that I would be just fine, which I found reassuring. Shamanism is not "New Age," it is Stone Age, and has been living ever since.[4] It is the oldest form of spirituality, and I was ready to take the path.

Under the guidance of Maestra-shaman, my first important realization was that reality is multidimensional and that it expands beyond what human beings perceive. This has been a key feature of shamanism throughout history. Shamans travel to other dimensions to gain understanding of what happens on earth. With the knowledge and power gained from these non-ordinary experiences, they come

---

4   Michael Harner, *Cave and Cosmos: Shamanic Encounters with Another Reality* (Berkeley: North Atlantic Books, 2013)

back to ordinary reality and release suffering. Shamanic wisdom includes an original awareness of unity and the understanding that perception is based on our own fragmented belief systems. Embracing the path of the shaman, therefore, consists of learning to release the ego structure as much as possible, allowing the whole to be manifested in the process. This is the spiritual dimension of the practice, which is accessible to absolutely anyone.

Some might state that I am just a lunatic. I jumped out a window dressed as a yellow canary perched on overpriced stilettos. Fair enough. Let me remind you, however, that the only ritual that I ever performed under such avian circumstances comes down to a daring escape from life. I tried to commit suicide. There, I said it. Tony was being unfaithful to me, and LouLou had just died. I am not selling patchouli sticks for an equinox new moon in Sagittarius conjunct with Chiron. As much as I believe in experiential astrology and enjoy incense, one must face the fact that too much patchouli killed the patchouli. I must, however, still have lavender in my handbag. Unless Omar smudged it all in an attempt to clean energies, which he did each time he ran out of Rescue Remedy. My pharmacist once told me that if you're having over forty drops a day of the magic potion, you might as well just have a glass of whiskey. Her recommendation did not fall on deaf ears. Did she really say that?

Although running high on lavender and other legal herbs – the community had strict anti-drug rules – my communication with Tony became erratic during my Greek escapade. He was the one cheating on me, but I could not help thinking that it happened because I was not good enough. I must have disappointed him. I was too predictable. Or maybe too unpredictable. Anyway, I refused to support him financially any longer. Most of the time I was just trying not to think about him. Or Stein. Or LouLou. Or everything. An ostrich-like approach. Very effective, to a certain extent. It got me out of Suicide Avenue, so to speak.

Upon my return to Brussels, I found out that Tony had contracted debts in our name. I was jointly liable under our prenuptial agreement. He was not making a living out of anything, but refused to scale down his opulent lifestyle. *Get thee a good husband, and use him as he uses thee*, Stein used to say, quoting Shakespeare. An option worth considering too, definitively. I wanted to see Frank. Who cares for an ideal husband when desperate? An email from Frank came in. He was also missing our psychosexual rendezvous and was impatient to engage further in them, especially now that I was recovering well. Of course, payment for the sessions was still due: Frank was a professional. In trouble with our national Ordre des Médecins Psychiatres, he was nonetheless to leave Europe soon and planned to open a new practice in Bangkok. But who cares about ethics? Human sciences are bound to feed on human flaws, and I was providing my not-so-honorable doctor with material of his own for his new patients. Doctor–patient relationship reversal, the loop was looped.

"Ma'am, we've arrived."

"What? I'm not going back to Les Acacias!" I protested, half-asleep.

"The airport. Brussels Airport."

"Ah... thank you." Two years to the day since I checked out of the madhouse, I was leaving my apartment again, but this time for Pisa.

We were preparing for landing. The extent to which my life had changed over the past two years struck me. I was getting divorced and was soon to be ruined. My uncle had kicked the bucket. I had abandoned the dream of a normal job. I had started to learn and practice shamanism. And I was about to journey around the world with Omar. We wanted to write a book on experiential shamanism that we envisaged as a path of spiritual discovery. And I still had fantastic hair and amazing blue eyes.

I rushed to the closest toilets before collecting my bags at the carousel. My bladder was on the edge of explosion. I continuously had the urge to pee, which sometimes put me in unpleasant situations. "This is just a phase to go through, you're going to be just fine," Penelope Eagle-Eye kept repeating. "You saw it coming too." The ladies' room walls were covered with mirrors of various styles and sizes. I looked at my image in a massive Venetian mirror. "Fuckable. You're still fuckable, Benedetta, and this comes as a pleasant surprise. What else do you want?" Good question. What did I want? I wanted love. Tony did not love me. I was not sure about Frank, either; he had evaporated in Thailand. I had tears in my eyes. *Enough*, I thought. I blew my nose and emerged into Pisa Airport hall.

Alfredo's coffee shop was open and still serving its legendary pastries. I collected myself and chose a table on the terrace. "Espresso, *per favore,* and a cherry pie," I said to the waiter, "and add one of your local brandies." Omar was due to arrive later. I was so looking forward to seeing him. I texted him that I had landed and where to find me. What was he doing in Amsterdam? Was he being naughty? My friend enjoyed cultivating a healthy dose of mystery, just like me. I was presented with a glass of peach-flavored brandy. Down in one. Or maybe not. *What do I have in my handbag?* I wondered. I could not remember. Characteristically, I had ended up packing in a rush a few hours before departure. As a consequence, I was not sure of the exact contents of my bags. I opened my handbag with curiosity: yellow candle, plastic lighter, small Buddha wooden statue, dry lavender, moon calendar, favorite sunglasses, red purse, and passport. And other items no one needed to know about. One can live with that and sit at an Italian café terrace – ground-floor-located, just in case.

"Hey yaa, what's up, sista?" I heard as I was lighting the candle.

"I'm doing coffee reading."

"What's that? Never heard of it."

"Are you kidding me? Coffee reading is such a powerful spiritual technique. Groundbreaking stuff. With an appropriate coffee blend and the needed savoir faire, which I happen to possess, one can make very accurate predictions."

"Are you serious?"

"Take a seat and see the miracle unfold in front of you. I always give the first session for free. It's your lucky day! Synchronicity of synchronicities, an espresso is waiting for you on this table. This reading is meant to happen."

"I don't have anything to lose, I suppose," said my visitor nonchalantly. He sat and drank the coffee in one gulp.

"I feel it coming…"

"What?"

"The prediction."

"And?"

"You're going to win the war!"

"Which war?"

"World War Two, of course."

"But… I won it already."

Looking at me as if our conversation was a non-event, my visitor gave me the V sign that made it clear he was not just anybody. Goodness me, it was Winston Churchill sitting at my table. Let me get this straight immediately: I do not really believe that Churchill was paying me a visit at Pisa Airport. Following my obscure encounters with David Copperfield, which propelled me to Les Acacias, I became careful at discerning which parts of what I see are real and which are not. I burst into cathartic laughter. Hopefully, next time I would be visited by a punk rock star or a disgraced client.

"I'm having visions!" was the first thing I heard Omar saying as he was rushing to me at Alfredo's.

"That's fantastic, dear! I've just had a conversation with Winston Churchill!"

"Churchill? I'm talking visions here, like ghosts, not historical characters!" Omar seemed puzzled. Why did he think this was such an issue? Winston Churchill is as good a conversation candidate as any other, isn't he?

"What kind of ghosts then?"

"I'm not sure, maybe the spirit of my younger self, something to do with sex and drugs."

"Oh, I love it! Do you want a coffee reading?"

"That's just what I need! You're so resourceful. I'm so happy I have you to talk to!"

"I can tell you all! Do you prefer the macchiato or the espresso option?"

"Give me the macchiato."

"Okay. That's the soft version then," I said, faking disappointment.

How could I possibly be disappointed? Omar was here, charming and radiant, and we were heading to Il Casolare, an inspiring place. And so was this journey that we had decided to undertake together. A journey in the here and now, a journey of the self, a journey of our souls. I was tempted to tell him that I had given up on my medication, but this would have opened the chapter of my nervous breakdown and my little vacation at the madhouse, which I had never mentioned to him. I had never told him about my jumping out a window either. Nor about Stein, though he knew about Tony. Maybe a little too much for our first macchiato.

. . . .

Belsedere, 19 June 2015, later in the day

Benedetta and I were staying at Il Casolare del Belsedere, a beautiful Tuscan stone house in the middle of the woods, the picture-perfect retreat spot. There was a blind cat able to navigate his way across the roof and a curious deer that grazed in the garden at times. It was remote, somewhere near the border with Liguria, a half-hour car ride from the almost non-existent train station of Belsedere–Baciadonne that, as its name suggests, serves the towns of both Belsedere and Baciadonne. The three-hour train ride from Pisa reminded me of a journey that I took as a backpacker in my early twenties in former Yugoslavia. There was no dining wagon, no drinks or sandwich trolley, and the toilet could euphemistically have been called a black hole. It was damp, rundown, and vandalized. We were entering unhip rural Europe, the type of life that glossy magazines never show. I felt at home.

During the train ride from Pisa, Benedetta alternated between happiness and excitement, occasionally verging on manic. In the middle of a tirade against her ex-husband, she interjected abstract comments about a YouTube channel on sexuality and then described in uncomfortable detail a lesbian relationship, though I was not sure whether this was something that she had watched on YouTube or whether it actually involved herself. I decided not to interrupt her and just nodded sympathetically. If she were having a lesbian affair, she would mention it again. Though I hoped she would not.

At Il Casolare I was offered a room of my own for the first few days of the retreat, until another guest arrived. This was luxury. The bathroom was shared among twelve of us. The ability to have a short shower was therefore essential to demonstrate community skills. More importantly, this was one of the few places in the world where my food neurosis was appeased: organic, vegetarian, no white flour or sugar, no lettuce, next to no eggplant, *gomasio* on tap, almond milk, and everything almost vegan, except for *parmigiano* on kamut spaghetti nights. Most guests had arrived before sunset. It was a pale early-summer night. We sat around the long table in preparation for dinner.

Benedetta was lost in the women's dormitory, negotiating a bed next to a window that was much sought after because of its good view of the moon. We actually had a full moon that night, which put us all in a particular mood. I was anxious, pessimistic, and tired. Not to mention the visions. On the contrary, in such planetary circumstances, Benedetta felt inspired, connected with nature, and prone to losing consciousness of her mortal status, all of which had demanded the intervention of the *carabinieri* during at least one previous Italian sojourn. Some of the spiritual experiences she had described to me, especially those involving communion with celestial bodies, showed strikingly similar symptoms to a nervous breakdown. I took a look at the content of the large *nécessaire* that she had left in the communal bathroom but found no prescription drugs. Either she was totally fine or she was off her medication and about to have a major crisis. I braced myself for the upcoming night.

I had no Benedetta to rely on for conversation starters, so I reached out and joined a conversation that was already happening. The usual round of introductions and some shamanic jokes. It was in this kind of environment that I felt less of an outsider. We were all a little bit lost and a little bit uncomfortable with the normal urban world where we inexplicably lived. We each had our own social handicap. I was a neurotic and a recovering addict, and Benedetta was not able to talk about her life if not in abstractions and generalizations. There was a middle-aged German woman who went by a spiritual Hindu name that we would never learn to pronounce, very well versed in the Mayan calendar, and two young Swiss girls, one of them afraid of cats. I could not understand how anybody interested in shamanism could be afraid of cats, though the logic of my reasoning escaped me. I chose to keep a low profile. In rehab I learned that people with high self-esteem do not talk too much.

I looked at them and felt proud. Not pedantic-proud, but rather a kind of pride that I would try to sustain for the duration of the retreat. I was doing something that was good for me. Spiritual retreats connect me with like-minded people and shelter me from triggers that may lead to licking drugs on toilet seats or having intercourse with ghosts. Moreover, spiritual retreats provided an understanding audience with whom I could share my ghost stories and expect attention and respect. This was a space neither to suppress nor to indulge in my pressing emotions, but rather to view them with generosity and acceptance. This is Sogyal Rinpoche off the top of my head, who is high on my recovery toolkit.[5]

I breathed: I should be fine for the week, one day at a time. I texted my twelve-step recovery program sponsor, telling him that I was calm and in a good place. I attached a picture of the blind cat. We both loved cats. The German woman had produced a pendulum and was making some of us uncomfortable as she lectured on necromancy. I moved to the other end of the table and tried to communicate telepathically with the blind cat, an art I had not yet mastered.

Maestra-shaman emerged from the woods with a basket full of wild mushrooms. She was a wise woman and had seen extraordinary things. I perceived a certain fatigue. Perhaps she'd had enough of this world. And yet she had so much to teach to the eager bunch of us who had come searching for a way out of the illusion of separation. We so much longed to be reunited again, and she would help us to aim there with her Oriental patience, enigmatic smile, and challenging teachings. She liked to contradict herself and taught us to love what we did not like about ourselves. Maybe this was the main reason why we had come to her that night, and the only way in which we could finally be reunited.

There was a warm round of hugs, *namastes*, and *wais*, before she quickly excused herself. We did not see her again until breakfast. Apparently she was observing a fast of considerable duration that had miraculous results. Before receding into her quarters, she looked at each of us and said, "Spiritual strength depends on going hungry and thirsty. In God's domain, hunger is a divine food." Benedetta made her appearance just in time to listen to the first teaching from our maestra. She had changed into a bright pink linen dress in an

---

5   Sogyal Rinpoche, *The Tibetan Book of Living and Dying*

attempt to look *campagnarde*, but she was definitively overdressed. Maybe it was the effect of the earrings and necklace made of conchs and tassels. Allegedly, the necklace was a powerful Polynesian charm. She would adjust by the time she ran out of clean clothes.

"Do you think fasting is optional?" she asked me, but I could not reply because my mind was absorbed in two events happening simultaneously: a steamy quinoa with *funghi* landing on the table and Carlito making his grand entrance.

Carlito must have been twenty-four, tall and strikingly good-looking, bearing a resemblance to my childhood hero, Corto Maltese. He wore sandals, loose white linen trousers, and a casually worn-out white shirt, halfway between an ashram hip and an Ibiza-cocktails outfit. A wooden eagle charm hung from his neck. He had a strong accent and a powerful smile. His arrival triggered a general shuffling of auras, as everybody wanted to become available to the newcomer. Except Benedetta, who was in a distant corner of the *loggia*, secretively talking into her mobile phone in the fastest possible argot. In spite of her efforts to hide the content of her conversation, I picked out the words "ex-husband," "lawyer," and *"espèce de con,"* the latter strongly emphasized.

Carlito traveled light. He threw his tiny backpack into a corner and was ready for dinner. He looked each of us in the eyes while rapidly accessing his akashic records. He placed a hand on the heart of some of us, including myself, retrieved the akashic file pertaining to the relationship that each of us had with him in a previous incarnation, and sighed with benevolence. Some stared intently back with a smile, acknowledging the millenary connection, and others cried in the presence of such an overwhelming presence. I fell in love with him.

Romantic fantasy is another of the many obsessions that I suffer when being sober from other addictions. I was blind to the fact that Carlito was a flirt, not within my ideal age range, likely not interested in the monogamous relationship that I aimed for, and he might not be gay. Although I bet he was heteroflexible. Those insignificant yet insurmountable details made him a desirable trophy for the compulsive-obsessive side of me that at times governs my mind. I took a deep breath and four more drops of Rescue Remedy, and said the serenity prayer to myself for about five minutes. *How we live now can cost us our entire future.* I was going to keep away from the snake charmer.

Meanwhile, Carlito had explained that he was born under an auspicious full moon in Leo and that the singularity was probably the relic of an earlier and collapsed universe. He was well versed in astrology and cosmology, had read Madame Blavatsky, trekked in Kamchatka, was on friendly terms with Pema Chödrön and was frequently embraced by Mata Amritanandamayi. Asked about the eagle charm hanging from his neck, he broadcasted that his helping spirit was an eagle. Carlito appeared to be of the type that opens up early. The German woman was already inviting him to stay at her home so they could together attend the next Thomas Hübl event in Hof Oberlethe.

It is for this reason that Milarepa stayed in a cave. He knew that once the deluded mind comes into contact with the object of desire, delusions arise uncontrollably. Oh yes, but I was two years, nine months, and one day sober, and I had learned one or two efficient tools to control my delusions. I felt proud of my conscious decision not to take part in the conversation and sat at the farthest end of the table. I silently gave thanks to the rain and the sun and to all those who worked to bring the buttery quinoa to my plate.

If I've survived today, I might very well make it into tomorrow, I thought. I went to bed early, after a delicious vegan chocolate cake, after checking on Benedetta, who was slightly agitated. She was on her second glass of wine and intensely engaged in conversation with the Swiss girl who was afraid of cats. I assumed they were discussing a girly topic that would escape my grasp. I gave her a goodnight nod from the opposite end of the dining room and disappeared into my room, where I sat in a corner and meditated.

Shortly after midnight, I woke to the sound of steps in the corridor. I stayed in bed, alert, and confirmed that some movement was taking place outside. Just before I left the dinner table, I had overheard something about going to a nearby power point in the middle of the night. I did not pay much attention to it, because I am easily convinced to partake in absurd expeditions and I needed a full night's sleep. I tried to go back to sleep, but the sound of steps in the corridor made me curious, so I went out through it to the terrace, from where I would have a good perspective on any nocturnal activities. A group had climbed the small hill next to the garden and were holding hands at the summit. A quick headcount resulted in the conclusion that almost everybody was there. I decided that whatever impromptu ceremony was happening, it had started without me and could therefore very well end without me.

On the way back to my room, I noticed that the door to Benedetta's dormitory was slightly open, allowing the moonlight to filter into the corridor all the way to my bare feet. I looked inside the dormitory and caught a glimpse of Benedetta in bed, dressed in a prudish nightgown. Her eyes were half open, with the strange serenity of those who see spirits or of the epileptic after a seizure. She was not the kind of girl to get seriously drunk at a retreat. Or was she? I was about to whisper her name when a shadow moved across her. It looked like a large bird, but it turned into human form under the moonlight. I was presented with Carlito's naked butt. The light gave it an eerie appearance, as if it were the butt of a marble statue or of a ghost. It was, however, definitively Carlito, who was relentlessly humping my friend. Benedetta jerked her head back, ecstatic. After the initial surprise, I wondered whether she was conscious of what was going on.

"Should I join them?"

"What the fuck…" I said as I turned around to find the German woman with the long spiritual name. The first thing that I felt was embarrassment at being caught spying on the spontaneous lovers.

"Oh, you… I'm worried. Did you see, like, an eagle in there?"

"An eagle? Oh yes, the eagle. Look. They are journeying to the sky."

The German woman confirming there was an eagle convinced me that there could not have been any bird at all. Maybe the presence that I felt was a small bat. Or a flashback. Maybe I sensed the archetype of an eagle. I could not accept that a pretentious flirt like Carlito could turn into an actual eagle like the shamans of old times. Once the supernatural concern was clarified, I turned to my other, more mundane concern:

"Is he abusing her? Was she drunk?" I said, hushed, short of breath.

"They are cosmic lovers. A shaman shall be born."

"Born? Oh no. No, no, no. Do you think he is using a…?"

"I think I should join them."

Desire was here! The deluded mind coming into contact with desirable objects leads to superstition, producing more and more delusion. I thought that I was getting the message. Thank you, Rinpoche, for presenting me with so many examples of your teachings. *All right*, I thought, *if this freak German woman thinks this is a sex party, maybe they're having consensual intercourse while the codependent in me is brooding on a drama. What do I know about what faces women make when they fuck?*

"No, I don't think you should join them," I replied firmly. "My friend has a very sensitive aura. What was your name again?"

"Ambaambalaambalika," she whispered flirtatiously.

"Isn't that three names?" I enquired, suddenly distracted from the cosmic lovers.

"I'm the mother of God."

Was I tripping? Maybe it was the flashback. The German woman had henna tattoos on her hands and feet, and I could smell a flowery tincture coming from her red hair. She was no ghost. Western culture sometimes is too much for me. "We should go." I grabbed her firmly by the arm and took her to the terrace. Once there, she tuned in to the moon and started humming the Gayatri mantra. I recited with her for a few minutes to keep her busy. After maybe a half hour, the party at the top of the hill started hugging and then walked back to the house. I sneaked back into my bedroom and dove under the duvet.

I had a view of Carlito's ass without jeopardizing my two years, nine months, and one day of sobriety. What else could I have hoped for? Tight, firm, prime faun's ass. There were so many things that I did not understand. Like the eagle and the rest of the visions I was having. Maybe it was a flashback. I was confused; it seemed easier for me to believe that Benedetta had had sex with an eagle spirit than to accept casual sex in the dormitory. Welcome, this bizarre opportunity to face misogyny. Yes, Benedetta was a woman, with vagina and all, and entitled to a rewarding sex life, even with guys I fancied. The fact that she listened to the most lurid details of my anecdotes, romantic dramas, and eternal obsessions without sharing almost anything on her part did not deprive her of her human nature. She had a life of her own, independent from me. That hurt. How difficult it would be not to treat her as a eunuch any more.

But who cared if Benedetta was on medication, Carlito was the reincarnation of the Siberian father shaman, or Ambaambalaambalika the mother of God? After all, we are all addicted to the medication of illusion, and we are all relatives of God. I meditated for a long while. It was warm under the duvet, and I was grateful to have a roof over my head. What really mattered was that the next day we would all share breakfast and be ready to journey. We would make drumming arrangements and listen to the wise words of our maestra. I would feel blessed for joining this party.

All the academic information about physics and other laws of the cosmos, all the metaphysical information about religion, my petty grievances and selfish deeds, would evaporate by the second beat of the drum. Our bodies would be dismembered. We would experience a feeling of oneness that no words can describe, because language is the child of separation. Each of us would be thrilled and soothed as we dissolved into a larger consciousness. All the knowledge that there is would be unveiled. Who needs to lick ecstasy from a toilet seat once all this is revealed? I slept like a log.

The following morning, Carlito offered me an espresso. I tried to detect some sign of the shamanic conversion that he had experienced the previous night, but I found nothing. His hands were perfectly clean and steady, he was able to pour coffee and talk at the same time, the form of his nose had not changed, his hair was casually combed, no feathers, no shining aura, a normal mortal guy. I should investigate further.

Benedetta appeared from the woods in her nightgown, completely soaked. She made a signal with her head for me to approach. In spite of the bizarre circumstances of her roaming the woods drenched, she looked perfectly fine to me. Carlito had just started discoursing about shamanism in Siberia. I would have liked to stay with him to identify any hints that his Siberian stories might present about his apparent ability to turn into an eagle and mate with humans for the sake of preserving the shamanic lineage, as is the tradition among the Buryat people in Siberia. However, I had painfully learned that dwelling on that kind of obsession did not help my sobriety. I reluctantly excused myself and walked toward Benedetta, committed to being attentive and non-judgmental. I greeted her, and we walked arm in arm. My arm got soaked.

"Darling, where is the meditation room?" she asked, casually squeezing the excess water from her hair.

"Darling, are you on medication?" I whispered in a friendly tone, as if talking to a child.

"Of course! Take me there. You are late!" she commanded in that affectionate yet conclusive way of hers that demands action and admits no further distraction.

Wherever you are, enlightenment is there. This was the odd family that I had now; this was my *sangha*. It was a blessing, and I had to cherish it. A song by Los Fabulosos Cadillacs had been in my head all morning. It had something to do with the moon, false promises, and illusion about the nature of reality. Or maybe not. Perhaps it was just me feeling lonely, trying to convince myself that I had found my *sangha* and that life was not a mere illusion. Anyways, it all seemed real to me.

. . . .

Belsedere, 19 June 2015, later in the day

Omar and I entered Belsedere–Baciadonne station after a lovely three-hour train ride from Pisa that gave us a welcome opportunity to catch up. Actually, for me to hear his many stories and anecdotes. A resident from Il Casolare was waiting for us at the train station. "Hello, I'm Benedetta. Can we stop at a bar please?" Our resident seemed startled by this way of introducing myself.

"No, she doesn't need a drink. She has medical issues," Omar whispered to him. I would have preferred for our resident to believe that I was a terrible drunk. How was my bladder, always edging explosion, supposed to help me find true love?

When we arrived at Il Casolare, the dinner table had been set with flowers and candles. Omar and I had decided to kick off our trip with a shamanic workshop that took place there. This was the welcome dinner. Another resident turned up with a basket full of organic zucchini. With him came Meravigliosa, a young deer who had made this place her home. Three cats were snoozing undisturbed on the sofas. Enticing Spanish music, which resonated as a liberating invitation to dance, was coming from the kitchen. We were offered a glass of wine and rolled cigarettes. Omar politely refused. I accepted.

I made my way up to the dormitory where women usually slept at Il Casolare. From my previous sojourn, I remembered the private alcove, which contained a creaking four-poster bed offering exquisite views of the mountains and surrounding nature. I claimed to my roommates that I had sleeping disorders and would therefore appreciate the alcove. But many of them had sleeping disorders too. I had to upgrade my game. I confessed to sleepwalking stark naked, especially on full-moon nights. "I cannot help it; I have my moon in Scorpio," I added. No response from the female gang. When I started to undress shamelessly, it was unanimously decided that I should be the one getting the alcove.

Roaming around naked in a women's dormitory comes naturally to me. Tony erased any modesty that I might once have had. That being said, I usually do not engage a third party in the kind of practices he initiated me into. I also avoid telling people the exact nature of my relationship with my psychiatrist at the madhouse. I am not ashamed, but I do not want people to think of me as a slut, which I certainly am not. I simply enjoyed bending the borders of what I thought was socially acceptable. Acceptable is an illusion and a curse.

The beauty of LouLou was that he never cared about opinions. He wanted to live as a free man and was kind to everyone. For me, this placed him de facto in the realm of some sacred authenticity, despite his illicit activities. I was blind to their real nature, and I never knew whether he had blood on his hands. I preferred to believe he did not. I was naive. My uncle was nevertheless moving into life with grace and a true sense of adventure, until the Hanged Man moment came. I am not my uncle. Others' opinions mattered a lot to me, until I hit rock bottom, because I did not know myself and was scared to death of being rejected. Because of the spiders, too. But rock bottom is a nice place to start all over again. Appearances are everything, appearances are nothing, and long is the road to liberation. But please, give me another tarot card.

Back on the terrace, savoring my alcove victory, I greeted the other guests and participants in the workshop. They were showing up one by one. Suddenly, an awful *Mission: Impossible* ringtone invaded the space. Who the hell was still using this? A little louder, please? My goodness! It took me five full seconds to acknowledge that it came from my phone. Could it have been more embarrassing? I was horrified at the poor first impression this situation was creating. I would have to work hard to restore my spiritual credibility in the next hours. I picked up my phone. It was Tony, arising from ghost land.

"*Connard! (…) C'est en taule que je vais t'envoyer. Tu croyais que j'allais te laisser filer? (…) Un village de merde avec trois vaches, deux moutons et la cajole du coin. T'es vraiment le plus grand loser du monde. (….) J'en ai vraiment rien à foutre. Tu me prends vraiment pour une conne. (…) A partir de maintenant, c'est mon avocat qui t'appellera directement. Putain de bordel de merde!*"

I hung up in a fury and vomited another series of enraged "*putain!*"s. The terrace had become dead silent. Everybody was looking at me in dismay. Or were these compassionate eyes? I could not figure out what was worse. Out of the blue, Lola's arms surrounded me warmly. I could not see her, but I recognized her bracelets and perfume. She gave me a much-needed hug, bringing me to the brink of tears. I did not want to cry, not then, not there, not in front of strangers. Fortunately, conversations resumed quickly and dinner was announced. I took a seat beside a middle-aged Italian man who seemed so absorbed in his thoughts that he might have missed my eructation.

"Hello, I'm Benedetta, from Belgium," I said, putting an end to his reverie.

"Oh! Hello! I'm Cylindro Anarchia, from Piemonte."

"I beg your pardon?"

"Cylindro Anarchia. But everybody calls me Indro. And I live in Piemonte." Not quite what I expected.

"Cylindro Anarchia?" I asked with an encouraging yet doubtful smile.

"My parents were into *futurismo*, and we were all given that kind of name."

"Interesting."

"My sister is Veritá Dynamica. But everybody calls her Vedi."

"Oh, marvelous… does she live in Piemonte too?"

"No. She lives in Roma. She teaches *gladiatore* to tourists." This sounded rather obscure to me.

"I'm wondering… how does it feel to have such a name? For you, I mean," I hesitantly enquired.

"You know, this is just a name… I'm transitioning to a new identity."

"Tell me more about it," I said, not really knowing how to respond.

"I'm transitioning to Vittorio Emanuele. I'm a royalist!"

"A royalist? This is a big shift from where you come from, isn't it?"

"I believe that everybody should live according to his true nature. I ain't Indro any more. I'm Vittorio Emanuele." He then stood up, raised his glass, and said something like "*Forza Italia.*" Was he a Berlusconi fan too?

I was getting confused by the odd turn of this conversation. Too much information. How can such a thing as a royalist-shaman be? Jesus himself was a powerful shaman, meaning that all possibilities remained open as far as mixing genres went, but Indro's political references seemed rather wild to me. I sought solace in Omar's warm smile. He was sitting in front of me, chatting with a young hottie. The guy's psychic energy seemed to be able to bend spoons. To be a bended spoon, or not to be a bended spoon: that was my question. I drew inspiration from this realization, and I declaimed to Indro-transitioning-to-Vittorio-Emanuele the *Hamlet* soliloquy that I had painfully learned at Les Acacias under Frank's supervision.

Apart from exploring the possibilities offered by Frank's sofa, my treatment had consisted of learning Shakespeare quotes suitable for cutting my negative emotions in a variety of situations. Instead of looking for the closest window, my mind would be trained to retrieve an appropriate quote that I was invited to recite as a mantra until the storm had passed. If nothing came to mind, the *Hamlet* soliloquy was to be used. *Though this be madness, yet there is method in't.*[6] I proved to be terrible at learning lines by heart at the madhouse; the drugs that I was ingesting on a daily basis, if relaxing, were hardly supporting any decent focus, let alone intellectual activity. This was the price of my relative peace of mind.

My Shakespearean outing put an immediate end to my conversation with Indro, who drifted back to meditative mode. A piece of veggie pie landed in front of me. The red eight-sided plate was marked with a small heart-shaped *I'm in love with a mathematician*. I am sorry, but I was in love with a gigolo, and with a psychiatrist at risk of a malpractice lawsuit. Can I get another plate? This was the moment that Lola chose to invite me to the *collina* to observe stars with her and establish connections with UFOs. For one second I felt completely desperate. Seriously, was there anyone in this place with whom I could have a normal conversation? Or was I precisely just like them? A freak among weirdos. "A glass of wine. Red. Now," I begged one resident. I urgently needed to recover. He detected my distress and gave me the full bottle. Amen.

As a good Cinderella, but without charming prince, I left the welcome party before midnight with mixed feelings. What was this about? A solar plexus chakra-opening experience stirred up by Maestra-shaman? A shamanic happening on overcoming loneliness

---

6 William Shakespeare, "Hamlet" from *The Complete Works of William Shakespeare*, edited by Stephen Orgel and A.R. Braunmuller (London: Penguin Books, 2002)

by means of compassion? "I have Buddha nature, that alone is not enough to make it work. If you do not have a friend or a *sangha*, it won't work." I had read that on Facebook while waiting for Omar at Pisa Airport. Daily quote by "Buddhist Wisdom". I had to mention this to him – but he had drifted off already. Was he aware that an introspective Indro was going to share his bedroom? Believe me, no matter how well advanced in his *zazen* Omar liked to appear, he would need all the Buddha nature available to endure this roommate.

Anyway, I was certain that establishing connections with UFOs would not get me any farther on the spiritual path. "Lola, about your *collina* proposal, another time maybe. I need a good rest." I planted a kiss on her third eye and headed to the dormitory. It looked as if someone had gone through my belongings. "Welcome, friends and weirdos, you will be my *sangha* this week, and I'm volunteering to be your queen," I whispered. Sun in Capricorn or in Leo. Besides, I had nothing to hide. Nothing except Valium ensconced in a Fisherman's Friend box, just in case I would see a halo of fluorescent green light and feel like flying again. No more canaries, thank you very much. I was never completely sure about Frank's methods: too much Shakespeare killed Shakespeare. That and patchouli.

Abruptly interrupting the stream of my reflections, I noticed the presence of the spoon-bender hottie right in the dormitory doorway. Almost naked, he said something about having had a shower and not being able to find the way to his bedroom. He was obviously looking for someone, and that someone happened to be me. "By the way, my name is Carlito. Nice to meet you," he added with a mischievous smile aimed at erasing doubts about his immediate intentions. To be or not to be a bended spoon: this is always the question. Because God is merciful and the world abundant, I decided to show our local Adonis into my alcove of intimacy. I could not deny the sexual nature of our akashic file. *Graze on my lips, and if those hills be dry, stray lower, where the pleasant fountain lie.*[7] Did I really say that? He went down on bended knees.

It was 4:45 a.m., and Carlito was sound asleep. I contemplated his vigorous body. He was just a boy. I decided to leave him to linger in his peaceful dreams and go for a meditative walk. This was a perfect time of the day to go down by the river. The last twenty-four hours had been a whirlwind. "Could it have been more bizarre?" I nervously questioned the fading moon while walking along the steep path leading from the house to *la piccola piscina*, a natural pool formed by the river. No, it could not. I was feeling overwhelmed. Since our arrival at Il Casolare I had been floating from one absurd conversation to another, without ever stepping back on their meaning whatsoever, to the point of allowing a stranger into my bed. I entered the pool. The water was cool, and I started to swim, which created ripples. *Glory is like a circle in the water, which never ceaseth to enlarge itself, till by broad spreading it disperse to nought.*[8] Another of Frank's findings. For rainy days. A moment of glory never lasts. The magic of the night had dissolved.

I continued swimming, hardly noticing the beauty and quiet of the pool and its surroundings. I was in overthinking mode, stubbornly trying to make sense of the last twenty-four hours. I recalled the message that I had received at Pisa Airport from my lawyer: Tony and his new wife had just become parents, and I would have to be in Brussels the next week to sign documents related to the financial settlement of my divorce. I hated the prospect of having to travel to Brussels. I was not sure that I wanted to stay at Il Casolare either. But nothing ever really goes away until the lesson is learned. Who needs Valium once this is revealed? Probably everyone. Probably me.

"*Un, deux, trois, allons dans les bois. Quatre, cinq, six, cueillir des cerises.*" What was this? "*Sept, huit, neuf, dans mon panier neuf. Dix,*

---

7 William Shakespeare, "Venus and Adonis" from *The Complete Works of William Shakespeare*

8 William Shakespeare, "Henry VI" from *The Complete Works of William Shakespeare*

onze, douze, elles seront toutes rouges." I knew this voice, and this French children's song, which gave me a twinge of sorrow.

"Gail?" I asked. No answer, but she was a bit deaf at times – or pretended to be so. "Gail, is it you?" I insisted.

"Hello," said the familiar voice.

"What are you doing here?"

"I saw you walking down to the river, and I thought you could use some company. How are you doing?"

"All right. What about you?"

"Oh, not too bad I suppose, considering I've been dead for almost two years," she said in laughter. I laughed too. It was good to talk to her. "And now, tell me how you are really are doing." I breathed deeply and told her everything that had occurred since my arrival in Italy, including the news about Tony. My lawyer had also told me that the new wife did not have any money and that she used to be a maid. Could it be that Tony loved her? I was profoundly upset. "Maybe, after all, I should also have a baby," I finally said, ending my lament. Gail laughed again, which upset me even more.

"Oh, Benedetta, don't be so serious. Even you should be able to see how comical you and your stories sometimes are."

"Seriously? You will have to explain that to me!" But she did not explain anything.

"*As I was going down impassive Rivers, I no longer felt myself guided by haulers: Yelping redskins had taken them as targets and had nailed them naked to colored stakes.*"[9]

"What is this again?" I asked, irritated.

"French poetry. You are now able to navigate your life on your own. You are free to go wherever you want and to do what you like. And without blaming others for what upsets or irritates you. I will still be by your side, Benedetta, but my teaching to you ends

9 Arthur Rimbaud, "The Drunken Boat" from *Complete Works, Selected Letters,* translated by Wallace Fowlie (Chicago and London: The University of Chicago Press, 2005)

here: your life is what you make of it. Your responses to what has happened since your arrival in Italy, including to your ex-husband's new situation, depend on you. Besides, this Italian guy did not force you to have sex with him. He would have left should you have asked for it." She paused and observed her words slowly landing into my consciousness. "Goodbye, darling. Be strong." She left without notice. Evaporated.

The last thing I had expected was Gail's visit. The last time we talked had been months ago. So why today? Why here? She for sure did not care about my sexual life. She had always found my relationship with Tony amusing. This was her way of helping me not to overdramatize. And I was not serious about having a baby. I was not stupid enough to think that motherhood would solve any of my problems. It then struck me that Gail had only ever visited me for one reason: teaching me that I was responsible for my own life and that my choices were entirely mine, whether I liked it or not. If there was a joke, it was precisely that of having moved through life without acknowledging that reality. "My life belongs to me," I said aloud. My voice echoed, and I liked it. I repeated the magic words slowly. Could it be that my life actually belonged to me? That felt strange. "Oh my God, it does!" I was exhilarated. If LouLou had been alive, he would have been proud of me.

I recalled my first meeting with my uncle. I had met him during my first year in college. I was living on campus. I could not camouflage my weight issues – I had been battling anorexia since the age of fifteen – but I was trying hard to hide my other disorders. My uncle had no children but had lived enough to perceive the kind of drama I was going through. LouLou had avoided asking me questions regarding my health. I would have ignored them anyway. "Hopefully, one day you will start loving yourself and appreciate the beauty of this world," he told me during our first meeting. I had not known how to respond. But in the meantime, he would love me even when I hated myself. By the end of college, I had recovered from anorexia, but my eating disorders were far from being solved. My weight had not stabilized, and I was yo-yo dieting. For several years I alternated between overweight and normal weight. I was accustomed to gaining or losing three to four sizes in record time.

My peculiar association with Tony did nothing to improve my general condition. Our marriage served the illusion that I could hold on to something real, only to catapult me out a window, together with other propellers of the same kind. I had made a mistake when marrying Tony. I could now make new choices, better choices. I could take a new route. I noticed that the sun was high in the sky. What time was it? How long had I been floating in *la piccola piscina*? It seemed that several hours had passed. I hoped not to have missed breakfast, for I was hungry. I rushed back *pronto* to the house. I made my way soaked to the terrace, leaving a dripping train. Meravigliosa the deer was licking the water from my drenched goddess-tunic. Or was it a nightgown?

Looking like the cat that ate the canary, Carlito welcomed me with a warm smile that I returned in a mirroring effect. He obviously had a direct approach with women, but there was nothing of the devil in him. He was just a boy. Lola accosted me.

"Benedetta, you really missed something last night. We saw the most amazing shooting stars!" she exclaimed with eyes full of excitement.

"Oh, wonderful! Did you make a wish?" I asked curiously.

"Of course, many wishes. For me, for you, for everyone. And, guess what, we might have opened a new channel leading to a connection with UFOs. It could not have been any better! You would have loved it so much! Do you need a hair dryer, by the way?" Lola's happiness and generosity were genuine.

Maestra-shaman made a discreet entry through the kitchen door. After greeting each of us, she invited the group to join her in the downstairs meditation room for a release practice in preparation for our first shamanic journey. We had all been longing for this moment of journeying together to multidimensional realms of unconditional love, where there was no right or wrong. The collective experience would make it stronger. Whatever the past twenty-four hours had been, they had opened my heart. I was feeling immensely grateful to be in this place of beauty, surrounded by this motley crew of good-hearted people. None of us might just be normal, but then normality is overrated. It is a variable moral standard intended to take the lead on our individual and collective destiny to the benefit of a few, and to kill one's inner child and soul. I did not want to be normal. I did not care about morals, either. I just wanted to be me. This was the only thing that mattered. That and the beautiful friends I was meeting along the way.

Where was Omar? So much had happened overnight. I wanted to know whether his ghost from the past had visited him again. At times my friend looked very fragile. From the abyss of my own shortcomings, I vowed to keep an eye on him. Maybe he just needed someone to take care of him. I might never become a mother, but I could definitely take care of my friends and the people I loved in the best possible way. And Omar was worth it. As a matter of fact, Maestra-shaman told me that we all were. Seriously, dude? Valium, please. Oh, chill out, only joking.

I saw Omar walking toward me. I wondered whether he had noticed the eagle flying unusually low over the house under the moonlight. Maybe I had just eaten too much broccoli-rosemary pie, a devilish combination. Vegans can trick you badly, but they will not ever repent. Where is my Valium, please? Oh, really joking. Xanax will do too. *Perhaps perhaps perhaps!* And Lexomil. Would I like some tea? Or an orange maybe? Or a Cuban cigar perhaps? I beg your pardon? I would rather have one of these juicy peaches. Do I want to play the guitar? *Tu vuo fa l'americano?* Sorry, I am only the bird that was eaten alive by the cat. *Yea, man and birds are fain of climbing high.*[10] Oops. I did it again.

---

10   William Shakespeare, "Henry VI" from *The Complete Works of William Shakespeare*

"Darling, where is the medication room?" I asked Omar, smiling.

"The medication?"

Here we go again, I thought to myself, but I could see that he really cared. "The meditation, meditation room, darling. Of course. Take me there. You're late!" Omar then took my arm and sang in Spanish. Something about Cadillacs and moons. I did not really understand the lyrics, but I liked the melody. We both laughed. At that moment I realized that our journey had started and would take us exactly where we needed to go. I got a bit scared.

"Benedetta, don't worry. The spirits are good. Everything is going to be all right," Omar murmured in my ear as we were entering the room. This was a rite of passage in its own right too.

. . . .

Belsedere, 22 June 2015

One by one we entered the cellar that was used as meditation room at Il Casolare del Belsedere. Benedetta and I sat next to each other. It was the fourth day of our retreat, and we already felt part of a well-established community. Over the years, the spacious meditation room had acquired a solemnity that made us quiet and appreciative of what was about to happen. Our Maestra-shaman casually enquired whether anyone wanted to do the drumming. We looked at each other with embarrassment, for it was too great a privilege. In pure honesty, none of us felt up to the mark. To our surprise, Ambaambalaambalika stepped forward, blinking nervously. The embodiment of divine motherhood. We had expected Carlito to rise to the occasion. To his credit, he stood humbly in a corner, looking at his bare feet. Maestra-shaman gave Ambaambalaambalika a small frame drum. They would do the drumming together.

We were reminded that one should always journey with a clear intention. Our guided journeying procedure would offer us the needed protection. Maestra-shaman called, in a gentle voice that had a soothing effect, the spirits of the seven directions to be present and support us in the ceremony.

We lay down on yoga mats, using blankets and pillows. We covered our eyes and prepared to journey to the non-ordinary reality. Three deep breaths, and the powerful drumming started. From the snug darkness into which we had sunk, drumbeats seemed to dissolve into metallic and vocal sounds.

I stand in my mind at my usual starting point for shamanic journeying: the slopes of the Popocatépetl volcano. I run as quickly as I can, with greater energy than in ordinary life. I jump over turtles, geysers, melting glaciers, and sleeping whales. My step becomes lighter as the relentless drumming gradually invades my consciousness. I approach the point where I leave the ordinary reality and enter the spirit world, such a precious and inexplicable moment. I do not have a body any more. The laws of physics become a derelict set of limitations, and the force of gravity is left behind. Logic turns into a velvety flower garden.

I feel at home, in the best imaginable *sangha* ever. The volcano turns into soft dunes. I climb gigantic cacti with the ability of a monkey. There are clouds, cotton candy clouds that I lick and that are sweet to the taste. My heart throbs with the power of a million drums. I am pulled upward by a magnetic vibration through layers of these clouds. I emerge in the vast expanse of an Antarctic pebble beach. My spirit guide is waiting for me. He appears to me under the form of the Yamana people of Tierra del Fuego, the native inhabitants of the southernmost part of Argentina. "Are you my spirit guide?" I ask him each time we meet. I look at him from three different angles to make sure it is really him.

My spirit guide greets me warmly. We hug, and I stay in his embrace long enough to feel the thickness of the animal hides in which he dresses, their smoky smell, as well as his radiant and reassuring presence. There are no words between us at greeting time, though my heart systematically receives the message "You are sacred and I love you."

"Spirit guide, master, I have come today to ask you what I need to know to heal my soul. What is it that I need, medicine or action, to be able to heal my soul?" The mere fact of having the opportunity to say these words is the starting point of the healing process. My spirit guide holds my gaze lovingly. He fills me with potentiality and hope. I can sense his imperturbable patience. For many years, my spirit guide has silently looked after me, preventing accidents and instilling messages through dreams or casual synchronicities – anything, really, that would not frighten me in my ignorance of the spirit world.

The day that I climbed those stairs into the attic of an old house to take part in my first shamanic session, he was able to make himself visible to me for the first time. He had been patiently leaving bits and pieces of spiritually stimulating information to entice me to that day. It marked my birthday, my real birthday, the day on which I recognized the existence of the spirit world and started to trust it. I had a glimpse out of the matrix to an infinite world and a new and more sustainable sense of purpose, something that became more meaningful to me every day. It was impossible to get tired of this.

The cold and windswept beach disintegrates under our feet, and we float in the darkness. I see planets, stars, and constellations.

"What is this?" I ask my spirit guide. He nods at the constellations.

By connecting the dots among the stars, I can see a bear, a warrior, and a crab. My spirit guide smiles knowingly.

"You know what you have to do." He communicates telepathically, his kind smile unperturbed.

"I don't understand. What is this? Can you say it in another way, please?"

By way of response, in the middle of the dark universe in which we float, fine phosphorescent lines appear along my arms and legs, which also become slightly dotted. A small star dawns behind each of my fingertips. I look at my body in awe, as if I am becoming an electrical Christmas decoration. The matter between the dots and the stars begins to dissolve, and gently, I realize that there is nothing left of my usual self any more. Instead, I have transformed into a bright constellation. I touch my spirit guide with one of the tiny stars that I now hold in my hands, and we start orbiting the vastness of the dark universe.

I can hear my voice, but I am pure space, completely expanded into unfathomable galaxies that I can only imagine. There is no more *I*. Just a feeling of lightness, of permanence, of reaching what is and what is not. There is always the vibration of my spirit guide nearby, or rather, across everything there is. For a fraction of a second I am everything in a totality, where there is no separate *I* but merely the blessing of experiencing a state of pure energy non-attached to the physical form, what I will be one day.

The totality into which we have dissolved acquires a liquid nature and transforms into swirling water. We surf a cataract of quartz crystals and slowly plane down toward my hometown. We fly across concrete buildings that we cannot see, but we do feel the thermal radiation of living creatures as we get closer to them. My spirit guide leaves me floating close to the ceiling of a crowded room. He sits on the floor in a corner of the same room, away from the intense traffic and exalted conversation of people busy around an unconscious man lying on an operating table. It is I, lying there. I had an overdose and was taken to a hospital. I am intubated and about to undergo a gastric lavage. These people are listening to the radio, some familiar pop music that makes me feel sick. Floating up there, I experience profound love and gratitude for that team of doctors and nurses trying to bring me back to my so far bored and inexplicable life.

The drumbeats become stronger. My spirit guide has brought his whole tribe with him. They are gathered beyond a transparent wall of the operation theater. They light a bonfire. Some of them start dancing and rattling around the glowing embers, and elders are chanting a monotonous and repetitive song. A large grizzly bear comes down a mountain behind the chanting and dancing tribe. The tribe is not scared, since they know this bear well. My spirit guide welcomes him with a warm smile. The bear, in turn, rubs his muzzle against the clothes of my spirit guide. I notice that my spirit guide has charms made of conchs and rattles made of seeds. He starts a little rattling close to his head, prompting the bear to dissolve into a deep roar and enter my body on the operating table through the vibration of his energy traveling through the air.

The doctors and nurses notice a change in the vitals that they scrutinize through their medical equipment. They give each other approving nods and continue with the job of rescuing me. I am empowered by the spirit of my power bear. I have recovered the vital force that left me on the verge of succumbing to a life without a spiritual purpose. I am alive.

My spirit guide grabs my hand, and we fly across the roof into the most picture-perfect woods. My bear is happily rubbing his back against a tree. I walk to him and lie down on top of thick moss. My bear and I lock eyes until I understand that the bad times are over and that the great adventure of my life is about to begin. I am strong now, and I have clear sight. There is no need to go back to old patterns. It is impossible to grasp the iridescent, inexpedient desire because it no longer has any substance for me. It is a perfume of a past season, of something that went by and is gone. It shall no longer flourish here. I have to get out of the cave, the cave that gives me the false belief that I am alone. I can fly above all that. *Like the soaring Garuda.*

My bear is looking into me while I digest these revelations and hug him. I hug this enormous furry beast. I feel his warmth, his paws, and his heartbeat. It is the most real thing that has ever happened to me. I lie back in the moss that feels like a soft mattress. My bear licks me with a thick, warm tongue. He licks my feet, knees, genitals, heart, palms, and face. I feel blissfully bathed in the archetype of the love of animals for their offspring. I get a glimpse of fatherly love.

My spirit guide kneels next to me while his tribe continues drumming, chanting, and rattling by the bonfire in the foreground. He thrusts a hand into my solar plexus, as if thrusting a hand into a pocket. My sternum collapses and opens a jewel box inside my chest. I feel the warm and leathery hand of my spirit guide inside my organs, grasping my heart with the accuracy of a surgeon. He takes my heart out and cleans it in a stream of orange light. He removes rusty nails and screws, swarming insects, rotting cords, and opaque stones. This cleansing procedure goes on for what seems an eternity, but it feels good, as if I am receiving a massage. The drumming and chanting of the tribe makes me feel secure. Once the ritual is finished, my spirit guide puts my heart back into my chest, together with a huge red crystal that will replace all the junk that was cluttering it. He seals my chest with bright marigolds and purple stardust.

I stand up and walk by him down a path across a tropical rainforest until we reach a palace made of glass and ice. A thick forest protects the palace and its contents from unwanted visitors. Ice and tropical forest appear to coexist in harmony. Right below my navel there is a keyhole: my spirit guide gives me a bright and heavy key that fits into it. The key unlocks the vault of the glass palace manifested to us in the form of an immense library.

I understand that the book has already been written. It is the right time to take it out of the vault into the ordinary reality. The book is the medicine. *Writing the book is the medicine.* It is a healing experience that has a glowing light of its own. My spirit guide radiates encouraging energy. Recovering from addictions is part of the way, and more and more shall be revealed as I write. This is the path to find my life purpose. *Walk close to the spirits.* I sense a bright orange Hanuman in the foreground establishing a vibratory connection with me. What remains unsaid, what is purely of a vibratory nature, is of the utmost importance. All dirt shall be removed, and the loving and compassionate power of the spirits is the strongest force there is.

The drumming becomes more intense: it is the callback signal. I have to take leave of my spirit guide, my power animal, and all the helping spirits that were so generous on this journey. My spirit guide kisses me lightly on the forehead while my bear rubs his head against my shoulder.

I disintegrate back into stardust, and my particles reach far away, rolling in an infinite and all-encompassing purple bubble. I dissolve into water and fall in the form of rain all over the earth. I touch the porosity and smell the humidity of the Popocatépetl slopes over which I have just landed. I come to the surface and feel a slight pain in the back of my head, right on the spot where I have been resting against the floor during the journey. I feel my skull. My mouth is dry. I can feel my tongue inside my mouth. I can touch my teeth with the tip of my tongue. I feel the air in my lungs, the heaviness of my stomach. I am completely in my body again. I am back.

. . . .

Belsedere, 22 June 2015

I entered the meditation room with much excitement. I took a blanket and sat next to Omar. I would not do the drumming, for I preferred journeying. Omar was right: spirits were good to us. Comfortably installed on my mat, I closed my eyes and formulated my travel intention or question. Soon the drumming started.

I stand in my mind in front of a cave that I have been to in Greece and that is only accessible by sea. This where my shamanic journeys usually start and end, but I could use any other place that I like and feel connected to. As soon as I enter the cave, the ceiling breaks open. I am invited to climb a staircase that reaches the stars. I will not go down this time, I will go up. Far above the clouds and the galaxy, I reach a platform from which I am used to calling my spirit guide. He shows up without delay. He often appears to me as a mischievous child, a genderless carefree child, dressed in an old piece of gray canvas jute. He walks barefoot too. I tell him that I love him, and we warmly greet each other. I have missed him. "Spirit guide, I have come today to ask you what I need to know to heal my soul. What is it that I need, medicine or action, to be able to heal my soul?" We look at each other silently for a couple of seconds. He smiles fondly at me.

"Dear spirit guide, I need your help. I feel so sad and helpless at times."

"I know," he answers.

He warns me that I am going to experience a peculiar journey during which I will have to make crucial decisions. He will not open the path ahead of me. He will, however, stand by me, ensure my full protection, and intervene should circumstances become too challenging. I am intrigued. I might just not be up to the challenge.

"Are you ready?" my spirit guide asks warmly.

"I'm not sure if I want to do it. I'd rather have you lead the way, as we normally do," I reply in a doubtful tone.

"I'm here to guide you only. I will protect you under all circumstances."

"You've just said that I would have to do it all on my own this time."

"No. That isn't what I said. Let's get started now."

My spirit guide grabs my hand, and the next moment we land on a frozen sea. It seems to me that we have traveled for days, even weeks or months.

I am naked and walk straight ahead in the direction of the sun that is about to set in this landscape of ice. The scenery is magnificent. My spirit guide follows me carefully, as promised. I am not cold but am aware that I have somehow become insensate. I feel beautiful but desperately emotionless. I hear my spirit guide whispering inside my head that I am doing what needs to be done and that I should not be afraid. His words reach the little part of my heart that is still vibrating. He adds that he will stand by me, whatever happens. He always has and always will. His love is unconditional.

All of a sudden my body is covered in thin cuts, all of approximately the same length. They are open but do not bleed, giving me an imposing tribal appearance. My eyes turn white for a second and then return to their regular blue. I continue walking straight ahead like a porcelain automaton. I know that if I interrupt this ceremonial march, I might die, and I am not ready to die yet. My spirit guide walks by my right side, observing each of my moves and silently supporting my progress. I reach a white door, which I open without a thought about what might await me on the other side. I have become fearless because I am emotionless. Beyond the door, an ancient and powerful god of the sun is resting on a stone throne. His name is Apollo. As we are approaching him, the landscape turns into a field of cotton clouds perched in the sky. "Hello and welcome," says Apollo. "I've been waiting for you. I'm happy that you've found your way home." I have difficulty grasping what he is relating, my attention being solely directed to my cuts that are now bleeding. "Obviously, you enjoy harming yourself in diverse ways," says Apollo in a nonchalant tone. "Here is a set of knives. Which one would you like to use in order to finish your work?"

I fail to answer and stare at my bare feet in confusion. My spirit guide telepathically lets me know that Apollo can be trusted. A knife lands in my right hand without notice, causing my heart to beat faster and faster, while the excitement of using it builds up inside my lower belly. My body becomes alert, but I keep bleeding from all parts and soon enough – bang! – I pass out.

I wake up and wonder how long I have been unconscious – days, weeks, months, years maybe. A whole lifetime. I am still journeying and lying on a velvety surface of white clouds. My spirit guide is sitting beside me, chewing mysterious yellow grass. Apollo is slumped on his throne, seemingly bored to death. Another spirit joking around, I suppose. A never-ending story. I try to get up in an attempt to get noticed, only to fall again. Apollo, however, raises an eyebrow: my goal is achieved.

"Oh, she's awake," says Apollo. "You took your time, but welcome back."

"Yes," I answer inaudibly. My spirit guide strokes my hair tenderly. I find comfort in this heavenly touch.

"Your situation is simple, Benedetta. You must choose between life and death. You must hurry though. Gates will be closed in a couple of minutes. Past that stage, you must prepare yourself to die soon." This seems unreal to me. I am speechless. I am not even sure that I am having this conversation.

"Let me tell you what's going to happen, Benedetta. If you choose life, you will continue your journey from a place of healing, as if the past had never existed. What damaged you will stop controlling your life. The path will be challenging at times, but this is one of joy and fulfillment that can make you happy." A heavy silence invades the space. Apollo pauses to let his words land into my ever-fading consciousness. "On the contrary, should you favor death, which you are attracted to, you will die, cold, alone, and sick. Until that moment, you will manage to create pleasurable yet shallow diversions for yourself, but all that you will ever really do is dig your unhappy grave a little more every day." Is this real? "No one will be in a position to save you this time. So, what do you choose?"

Almost unconsciously, I stand up and walk toward the gate of life. I refuse to die like an abandoned beast. Immediately after going through this gate, my cuts stop bleeding and transform into scars, which soon evaporate. My wedding ring falls on the dusty ground and vanishes. The gate of death has disappeared. I see nothing but high desert plains surrounded by distant mountains and a glorious sun. Big birds are dancing high in the sky in some sort of joyful parade. An eagle approaches me and lands on my right shoulder. Apollo appears in front of me. "I know that you want to die sometimes," he says. "Hopefully you will learn over time to let go of this feeling. You have chosen life, and this is sealed now. It was a difficult choice. We're proud of you. You're on a new journey now, a journey of light. Enjoy it, and never forget that the spirits always answer positively when you ask for their help." I am not convinced that there is anything to be proud of. I nonetheless feel healthier. The wind blows, and shining rays of light nourish me. I am not hungry, and my foot stands firmly on the ground.

After having consulted my spirit guide, I follow the road that is presented to me. It leads toward the east and divides the high plains into two equal parts. I feel my muscles in motion and my heart expanding. I smile for the first time in years, a smile that comes from deep within. The girl with the cuts, merely an old ghost of myself, is nowhere to be seen. At some point I might no longer be able even to recall her existence. Progressing on this road of liberation, I empty myself of the stories not serving me any more, and I regain the ability to see and sense the surroundings. I stop being focused on myself. My whole being relaxes from this new perspective. I feel blessed.

A luminous shape can be seen farther down the path. I know that this is the point that I am meant to reach today. I accelerate my pace, taking my spirit guide by surprise, and start running. The shape unveils itself as an eight-sided high table made of violet fluorescent light, radiating powerful energy. A red-covered book lies on the table. I open the book, which has increased in size, and release the huge flow of light in the center of the first page. People, colors, landscapes, places are streaming out and being projected on a dynamic wave of fireworks and rainbows. They are the movement, the joy, the story, the stories within the story, the release of grievances, the adventure, the new. Alive.

Omar shows up by my side. We both look at the book, the pages of which we turn with care and excitement. The content is precious and reveals an eternal truth. We have both transformed into young children. I wear a knee-length red dress with short sleeves and a matching hair ribbon. I hold my beloved teddy bear in my arms and suck my thumb. Omar looks like a carefree and happy boy of six or seven years of age with a healthy amount of tousled hair. We are entirely absorbed in this mysterious and enchanting book. It is our own lives and stories that are being told. Writing the book is the medicine, and it can only work because we are together. Nothing of this would be possible if we were on our own. Being witnessed with love, we heal and let go of suffering, enabling us to move beyond the fragmentation of our individual egos and touch the realm of wholeness. This is a most sacred work that carries the potential of ritual death and rebirth. "Trust the spiritual path," I have often been told. This is exactly where I have landed. Omar and I look into each other's eyes and know exactly what we have to do. Words are useless when magic operates. *Writing the book is the medicine*. My heart is filled with the love of the world, which brings me to healing crystal tears.

We recover our adult shapes. The time to leave our wonderland has come. This journey has already revealed its sacred mysteries. I send love and light to my friend and let him continue his own journey. For a second, I wonder if I should go back to the gate of life. My spirit guide, who has been watching the whole scene from a short distance, indicates with a single nod that I should rather continue walking toward the east. I follow his advice. I am struck by the immensity and the possibilities of this new world that has just been disclosed to me. I am right where I am supposed to be.

I hear Maestra-shaman drumming the callback signal. As a consequence, we rejoin the magic cave at cosmic speed. I wholeheartedly thank the spirits that have supported and guided me in this journey. I hug my spirit guide before leaving this non-ordinary realm of bliss and contentment. I am still lying on the same yoga mat, covered with a blanket. I am back.

Was this real? Omar opened his eyes and looked at me with excitement, grinning like a Cheshire cat. After a couple of seconds suspended in eternity, he whispered to me, "Benedetta, writing the book is the medicine!"

"Yes, my dear, I know," I answered shyly, almost in a state of shock, "and I believe we should consider heading east for our next destination." Yes, this was really real. I smiled. Our wounds were ready to sing.

DEAD

PART 2

Leave the past behind
abandon all thoughts of the future
and let go of the present.
You are ready then to cross to the other shore.

THE DHAMMAPADA

Ulan-Ude, 7 July 2015

We left Irkutsk in the middle of the night. Benedetta and I were frustrated, but we agreed that what had happened was a trial to test our resolve. I was still under the impression that on that night of debauchery at Il Casolare, Benedetta had been impregnated by the eagle spirit that the Buryat tradition considers to be the origin of shamans. For my pathetic lack of more pressing matters to attend to, I felt an urge to take Benedetta to Buryatia and witness a miracle. I was hopeful that the appropriate events would unfold naturally once we were in Buryatia, the Land of the Shamans. Although I could find no plausible excuse to persuade Benedetta to go to this part of Siberia, we received consistent guidance that we should go there.

Guidance, however, came in unreliable forms. We both had dreams about Siberian shamans. Carlito talked copiously about Siberian shamanism. We walked to the nearby town of Baciadonne to get strawberries and found the local grocer watching *Battleship*

Potemkin on a battered TV. My roommate Indro got drunk and started singing "Ochi Chornye." So we decided to take a leap of faith and go to Siberia. In any case, it would be good for the book we were supposed to be writing.

Siberia is, however, quite large and rich with shamanic tradition. I casually mentioned Ulan-Ude, the capital of Buryatia, a couple of times, but Benedetta did not seem to acknowledge it. We discussed the possibility of journeying to consult the spirits about our Siberian expedition, but we both agreed that they would not be interested in revealing much about the possibilities of our limited three-dimensional geography. We needed to make a decision based on our intuition.

By the end of that week we were still at Il Casolare, checking flights to Russia on the Internet, when Benedetta found a YouTube video about a former Bulgarian TV presenter who had turned to shamanism. This curious woman was promoting workshops in Siberia where the participants would meet "real shamans." These dubious workshops took place twice a year, and the following one started in two weeks. This was the type of workshop that I would normally condemn: a colorful pamphlet of spiritual clichés aimed at the European middle-aged middle class who have already trekked in Patagonia and drunk champagne on Amboseli balloon safaris. However, the starting point of this workshop was Irkutsk, conveniently close to the Siberian Republic of Buryatia. I could put up with whatever fake shamanic attractions our TV presenter would concoct and then find a reason to extend our excursion to Buryatia. *Come fate into the list,*[11] Benedetta would say. Things fell into place, or so I thought.

Benedetta needed no encouragement; she was already on the phone with her lawyer, discussing money and the status of her divorce proceedings. Yes, she would need to be in Brussels the following

---

11   William Shakespeare, "Macbeth" from *The Complete Works of William Shakespeare*

week to sort out money and ex-husband matters. She would fly to Moscow from Brussels, and I would fly from Milan. We would meet at Sheremetyevo Airport to continue together to Irkutsk. She kindly invited me to stay at her place in Brussels, though I chose to spend the week in Italy near the Damanhur community. An acquaintance from my Vipassana days had a cottage there and let me use it for a few days.

My journey from Il Casolare to the cottage near Damanhur was uneventful. I spent the week dancing to my power animal, brushing up on my Russian grammar, and in contemplative meditation. At times I was depressed about the thought that this entire trip was an expensive manner of denying my loneliness, my many failures at an emotional level, and my firm interest in being peculiar. However, most of the time I was excited about the deep uncertainties that the quest for the homeland of the shaman-messiah might pose. That is, if Benedetta was in fact carrying the embryo of the hypothetical messiah. My whole raison d'être was, once again, built on a flimsy speculation, though it was providing a reasonable level of adrenaline without jeopardizing my two years, nine months, and sixteen days of sobriety.

I resolved to sit in meditation for longer hours and prayed to be rid of depression as well as of excitement. I was hoping to achieve a sustainable level of contentment to be a good traveling companion for my friend. I spent the entire day and night before my flight to Moscow fasting and in meditation. *What remains unsaid, what is purely of a vibratory nature, is of the utmost importance.* Recalling my last night in Amsterdam, this time I took every spiritual measure to prevent visits by unwanted ghosts. I did little journeying, though all the signs that I received from the helping spirits were encouraging. I stopped doubting myself, one day at a time.

Our reunion at Sheremetyevo Airport was epic. Although we had only been apart for one week, we felt that years had passed. We chatted for hours while waiting for our connection to Irkutsk.

Benedetta gulped an alarming number of vodka shots, I had *chornyy chai* in a fake Lomonosov tea set, and we shared blinis with orange marmalade. We also shared this curious approach to foreign lands: we flew unreliable local airlines, never stayed at international hotel chains, shopped and ate local, learned at least a few words of the language of the land we were in – at one time I could count up to twenty in Uyghur. Sitting at the airport's Shokoladnitsa Café was an act of affirmation of our search for diversity. We looked at the passengers having sandwiches at Subway with a little contempt.

After the vodka settled in her system, Benedetta came up with an incredible story about a Russian lawyer helping her to obtain a Russian visa waiver based on false medical grounds, at a hefty price. A very bad solution, considering that her visa would be scrutinized not only upon arrival in Russia, but also in each city or town where we would sleep. Apparently, Russian visas for EU passport holders took thirty days to be granted. Learning that Argentine passport holders needed no visa to enter the Russian Federation for up to ninety days, Benedetta did not have the courage to tell me that our Siberian expedition would be delayed due to her. I seemed too eager to get to Siberia as soon as possible – true, because I wanted to bring the shaman-messiah in her womb to his shamanic homeland.

The Russian lawyer with an improbable name, something like Abraxas, Merlin, or Siegfried, was also taking care of her divorce. Most likely ripping her off. I would not be surprised if he were in collusion with Tony, the ex-husband. Why was Benedetta surrounded by abusive men? And more importantly, was I one of them? I was relieved to hear that Tony had not shown up in Brussels. I was worried that there could be some last-minute farewell lovemaking that would blur the legitimacy of the shaman-messiah. I felt horrible, but instead of coming clean and telling Benedetta my hidden reasons, I got angry. Bad Karma: 1, Spirit League: 0.

A brand new Aeroflot Airbus landed us non-stop in beautiful Irkutsk, "the Paris of Siberia," five and a half hours and three time zones later. We had wanted to take a lesser-known airline that would fly Tupolevs and make at least two stopovers, but the hassles of changing airports and unpredictable schedules would put at risk our timely arrival at the workshop. Arriving in Irkutsk on time for the first morning "Shamanic Orientation Conference" (*sic*) was a *conditio sine qua non*. To compensate for our craving for unpredictability, we made independent accommodation arrangements at a Siberian homestay. This meant lodging in a room in a family house, sharing one meal with the hosts, and mingling with the locals. The full *sibirski* experience.

And cheap, by the way. Benedetta and I had made plans to travel without a fixed destination for up to three months, starting at Il Casolare, and let the shamanic ebb take us to wherever it would be revealed more appropriate for our book project. I had roughly estimated that we would spend half of that time in expensive countries and the other half in more volatile economies, where our savings would last longer. So far I was within budget but would welcome any opportunity to spend my money efficiently and sustainably.

The financial institutions of the developed economies and those of my native Argentina were on reasonably good terms at the time, though the past had taught me that at any minute these relationships could deteriorate. A practical result of that would be my inability to withdraw money out of my Argentina bank account from foreign ATMs. Also, Argentine pesos are not the currency of choice at exchange bureau points in Central Asia. For that reason, I had left Argentina with two widely accepted credit cards and as much cash in US dollars as I was allowed to take out of the country without triggering reporting obligations. I gave half of my cash to Benedetta in Italy so she could deposit it in her bank account in Brussels. I could then withdraw that money from ATMs using her EU Basel Banking Norms Compliant Financial Institution card. Benedetta brought traveler's checks tucked in her money belt by way of an emergency fund that we could access in case of a catastrophe. We thought that we had safely covered access to funding under all weather.

The workshop hosted in Irkutsk by Bogdana Bilyana Dragovna, the Bulgarian former TV presenter, at the eponymous hotel (formerly known as Intourist) was indeed a tourist trap. In turn, the Irkutsk Hotel was a mammoth concrete post-Soviet example of architectural brutalism that did little to cheer us up. Irkutsk celebrates profusely the epic life of astronaut Yuri Gagarin, the first human being to journey into outer space. The city has honored this adventurous man by copiously naming streets, bridges, squares, schools, and most imaginable items after this hero of the Soviet Union. The Irkutsk Hotel proudly sits on the Gagarina Boulevard, with a fine view over the Angara River. The Shamanic Orientation Conference, however, took place in the Yuri Gagarin Room, a windowless dungeon in the deep bowels of the Irkutsk Hotel, where we were shown a lengthy PowerPoint. Halfway through it, we were depressed beyond recovery.

I was gaping into the void, absent-mindedly wondering if the first space journey of Yuri Gagarin would have borne any resemblance to a shamanic journey, and whether it was only by coincidence that the first human ever to journey to outer space was a son of Siberia, the Land of Shamans. It was in the middle of these ruminations that I caught Benedetta fidgeting with an imaginary *nécessaire* in what I deemed a Pavlovian classical conditioning movement to retrieve some equally imaginary sertraline. The situation demanded a summary escape plan. Since there were no windows, I smartly figured out our only chance of breaking free from confinement was through the only door. The moment I grabbed Benedetta by the arm, she sprang to her feet and we left the dark room unnoticed, with a synchronicity of movement that could not have worked better had it been rehearsed. We sat silently for a while at the Nostalgia Kafe, blankly staring at the extravagant fish tanks. By lunchtime we had decided to elope to the Autonomous Republic of Buryatia.

We left Irkutsk for Ulan-Ude in the middle of the night. We took the train that runs the Mascvá–Pekín stretch in seven days, though our trip in this part of Siberia only took eight hours. Although she did not speak a word of Russian, Benedetta managed to upgrade us to a first-class cabin after a hushed negotiation with a *pravodnitsa*, the bossy matrons who rule life in each wagon. It was still dark when I left Benedetta tucked in the cozy cabin berth. A few minutes later I brought her a glass of hot *chai* from the wagon samovar, only to find her happily snoring.

The sun was rising on one side of the train, while the moon, immense *Lunáa*, was setting on the opposite side. I was absorbed in the moment, lost in appreciation of the miracle that the sun still rose each morning. I felt a big wave of gratitude toward the spirits for creating that little space for me to acknowledge the vastly obvious fact that the sun rises every day. I then noticed a fellow traveler, a young backpacker who had been observing me with apparent compassion. She was so young, so fresh, so not yet damaged by what life might bring. I had to wipe a few tears from the corners of my eyes before our eyes could meet, and then we smiled. Without saying a word, she approached as if to kiss me, though what she actually did was to take out her earbuds and place them in my ears. I looked at her and slowly closed my eyes as a means to signal that I yielded to her move. Soon, melancholic ambient music flooded my consciousness. A deep, funereal voice appeared at times, as if glimpsing the fugitive moon with the same anxiety that I was experiencing at its imminent disappearance. Still without saying a word, she scribbled a few words on a minuscule piece of paper and put it in my hand. She held my hand in hers for a few seconds, long enough for me to feel the warmth of her palms and the pulse in her wrist. She took back her earbuds and sauntered back to the third-class wagon, lest the *pravodnitsa* scold her. Written on the piece of paper, the track that she made me listen to, "The Hills of Buryatia," was music inspired by the wild Siberian landscapes that we were traversing at that precise moment. We never saw the mysterious angel-backpacker again. Had this encounter actually happened? Were it not for the note that she gave me, I would have doubted it. Benedetta and I took an immediate liking to this music.

The *bagón restorán* was not yet open, so I took my *chai* to the corridor. We were riding the hub between Russia and the East. Although the train staff was mostly Russian, we had left European Russia a long while ago. I took a walk down the wagons to second and third class to find entire families of mixed Kazaks, Uzbeks, Mongols, and Uyghurs waking up to this new day on the train, greeting me with a mix of *priviet*s and *assalamu alaikum*s. A Han-Chinese old lady was eating out of a porcelain bowl. Homemade *pirozhki* were distributed by busy mothers to their children. A line was already forming behind the samovar to brew *chai* and the occasional instant noodle soup. The ubiquitous smell of smoked *omul* was a reminder of our close proximity to Lake Baikal. I felt the serenity and the contentment of being in the right place at the right time and gave thanks for the blessing of being in this millenary caravan.

This is one of the most scenic parts of the *Sibirski Ekspres*. As the sun rose, we bordered the southern shore of majestic Lake Baikal. Everything in it is superlative: it is the world's deepest lake and contains one-fifth of all fresh water on the planet. We were riding between the bluest waters of Baikal and a wall of rocky, tree-covered cliffs. Tiny settlements of wooden cottages or *dachas* appeared every now and then, painted with bright colors, submerged in a blue mist.

Several years ago in Buenos Aires I had an episode of acute stress that developed into pneumonia. That was only a couple of years before the overdose. My physician explained that more likely than not I was in need of a break from it all and suggested a prolonged vacation. I arranged to take four months off from my job of the time, but instead of doing the smart thing and relaxing at a beach, I traveled solo in Central Asia. It was stressful, but different from my everyday-life stress. Being buried in the anonymity of a remote part of the world proved soothing. I took Thomas Mann's *The Magic Mountain* with me. I wanted to write a novel of epic proportions. My main character would be a traveler, an atrocious mix of Siddhartha, Hans Castorp, and Sal Paradise, who would bring his enlightened self to the steppes to prove how life is but a futile experience. A pompous story, very much detached from my own life. *The book is the medicine. Writing the book is the medicine.*

The way in which I had changed had many facets, not limited to my literary aspirations. I stopped visiting the big capitals of the world and retreated to more meaningful places. Although I still lived in Buenos Aires, my world had become friendlier. Skyscrapers, marble halls, glass elevators, small talk, signature cuisine, potted palm trees: I got nauseated. Lately, my life had revolved around my garden, a carefully selected group of people, and local vegan eateries around my place. I had downsized to towns off the beaten track that had a soul I could tune into without being fried: Boissucanga, Yarinacocha, Phnom Penh, Urmiri. I roamed a paradise that I was only starting to understand.

Benedetta was coming down the corridor with a swollen face, her hair a total mess, a collage of different garments tossed on top of each other, and bare feet. She could have been mistaken for a lunatic just escaped from the madhouse. The *pravodnitsa* scurried after her with a pair of slippers in her hand. Benedetta found me and flashed the freshest smile.

"This is the most beautiful thing in the world! I'm so happy!"

"Yes, I know. I'm so happy too," I replied, as I bowed to say *spasiba* to the *pravodnitsa* and helped Benedetta with her slippers. "Can I buy you coffee? The dining wagon will be open just in time to have breakfast before we arrive in Ulan-Ude."

"That would be spectacular."

We walked arm in arm up the corridor toward the *bagón restorán*. The menu was in *russki* and *angliski,* though the waitresses spoke only Russian. My veganism had to yield to the limited choices. We held the coffee cups with both hands to appreciate the warmth and homey smell. We devoured the bread and scrambled eggs with gratitude and enthusiasm.

We arrived in Ulan-Ude around mid-morning. We instantly fell in love with UU, as the local hips appeared to call it. We found a homestay with a Buryat family at a spartan apartment. Upon careful inspection we concluded that at least Olga and her husband, in their early forties, and the old *babushka* living with them, professed Tibetan Buddhism. Their two teenage sons ignored us; their spiritual leanings were unfathomable.

Homestay in Siberia appeared to be very much a mother's responsibility. The father went to work early, the children were at school or hanging out with friends, so it was ultimately Olga who took care of us. The accommodating party was responsible for registering the guests with the local authorities, a custom probably inherited from Soviet times. Dear good Olga offered to make photocopies of our passports, fill in the *migratsionnaya forma*, and deliver the documents to the Local Migration Office by mail after having them scrutinized by the post office clerk. We were happy to keep a prudent distance between the immigration authorities and Benedetta. We let Olga take care of the red tape.

Olga was extremely busy, what with being a schoolteacher and also a part-time seamstress to make ends meet. She woke up earlier than us to present a full-course meal for breakfast. Benedetta and I sat at a sunny corner of the tiny kitchen; fruit, *kasha*, toasts and blinis with *tvorog* and marmalade, as well as leftover *pelmeni*, were artfully piled on the minuscule table. Her husband and children had all had breakfast earlier; we never saw them in the mornings. She stood busily between the sink and the stove, doing the dishes and pouring endless hot water from the samovar into our teapot.

It was also a good time for her to practice French with Benedetta. Olga was a courageous entrepreneur, always curious and willing to learn. She proudly displayed postcards sent by previous guests from the four corners of the world thanking her for her legendary hospitality. She regretted that the economic reform that brought wealth to many in the large cities of the Russian Federation had not filtered down to her remote abode. She joyfully explained that when she was a young girl, her mother took her to ballet and French lessons that were offered by the government to all residents of the Soviet Union. Nowadays she had to work hard to pay for her children's English classes and dental procedures.

We happily agreed on settling in UU for a while. Although our sleeping quarters were rather dismal, we found a peaceful *letnii sad*, a summer garden, down Lenina street, where we could sit for hours, have endless *chornyy chai* and light meals, and enjoy the delightful breeze of the brief Siberian summer.

We made shallow acquaintance with other patrons who came for *chai* at the garden, all the fault of our shallow knowledge of their language. Our limitations did not prevent the Buryats from warming up to us, though. We were introduced to an elderly professor of literature with whom we exchanged enthusiastic thoughts about the beauty of Siberia and how we were enjoying its serenity. He stood up gravely and recited from Nekrasov:

The capitals are rocked with thunder
Of orators in wordy feuds,
But in the depths of Russia, yonder,
An age-old awful silence broods,
Only the wind in wayside willows,
Coming and going, does not cease;
And corn-stalks touch in curving billows
The earth that cherishes and pillows,
Through endless fields of changeless peace.[12]

---

12 *Modern Russian Poetry*, chosen and translated by Babette Deutsch and Avrahm Yarmolinsky (New York: Harcourt, Brace and Company, 1921)

It was certainly these endless fields of changeless peace that Benedetta and I were tuning into without fully realizing their healing power. The days at UU came as an unexpected gift. We were like patients at a Waldsanatorium, fighting tuberculosis with the gentle source of energy that surrounded us. Like a good mother or father, our helping spirits were feeding us nutritious spiritual food to strengthen us for what tomorrow might bring.

I started to feel available to listen to the stories that Benedetta wanted to share, especially the bits and pieces of her life that she casually dropped into the conversation and that I had not paid attention to before. I was learning to encourage her to share more. She had some sad but profoundly enlightening stories to tell that revealed more about her spiritual path. I stopped thinking that she was a bourgeois who turned to shamanism out of boredom – that had probably more to do with myself. She was, as most of us are, a hurt child who had not yet felt requited love. *The suffering of the ill person could evoke pity by a spirit. In this way, a shaman is sometimes created.* [13]

A few days went by. Some people started nodding at us when we walked arm in arm down Lenina street on our way to and from our homestay, the exchange bureau at Hotel Geser, and the *letnii sad.* The literature professor offered Benedetta a small *buké* of flowers.

We needed to identify shamanic practitioners to engage in activities with them. We knew that shamans are reluctant to share information with strangers and that only when a firm commitment to stay and learn for a long time is made can a flow of communication happen. We were no anthropologists, we had no scholarship money, no relevant academic credentials, but we were traveling in good faith and felt uplifted by the wide array of possibilities that the Buryat wilderness could bring.

Also, we wanted to review the quaint notes we had about our experience in Italy and start gathering material to write about

---

13   Michael Harner, *Cave and Cosmos: Shamanic Encounters with Another Reality*

Siberia. We needed to feel that we were actually writing the book that had launched us into this expedition. After our first hours at the *letnii sad*, I started feeling more grounded. We were no dilettante tourists any more; we were researching and writing a book.

We identified an *etnografichesky muzey* that displayed a shaman hut with totems in the yard and teepees of the Tungus people of Siberia. We interviewed museum staff, only to discover that our interviewing skills in Russian got us nowhere beyond being photographed by the teepees with the friendly staff.

We sat at the Hodegetria Cathedral in an attempt to befriend locals willing to discuss spiritual matters, also to no avail. Even after it was obvious that we would obtain no intelligence from our Hodegetria operation, I continued to sit in meditation in front of the icon of the Lady of the Way. Benedetta was surprised about my willingness to visit the cathedral, knowing my deeply rooted aversion to Catholicism. I could not stop thinking that the Lady had also been impregnated by an eagle spirit and given birth to a powerful shaman. If I could convince the Lady to give me some direction while journeying, I could achieve the most spectacular ecumenical cooperation. But I was in no position to disclose this to Benedetta without bringing up the shaman-messiah in her womb.

We made two long visits to the Ivolginsk Datsan monastery, the center of Buddhism in the Russian Federation. It was not far from UU but not close enough to walk. This place provided an atmosphere of serenity that I learned to enjoy and to look forward to on ensuing visits. We made a first reconnaissance survey under the guise of a tourist excursion arranged at UU.

On our second visit we hired a driver, and once in the monastery we sat to meditate and pray. Later that day we had a preliminary conversation with a monk who spoke a little English and was willing to communicate in spite of our limited ability to reciprocate in Russian. We vaguely explained that we were researching spiritual matters, but the nuances were lost in translation and the monk deemed us to be Buddhist pilgrims. As a matter of fact, I had studied, adhered, and lived according to the Four Noble Truths. I have my fair share of *sak yants*, Thai Buddhist sacred tattoos that my friend Pak had suggested as a form of divine protection. I had stoically sat at Thai temples and endured being inked with a bamboo and steel needle by a monk with a firm belief in their magical qualities. However, the fact that Thai Buddhism is Theravada and that, to the best of my knowledge, Buryat Buddhism is a variation of Mahayana meant my tattoos might not have worked in our favor. We left the monastery with mixed feelings; we were happy to have made a connection, but we were not happy about having misled the monk. The language barrier was proving too difficult to overcome.

Back in the cool shade of our *letnii sad,* we indulged in lemon tea and sweet *gogol-mogol*. In fact, I ate most of the *gogol-mogol*, because Benedetta was affected by nausea. I was totally absorbed by her health and tried to follow her bowel movements and morning vomits with the attention to detail of an anthropologist. It was most decidedly a sign that the shaman-messiah was incarnated and kicking.

On the book front we were silent and slightly perplexed. We started wondering whether we had reached a dead end. We journeyed routinely to ask for directions and information from our helping spirits. The reply was monolithic: *Writing the book is the medicine.* That was too powerful a message to give up. We were discussing this matter when we were surprised by the arrival of a young Buryat woman who addressed us in English.

Bolormaa was the eldest daughter of the owners of the *letnii sad* where we stayed most of the day, scheduling, postponing, and rescheduling our activities. She was a tall indigenous Tungu of Mongolian complexion, with high cheekbones and glittery black eyes. Bolormaa lived and studied folk music in Irkutsk and was back in UU to visit her family for the summer. We learned that Bolormaa was a Mongolian name intermingled with Tibetan that meant "Crystal Mother." More importantly, Bolormaa spoke decent English.

We clung to Bolormaa like castaways in the middle of a storm. We acknowledged that Crystal Mother had been sent by the spirits to encourage us in our shamanic-literary quest. However, the actual nature of her gifts, beyond her role as interpreter, was still obscure to us. I made convoluted associations between the arrival of Bolormaa and my meditations on the Lady of the Way that had Benedetta in tears of laughter for my speculative praise of the Orthodox Church. Benedetta in turn had her share of abstruse associations bringing up the "crystal" nature of Bolormaa's name and the quartz crystals used by some shamans for divination. I could not help mentioning that Nirvana Chrystal was a White Widow cannabis hybrid that, many years ago, I had abused, repeatedly causing me visions that I was neither able to decipher nor remember.

Bolormaa laughed warmly at our excitement. She explained that she was busy catching up with family and friends in UU, visiting her beloved grandfather in his *dacha* in the woods, and participating in religious ceremonies pertaining to the summer season. However, she would be happy to drive us to the Ivolginsk Datsan monastery the following day and act as interpreter for our friend the monk. Seeing that we were engaged in intense conversation, her mother brought us fresh *chornyy chai* and warmed up the samovar. Bolormaa lingered with us for quite some time, as if enjoying the chance to talk to strangers, or just out of the good-heartedness with which her family and her fellow Buryats had already showered us.

Access to language would bring clarity to our relationship with the *sangha* at Ivolginsk Datsan. I had to face the moral decision whether to disclose to the monk that we were not, formally, Buddhists. Over Uzbek dinner at the trendy Chai Khana, Benedetta and I quickly agreed to come clean to the monk upon our next visit to the temple. The Chai Khana was beyond our budget, but we felt like celebrating the promising arrival of Bolormaa in our lives.

We hoped that the doors of perception would open slightly through her intervention.

The monk at Ivolginsk Datsan monastery turned out to be a close assistant of the head lama. He cackled lovingly when Bolormaa explained that we were not Buddhist pilgrims and gave us a tender look. *Live your life well in accord with the Way – avoid a life of distraction. A life well lived leads to contentment, both now and in the future.*[14] "Did he actually say that?" I asked Benedetta, but she was unreachable, deep in her emotions and on the brink of tears. Definitely pregnant.

Benedetta and I listened attentively, made notes, recordings, and sketches. We brought offerings to the Buddha and the monks, shared *tsampa* soup at the monastery, and started spending longer sessions in meditation when at home. Over the following days we learned from first-hand experience that the Buryat have embraced Buddhism, though they have retained and integrated magical practices that have been with them since older times. In blissful syncretism, Buryat Buddhism assimilated traditional folk ceremonies, rituals, and beliefs associated with honoring the spirits of the land, mountains, rivers, and trees. *Walk close to the spirits.* That was what the Buryat Buddhists were doing. We had gotten to the point where we could start enquiring about shamanism.

We had just reached this juncture when Bolormaa announced that she was going away for a few days. She had to drive to Irkutsk to take her grandfather back to his *dacha* in the woods outside UU. Benedetta and I assumed that the grandfather was paying a visit to a doctor in Irkutsk, though we later realized that we had misunderstood Bolormaa's explanation. We were going to be left on our own, as far as efficient communication was concerned, until Bolormaa's return, so we sat at the *letnii sad* and discussed how we could best use the following couple of days. Getting away from UU to visit the spirits of nature in the surrounding area was high on our priority list. We could

---

14   *The Dhammapada*, n.d.

take our notes, continue working on the book draft, and do some extensive journeying and meditation. We were thrilled.

"My dear, listen to this," said Benedetta as she artfully stuffed sauerkraut inside a rolled blini with one hand and held the *Lonely Planet* guide in the other. "'The eastern shore of Lake Baikal is some of Buryatia's wildest and least explored territory, not only untrodden by backpackers but also relatively uncolonized by Buryats and Russians. Farther north there isn't the slightest trace of civilization for hundreds of kilometers.' We have found our paradise!" Bolormaa's parents were happy to arrange our escapade to the Buryat wilderness. It was decided that Melscho, a distant relative of Bolormaa's grandfather, would take us in his boat down the Selenga River into Lake Baikal and leave us somewhere on the eastern shore. We were going to camp in the vicinity of Bolormaa's grandfather's *dacha*. We brought provisions for four days; Bolormaa would pick us up on the last day, and we would have a chance to meet her grandfather. A perfect plan.

On the day before Bolormaa's departure to Irkutsk, she offered to drive us again to the Ivolginsk Datsan monastery. She was going to light an oil lamp, burn incense, bring flowers, and pray for a safe journey. We brought our small share of offerings and sat there for a good couple of hours. The ride back happened in silence. The sky was overcast, and the clouds were hanging like a huge silver Mongol tent spread over the horizon. As we were nearing our homestay, the most extraordinary thing happened. "Are you interested in shamans?" Bolormaa asked out of the blue. Benedetta and I had had lengthy discussions about what would be the most respectful way to approach the subject, knowing how reserved people who live in shamanic cultures are about divulging their practices. Bolormaa laughed at our surprise and explained that she had heard us mentioning the word "shaman" between ourselves several times over the past days.

Bolormaa explained that her grandfather, Bulagat Buchacheyev, was a most revered shaman. She had mentioned that he was in

Irkutsk "delivering medicine." Of course she had; Benedetta and I had wrongly assumed that he had gone to see a doctor. He was in Irkutsk to assist his shaman-brothers in certain ceremonies and see old Buryat friends living in Irkutsk who had asked for help. He was supposed to make a cameo appearance at a workshop organized by a Bulgarian woman, though he had to cancel to see to the child of a factory worker who was seriously ill. Eliade's description of the Buryat shamanic initiation came to my mind: *If a rich man and a poor man summon you at the same time, go to the poor man and afterward to the rich man.*[15]

Michael Harner says that in shamanic work it is important to be on the lookout for the occurrence of positive synchronicities, for they are signals that power is working to produce effects far beyond the normal bounds of probability. It was the synchronicities that finally made me surrender to the book project and stop doubting the spirits.[16] *Act as if...* is one of the slogans in twelve-step recovery groups. Act as if I believe, until I start believing. Benedetta and I entered a perfect space where our actions finally aligned with our life purpose.

That perfect space did not last long. It was a cold and gray morning in UU, and the middle of the night in my hometown's time zone. People in Buenos Aires were sleeping, recovering strength for a day ahead at the office, at the gym, at the yoga studio. Coffee would start brewing in their kitchens in a few hours, lovers would part, parents would see their children off to school, newspapers would be sold, and the sun would warm up plants on balconies. I felt a sudden pang of nostalgia.

Through Bolormaa we met a young Mongol of mixed Buryat origin named Ganbaatar. His name loosely translates into "Steel Hero" in English. He lived in Ulaanbaatar, where he worked for a French tour operator; his job was driving tourists to *ger* camps, the

---

15   Mircea Eliade, *Shamanism: Archaic Techniques of Ecstasy*

16   Michael Harner, *Cave and Cosmos: Shamanic Encounters with Another Reality*

traditional Mongolian round nomad tents, where they stayed for a week to experience *la Mongolie profonde*: camel rides, throat singing, nights in the desert, and drinking *ayrag*, a spirit made of fermented mare's milk. Ganbaatar and I started communicating in French, and the language provided the basis for an incipient friendship. Ganbaatar was looking for a plot of land around UU to set up a *ger* camp and start his own independent business. Would I like to come with him on his motorcycle the following day so that he could show me around? Who could say no to a ride on a motorcycle in the Siberian steppe with a Mongolian steel hero? Aren't these the rare and precious rewards in exchange for a life that does not conform to capitalist heteronormativity? Benedetta smartly pointed out that she was the native French speaker. Would there be something beyond the pleasures of discoursing in *la belle langue* that Ganbaatar and I were interested in? Certainly. I had, however, been successfully keeping my romantic obsessions at bay since Il Casolare, and I valued the serenity that this had brought me.

As a consequence, I declined Ganbaatar's motorcycle excursion invitation. I knew very well about all the love that I was looking for all the time in the wrong places. I could then avoid that impulse most of the time, one day at a time. Ganbaatar might not be an unwanted ghost sent to provoke my fall, but a day roaming in the wilderness together, getting to know each other by grace of *ayrag* and swimming naked in the icy Selenga River, only for him to evaporate on the morrow to chase wild camels in the Gobi, would take away my serenity. In exchange for a fleeting brush with the millenary lifestyle of the son of Chinggis Khan, I would spend the following month daydreaming a life with Ganbaatar in Patagonia, where we would run a *ger* camp and live happily ever after. This was what codependency did to me, and, like we say in Spanish, I had watched this movie too many times. There was no antidote: I had to abstain from guys who were not available and not willing to share the lifestyle that I pursued. "Aren't you a nomad of your own kind, chasing spirits in the parallel reality?" asked Benedetta. Yes, but I do it while I am waiting to settle down. I want to write a book and find true love – did I say that earlier?

To compensate somehow, I took a long, solitary walk down the Selenga shore with the intention of meditating in the woods, but ended up with a bottle of freshly made *ayrag*. I drank it all. I smoked counterfeit Chinese Marlboro Reds that made me sick. I sat under a birch tree and started listening to "The Hills of Buryatia" again. I had been obsessed by this music since my encounter with the angel-backpacker. I took a few deep breaths and entered into a music-induced trance. I could feel my pelvic floor throbbing with each breath, and an electric vibration at the root chakra that sits loosely in that area. Like a tongue of fire, the *muladhara* or root chakra expanded toward the *svadhisthana*, or sacral chakra, immediately above. I could sense the sacral chakra rotating like a luminous compact disc, emitting electric sparkles that brought warmth to my genitals. For a second I tried to get out of the trance, but I realized that I had gone too deep into it, and coming all the way back required an effort that I was too lazy to undertake at that moment. I fell deep into the vibratory, seemingly infinite loop of those Hills. I felt entirely out of my body and floating in music. No – rather than floating, I felt like a seal trapped in a fisherman's net made of tone and atmosphere that was sucking all my listening attention like a vampire can suck blood. I yielded again to the nebulous music with some irritation, because it was entirely missing beats. My *svadhisthana* chakra started pulsing for a rhythm that was nowhere near.

I was trapped in a net of exasperating desire, where there would be no climax. Edging is the term most commonly used for that experience. It is a masturbation technique that involves coming nearly to climax, then purposefully stopping sexual stimulation in order to delay the same, so that the ultimate climax will be more intense. That is, of course, if there is an ultimate climax at all. Super-stimulation creates abnormally large influxes of dopamine to the reward centers of the brain. Now that I abstained from substances, I was very much afraid that I had become addicted to all possible manual techniques that could result in a release of dopamine similar to the one triggered by substances. Edging does it.

Edging is a widespread sexual practice in the bondage and discipline, sadism and masochist scene, commonly known as the BDSM scene. In this case, one person agrees to hand over control of his orgasm to another party, the dominant. The person about to be dominated is generally bound or restrained to achieve the purpose, and then the ordeal begins. There is always a safe word, utterance of which by the submissive indicates that they wish for immediate release. A respected player will, however, only resort to the safe word if he deems that serious damage to his health or life is imminent.

There are all sorts of gadgets to perform an edging session: cock-rings (leather, rubber, silicone, steel, or neoprene), cock-rings with attached ball-rings, finger-fuck textured latex gloves, dildos, and plugs (inflatable, vibrating, or rotating), speculums (they come in three sizes), bondage hooks, prostate stimulators (with up to seven speeds), anal balls (30 to 60 mm), urethral sounds (stainless steel, 4 mm up to 15 mm; standard, ribbed, or vibrating), Guyon Curves stainless steel sounding sets (not for the faint-hearted), hollow and/or rippled silicone or steel penis sticks and penis plugs, with or without glans-ring, sets of corkscrew silicone sounds, cock-locks with cock-ring, leather lockable solid chastity belts, about a dozen types of chastity cages, steel ball-weights (starting at 20 mm but hey, you aim at 70 mm), steel ball-splitters with frame, electro-stimulating units (high-spec, multipack, and remote-controlled) and their associated electro butt-plugs, prostate rockers, electro-stim intruders, metallic cock loops, electro-stim silicone balls and inflatable gold-plated anal probes, scrotal loops, bipolar clamp electrodes, unipolar clamp sets, tadpole flexi egg probes, bipolar "depth charge" dildos, Sacksling electros, electro ball-stretchers, and electro-stim jack-strokers. The latter come with their own sets of cables and adapters, plus sterile lubricant sachets or sterilizing wipes. There are about a dozen vacuum pumps for penises and nipples and around a hundred types of lube (water-, oil-, or silicone-based). A serious player will not do without condoms and gloves, douches and enemas, gags and blindfolds, truncheons, crops and canes, whips, floggers and paddles, bondage gear, rope, cuffs, restraints, and collars. If this is going to be a long session, you may wish to insert a silicone catheter (14 to 18 mm) into the penis to be edged, so there will be no need to stop to pee. This may come as a shock to some, but to others these are essential items kept at home next to the Advil, Band-Aids, and shampoo.

Because of the wide array of possible maneuvers, there is no way to anticipate how long an edging session may last. Four to six hours is not unusual, as I have experienced it. After all that time, the dominant may decide that the player does not deserve to orgasm at all, which is called orgasm denial. If he does, the player may be masturbated further to achieve two, three, or four more orgasms in a row, which is called post-milking torture. The dominant may alternatively decide to give the player a ruined orgasm. This happens when the player reaches the point of no return, but the dominant suddenly removes contact with the penis, meaning that there is ejaculation without orgasm. The player is physically drained but remains in a heightened state of sexual arousal. This usually happens as a way to satisfy the dominant's desires to erotically humiliate, though the one being dominated experiences the most explosive neural connections at the brain level. There must be some sort of parallel between this BDSM practice and tantra, though I claim no spiritual alibi to justify my own expedition into these sexual practices.

How many hours, how many dominants, how many dark alleys of the brain flooded with unusual stimuli, how much pain, how much ecstasy, how hard have I tried to escape the dull unfairness of life. How many mistakes, how many wrong turns, how many times have I been bitten by vampires, how many pieces of my soul have been shredded and lost. And this ethereal music was bringing fire to my sacral chakra, and I was again swamped in dopamine as the foreboding overtones of ambient music promised to edge me for ever and ever in this and in any other conceivable reality. I made a giant effort to move the throbbing of my chakras up my spine to my shoulder blade, into my biceps. It left a trail of scorching fire, and my soul was howling. I had a vision of red-eyed bats hanging upside down from the branches of birch trees, madly rubbing against each other with their webbed wings making a disturbing noise, masturbating and covering me entirely in thick coats of bat cum. I was still deep enough in a trance so as not to be able to open my eyes, though my biceps had regained control of my arm and started viciously masturbating me. Some distant level of consciousness and a burning pain made me realize that I might be hurting myself, but the unforgiving music was binding my soul with relentless ferocity.

The irony of life lit up like a bonfire. I hated this trip, I loathed the book project, I could not stand Benedetta one more day. I wanted to be someone else in a distant part of the world. I wanted a fresh start. I gave up on this quest. I had made too many mistakes, and I was ready to die. The cheap tobacco that I had smoked reeked in my nostrils, and the sourness of the *ayrag* that I had drunk came rushing up my throat. I came and I came and I came again in violent spurts of thick cum. My root and sacral chakras withered as I clenched my anus for enhanced intensity. I howled like a wild animal, and then I ground my teeth and exhaled a thick cloud of smoke through my nose. I regained consciousness and found myself half-naked lying against the birch tree, covered in vomit and saliva and cum. I looked incredulously at my dirty hands, as if they were covered in someone else's blood. Two loggers had sat down, axes in hands, at a prudent distance to observe me. As soon as we made eye contact, they stood up in shame and scurried into the woods behind them.

I crawled to the shore to vomit. I washed my face and hands in the bitterly cold Selenga and walked silently home. So there I was, once again, detached from it all. I had no lover in bed, no children to send to school, my kitchen was empty of perishables while I was on the road, no work to go to, no plants to water. I had a boat to catch down the Selenga to Lake Baikal, my laptop, sketches of a Buddhist temple in an Asian republic nobody at home had ever heard about, a tent to sleep in for the next few days, and a small backpack with all my worldly possessions. Would I ever be able to find my way back into the legion that was sleeping in Buenos Aires? Perhaps I had been cut out from my hometown for ever. Perhaps I was awake for a reason larger than a lover in bed and morning coffee. Or perhaps it was just a flashback. Two years, nine months, and twenty-nine days. I hated being sober.

"Are you feeling okay, my dear?" asked Benedetta, rescuing me from my thoughts.

"Okay, yes. We're going to camp on the Baikal shore. Isn't it an adventure? I'm just worried about the cold at night."

Melscho was an elderly man, a son of the Revolution. His name, not uncommon among the Mongols at the time of his birth, was composed of the first letters of Marx, Engels, Lenin, Stalin, and Choibalsan, the latter being a leader of the Mongolian People's Republic. Melscho was given lengthy directions by Bolormaa, who drove us to the Selenga River wooden pier, where we boarded Melscho's boat. "*Sputnik*" was inscribed in colorful Cyrillic letters on the stern. It was slightly larger than a dinghy, with a wooden hull and a modest outboard motor. I was alarmed at the fragility of our vessel and could not help recalling the dark atmosphere of "The Drunken Boat," the poem that Benedetta had declaimed in Olga's kitchen. I kept my preoccupation to myself. It was probably just me feeling fragile.

One could read the history of the world in Melscho's creased face and hands. A life of hard labor and a witness to dramatic changes in his homeland. He smoked cheap Kósmac cigarettes. He smiled at Bolormaa, as if to reassure her that he had understood all her instructions. He said a few encouraging words in Russian that escaped us and off we went.

The journey down the Selenga took longer than expected. Beautiful Selenga opens into an intricate delta, where we planned to stop en route to have a light meal. The shore was soaked from the persistent drizzle that had followed us since we left UU and that overtook us at the mouth of the delta. No shelter being in sight, we gave up on the idyllic picnic and hastily gulped a few garlic *grenki* and hot coffee from a Thermos that Bolormaa's mother had prepared. Benedetta and I were experiencing an introspective combination of reasoning and daring. We avoided each other's gaze so as not to comment on the hardships of reaching Baikal in this threatening weather.

We finally came out of the Selenga delta into the blue waters of Lake Baikal under heavy rain. We were facing a strong current that made Melscho zigzag his way into the lake, especially when the river widened and the water turned choppier. We had to start bailing out the water that was rising in the bottom of *Sputnik* due to clouds of heavy spray that the waves were scattering in our direction. We used the Thermos and a coffee mug to bail out, since there was no bucket in sight. I started to feel cold and gloomy; the experience was setting my nerves on edge. That did not, however, prevent me from acknowledging the grandeur of the landscape we were traversing and the overwhelming force of this limitless space that brought home to us our insignificant human dimension.

I was making mental notes for the book when the outboard motor failed. We were left at the mercy of the waves while Melscho fidgeted with the engine. He kick-started the motor; it cranked but it did not fire. And then it did. By that time the water coming aboard *Sputnik* was fearful, far more than what Benedetta and I could bail out. Melscho swerved the boat dexterously to dodge a larger wave, but the strong force of the backwash pushed us uncontrollably from the stern. The next moment, the wooden planks of the bottom of

Sputnik exploded under our feet. We capsized without realizing what was happening. In a fraction of a second I passed from appreciating the view of the pebble beach to experiencing the freezing grip of the Selenga in all its fury.

Everything disappeared. It was an instant death: I was suddenly wrapped in darkness and nothingness, then more nothingness and then some more. The nothingness radiated a solemn silence to the enveloping darkness. My consciousness started to dissolve into a thick, overcast sky. Before losing myself forever, I experienced a burst of rage. *So this is it*, I thought. *I fucked up again.*

. . . .

Brussels, 27 June 2015

The closer we got to Brussels, the grayer the sky became. Thunderstorms from the North Sea were expected across the country in the following hours. The air and my heart seemed equally heavy. I was in the worst of moods at the prospect of this confrontation with Tony and our disastrous association. The divorce settlement procedure required my presence in the city. The final agreement was due to be signed by both parties in five days. I had indeed been divorced from Tony for six months already, but a settlement on financial matters was still to be reached. He had gotten deeply into debt during our marriage, and I was jointly liable as per the terms of our prenuptial agreement. I would eventually have to surrender to those legal obligations.

My lawyer, Mr Isaac Merlin Volchebnik, had been preparing me for weeks for the likely necessity of selling my apartment to soak up those debts. My marriage was ending as a bitter fairy tale whose prince charming and princess had respectively mutated into a hideous frog and a turkey voting for Christmas. This was making me sick to my stomach. With the intention of helping me swallow the pill, Mr Volchebnik invited me upon arrival to the most select Russian restaurant in Brussels. He also intended to celebrate my upcoming departure for Siberia. He ordered caviar and vodka. We chatted the whole afternoon in an opulent lounge. Since I had filed for divorce, he had demonstrated the most unfailing support for me. I had learned to see him as a much-needed father figure. My lawyer was a friend of LouLou and had laundered money for him.

When Omar and I had decided by the end of our week at Il Casolare to attend a shamanic workshop in Irkutsk, I had to find solutions regarding my Russian visa. As I was a Belgian citizen, a minimum of thirty days was necessary to obtain the precious travel document; but our conference started in two weeks. Omar was so happy to go into silent retreat for a few days in some random cottage outside Milan that I decided not to mention this inconvenience to him. I did not want to worry him for nothing. I was determined to trust my lucky star in helping me find a way out of this situation, and my lucky star presently responded with the enchanting name of Isaac Merlin Volchebnik. He was not only a renowned divorce lawyer and laundry man, but also allegedly a close relative of the Russian ambassador to Belgium. My visa would be issued in three days by means of an exceptional waiver on medical grounds. I never came to know how he had managed to seal the deal. Certain questions are not meant to be asked.

He explained that I was supposed to be suffering from a most serious illness, the only remedy for which was to be found in Irkutsk. Given that my condition was abruptly deteriorating, I was allowed to enter Russia without delay. I would just have to remember to play my part with conviction at customs and immigration, and inform Omar in a timely manner, meaning preferably at the very last minute. I was up for the challenge. The results were worth the risks, and Mr Volchebnik was convinced by the success of the maneuver. Should things go wrong, however, he would deny any intercession with local Russian authorities. He had probably simply bribed a junior clerk to get the visa waiver – it is very unlikely that he would have involved the ambassador for the sake of allowing one of his eccentric clients to attend a shamanic conference in Siberia – but he understood human psychology well enough to know that his little miracles would work better if enrobed in a story that I could hang on to when entering Russia. Playing a role would make me focused and less anxious when passing immigration controls. I had never entered a country illegally and therefore accepted my lawyer's fantasy tricks without questioning them. Life was definitely either a daring adventure or nothing at all.

As much as I was trying to concentrate on those promising adventures, I was still in Brussels, about to see my ex-husband, our first encounter since I committed myself a little more than two years ago to Les Acacias mental hospital. Thinking about him, I was not feeling sad and nostalgic any more. With each minute that passed I was getting increasingly pale and nervous, but resisted quieting my nerves with anything but herbal tea and an occasional glass of wine, which for me was progress in itself. When the dreaded moment arrived, winter had invaded my heart, but my feet were steady. I was ready to face the consequences of my marital debacle.

The comforting thought of meeting with Omar at Sheremetyevo Airport soon provided some light at the end of the tunnel. I texted him that I was looking forward to seeing him and hoped that he was enjoying himself to the fullest in Italy. He had declined my invitation to join me in Brussels for the week, which was convenient. I was resolved to spare him my electrical moods and charged emotions due to the ultimate jolts of my divorce, which was mine to cope with and a file that demanded closure. I would not let our journey be polluted by my past mistakes and difficulty in dealing with them. I was, however, starting to understand the need to open up more to him about what my life had been and the person that I was, provided I had a clue on the latter.

The legal documents were signed without Tony. He was being held up in the south of France, where he had established himself with his new wife, our former maid, and their young child. Gigolo turned into shepherd. Really? My husband was unreliable and selfish, but my irrational fear of being abandoned and my genuine incapacity to trust him had been fatal to our awkward association. That being said, who would be stupid enough, except me of course, to settle down with a gigolo? I could not keep putting the blame on him. I wholeheartedly volunteered for chaos when I decided to marry him and ruin myself in our shaky relationship. *Be careful what you wish for, because you just might get it.* I loved the idea of loving Tony and being loved by him, but did that make it real love? Likely not. I began to feel grateful that he had dumped me, as it ultimately forced me to face the ugly reality of my addiction to him, as well as the true roots and nature of my pain and shortcomings. Addictions always die hard.

Within such context, my doubtful relationship with Frank suited me to perfection, because it was contained in a structure that was supposed to be therapeutic. But prostitutes, like gigolos, can be very professional, and the good doctor enjoyed mixing genres, just like me. That being said, aren't we all prostitutes to a certain extent? We sell different parts of ourselves, that is all. Down that road, I might be a prostitute myself too. The irony of the situation was that I was attached to Frank and had been missing him since he disappeared from the European radar. I sincerely wanted to believe that real love was possible between us, should we be reunited under a more favorable sun. I was, however, not certain I had the strength to survive another wreck. I did not even want to try it. Thirty-four years old, and so much to learn and unlearn.

If I wanted to be in a mature love-relationship, I had to grow up and stop looking for affection in the arms of shady men, especially when money was involved. I must enhance my ability to give and receive love from a healthy and luminous place. This was the big plan. And learning how to love myself unconditionally. It seemed to be a general truth of my new spiritual path and *sangha*. This was intriguing, and, in a certain way, frightening. Who would I become if I accepted forgiving others and myself for my many sufferings, shortcomings, and mistakes? Would I even be able to recognize myself and pronounce my own name? I had no idea, but I knew one thing for sure: true love only flourishes in a state of emptiness. I had just read an article in *The Buddhist Times* on the topic, containing interviews with great teachers and lamas. What did emptiness look like? How did it feel? How did it smell? How did it sound? And did it hurt?

In the meantime, the Brussels city hall clock indicated 11:00 p.m. sharp. My worldly goods had been officially transferred to the sole benefit of banks and a string of dubious creditors for six hours, forty-six minutes, and twenty-eight seconds. One step farther down the road of my material dismemberment. The last divorce papers had been signed. Was that a sign of emptiness? I was for sure getting rid of rotten branches and making space for a new something yet to be discovered. I wandered about like a lost soul in the so-called capital of Europe. Favorite restaurants and bars, museums and galleries, concert halls and libraries, ice cream shop, wedding church, office and pavement, Churchill Avenue, Acacias Hospital. Places that had meant something to me. I never really liked living in Brussels – not enough warmth and sun, too many unpleasant memories. I longed for some exotic destination. I nevertheless sat on the green metal bench opposite the madhouse entrance. It was 4:45 a.m. I had been walking for hours in an empty city. I had regressed to being a ghost on a pilgrimage to the past and was feeling like a stranger in this bizarre town.

A heavy summer rain burst out. I had no umbrella, but I stayed exactly where I was, motionless, my livid eyes gazing at the entrance to the madhouse, for I could not care less about my drenched condition. I have always been a pluviophile, which did not seem contradictory to any idea of emptiness that I was then able to formulate. Water has cleansing properties, and my tears were melting with the rain. The sun was rising. I assumed that I had been sitting on the bench for about an hour. An angular hand landed on my shoulder, interrupting my solitary contemplation in its gentle motion. I turned my head and saw green eyes, the same green eyes that had once taken care of me in the paramedic van.

"Are you all right, miss?" said the woman the hand and eyes belonged to. She was dressed as a paramedic. I remained silent. It could not be her.

"Are you all right?" she repeated in an ethereal tone.

"Do you like canaries?" I bluntly asked, tossing my head back in this odd way that reminded me of some patients at Les Acacias.

"I do, as a matter of fact… and I dare say that you like them too."

The rain suddenly stopped, leaving room for a bright summer sky. The woman grabbed a turquoise scarf from her bag and placed it around my shoulders.

"You should be careful. Soon you'll catch a cold."

"Thank you," I murmured.

"What are you doing here?"

"I don't know."

"Not true. You just don't want to look into your heart and be honest with me." Her eyes were hypnotizing. I was absorbing each of her words.

"Do you want to go back to that institution?" she asked.

"No. I don't want to go back there. Never."

"You should leave then. This place isn't good for you."

"Do you remember me?"

"I remember each and every one of you, fragile birds. That day you had jumped out a window. You should go now."

"I'm homeless," I painfully confessed.

"Not true."

"You don't understand me. I have lost my one and only home."

"That doesn't make you homeless. It only makes you free. You should be grateful for this. The world is your home now, and your heart home to many. If you accept, open it just a little more. Off you go now. You can keep the scarf." I was speechless. All that was ever needed was a change of perspective.

I arrived at the apartment rejuvenated. A fleecy turquoise scarf was enveloping me, attesting that the conversation was real and not a by-product of my disturbed imagination. A welcome thought. Same time the next day, I would be checking in at Brussels Airport for a new destination. I placed personal items that I liked in a box and left a note to my lawyer as to what to do with my belongings. I had given him power of attorney to sell the apartment. I then collapsed on my bed from emotional and physical exhaustion. I slept soundly until late in the evening.

I had not unpacked since my arrival one week earlier and was ready to leave. A pre-ordered taxi was supposed to pick me up at 5:15 a.m. the following day. The dawn of a new day and of a new story. When the doorbell rang, I gave a last glance at this place that I had considered my home for four years, my beloved apartment, and muttered an emotional *thank you*. I locked the door in haste and ran down the stairs with my bags. I never liked goodbyes. Besides, there was no need to rub salt in the wound. As the taxi was crossing an almost-empty Brussels, it struck me that I was not only taking leave of my home but also bidding a more permanent farewell to what life had been for me so far. A page was turning. By sunset, if everything unfolded according to plan, I would be in Russia. Was I crazy?

I passed the Sheremetyevo Moscow Airport's customs and immigration controls with the luck of the devil. My lawyer's tricks worked like a hot knife through butter. I think the whole gang of customs and immigration officers fell into the trap the moment they saw my horrible face. A provisional legacy from the past days; I was looking spooky, and playing the dying indeed came naturally to me. I went through controls feeling like Moses parting the Red Sea and entered the promised land of Rossiyskaya Federatsiya exhilarated.

Omar and I had agreed to meet at Chocolate Café or something like that. This was an audacious choice, because Belgians usually view themselves as international chocolate experts, which of course we are. Belgian patriotism shines at its zenith when expressed in culinary forms or songs. When I turned up like a bat out of hell in Shokoladnitsa Café, our place of rendezvous' correct name, the waitress perceived my need for an invigorating something. Omar was sitting on the other side of the room, seemingly lost in reverie. Putinka Vodka landed out of the blue on our table. The Boss's name was displayed on vodka bottles. Was he some kind of a magician too? I swallowed down the offered elixir, a matter of politeness. Thank heavens this place had little to do with chocolate.

"My dear, I'm very happy to see you, but you seem a little agitated. Is something happening?" Omar asked after I had had three vodka shots in a row.

"I'm very sick, and my condition is deteriorating from day to day. I suffer from the most serious illness, the only remedy for which is to be found in Irkutsk." I acted as if still at customs and immigration. I was overexcited and could not possibly hold my tongue any longer. Omar remained calm and focused, the temporary results of his one-week retreat, and looked amused in spite of his unsuccessful efforts to hide it.

"You're very lucky then, because we're traveling to Irkutsk today. We're going to be able to cure you," he replied with a crooked smile. Argentina wanted to play – fair enough. Belgium was ready to answer the invitation.

"I'm telling you that I'm dying, and you're not even shocked for a second. I don't know what to think. Even worse, you're shamelessly grinning. Boorish and scandalous."

"Darling, we're all going to die… it is just a matter of time and place. Chill out."

"Omar!"

"Yes?"

"You're sounding like the South American version of Winston Churchill."

"I thought you were dying…"

"I'm not sure that I will ever let you meditate on your own again. You know, too much Buddha nature kills Buddha nature. And you smell like patchouli."

"That alone!"

"Some people actually have to tell these stories to be allowed to enter Russia within half the time officially required to obtain a visa," I said in a rush, and a bit too loudly. Omar was surprised but kept his composure. I should go meditating with him next time. "This is the miracle my lawyer organized for me, and the story I have to hold on to until we're out of Russia," I murmured, as if on a secret mission. "Argentina has special agreements with this country, but Belgian citizens are bound by stricter rules. We need a minimum of four weeks to obtain a basic tourist visa by means of normal procedure."

"What's this? Do you think you're in a James Bond movie?"

"Do you want some vodka?"

"Benedetta, you should have told me, and I really think you should stop drinking before reaching the point of shouting that you're a special agent under cover." I ordered hot *chai* and blinis for both of us. Omar was not laughing any more.

"Next time you, actually we, have such an issue, talk to me. Please." I was fiddling with my hair like a little girl caught in the act of doing another damned stupid thing. Argentina was winning hands down. I remained silent. "I don't want to have to send you back to Belgium because you've had a nervous breakdown. Besides, if we could avoid ending up in some random prison cell in a country whose language you cannot even speak, I would really appreciate it." The word *really* resonated round the whole room. Calling upon all his advocacy skills, Omar added that it would take us much more than a phone call to my lawyer, Abraxas, to get us out of such a mess. Rules were different in this part of the world. He knew that Abraxas was not his name; he was just trying to be mean.

"I'm sorry," I replied, concentrating on my cup of tea.

"Come on, you've entered this country illegally. What are you planning to do if we're caught? You're not alone in this. Your actions have consequences for me." Tears were building up in my eyes. My triumphant arrival had turned sour, but Omar was right: whatever happened, we were in this adventure together.

"My dear, don't be sad. I'm not mad at you. I've told you how much I admire your resourcefulness. But what possessed you, seriously?"

"I don't know," I eventually managed to articulate. "I'm really sorry."

After a silence that felt like a century, Omar asked me to tell him the story of my visa and immigration breakthrough. He wanted all the details. I could not speak and became even paler than I already was. All I wanted to do was cry the hell out of my misery. "We'll send a postcard from Irkutsk to your magical lawyer to thank him for his creative services," Omar said in a playful and cheerful tone. I regained some color and began to narrate my sensational story, ensuring that no one could hear us, not even the Putinka Vodka bottle. I also told him the nightmare that my week in Brussels had been in reality and how I had lost my apartment for good. Omar was listening to me with great attention.

His reaction to my visa news could have been much worse. More than anything, he was helping me put my feet back down on the ground and digest the enormity of my days in Brussels and arrival in Russia. I was grateful for his discernment and kindness. I wondered by which miracle he was able to tolerate my borderline actions. I could hardly bear them myself at times. He was asking me to trust him and break that well-rooted childhood habit of doing everything on my own. I remembered what Apollo had said to me: *Never forget that the spirits always answer positively when you ask for their help.*

This probably applies to human beings too, I thought. Il Casolare seemed ages ago. I felt stupid and like the worst travel companion ever, but I had gotten the message. We were ready to navigate our shamanic waters farther east.

A couple of hours later, with many more stories from both ends, I was feeling like my old self again and preparing to board our plane to Irkutsk. I was patiently queuing in the economy line, whereas Omar was already comfortably seated in the cabin. Business-class seat, lucky him. We had come to the conclusion that my fraudulent condition was more credible if traveling alone than with an Argentine lawyer who carried shamanic musical instruments and healing herbs in a vintage flower-power bag. There was no need to arouse suspicion, and Omar wasn't ecstatic at the idea of playing my nurse either. We would keep a low profile until reaching our lodging in Irkutsk, where we would tell local authorities that we had met within the context of a shamanic workshop and made arrangements at the same guesthouse.

The 'Shamanic Orientation Conference' was absolutely horrible. It took place in the ballroom of the Irkutsk Hotel, a windowless room the decoration of which merely consisted of outdated olive carpets – had they been in touch with Frank? – and walls that had been painted in bombastic Russian Federation style. We were surrounded by monumental horizontal stripes, colors that had been selected according to the national flag, and massive pictures of the heroes of the Federation. Two hundred chairs covered with velvet-like fabric celebrating Irkutsk Oblast enhanced this visual aggression. Strangely, the ceiling had been kept white, although marks in the corners bore witness to it having been violet. Massive chakra-unbalancing. I wanted to vomit. When a participant sitting in front of us noisily opened a can of Diet Coke and started to devour popcorn, I felt on the verge of passing out or killing someone. Even without mentioning our conference host.

Bogdana Bilyana Dragovna was a former TV presenter seen on the Bulgarian version of *X Factor* until she resigned "to pursue her cosmic path" (*sic*). She served us a forty-five-minute speech about her stellar ascension as introduction to the day, which she followed up with a PowerPoint presentation addressing the roots of Siberian shamanism. The welcome package had a similar effect to two pills of Valium, on me and possibly on the whole room. Shamanic Orientation Conference? 'Manic Disoriented Hole' would have been more appropriate. And where were the advertised real shamans? Hidden behind the desk, preparing to jump around when the tension would have reached climax, or more likely when the participants had all sunk into a comatose state? Therefore, when Cosmic Agent Omar 007 grabbed me by the arm and led us to the ballroom entrance door, I followed him without hesitation. We had to escape this hellish place. By midnight we had left Irkutsk and were on our way to Ulan-Ude, an eight-hour train journey across breathtaking Siberia.

I woke up early from a short yet deep sleep. Covered by the warmth of the night, I looked out of the window from my berth and could see only cliffs. I found a note placed on the small table: Omar was inviting me to join him in the *bagón restorán* for breakfast. I grabbed random pieces of clothing and landed barefoot in the long corridor, stretching my arms and smiling with contentment. Captivating Lake Baikal was offering itself in full power and magnificence. It is estimated to be the oldest and deepest existing lake in the world and has been the scene of many natural and supernatural events. The latter include UFO-related incidents, inexplicable disappearances of vessels, stories of humanoid light and presence in the lake's depths, unexplained magnetic anomaly, and a mysterious lake monster feared by the native Buryat people. Locals call this creature Lusud-Khan or Usan-Lobson Khan, which means something like "water dragon master." Stories of Baikal monsters go back centuries. Carved stones representing these beasts can be spotted along the lake's cliffs.

Omar was standing farther down the corridor, admiring the view. Young children were playing in front of the door of our cabin. To their delight, I pretended one of the train hostesses was an elfish creature pursuing me, and rushed to Omar. The *pravodnitsa* was desperately trying to catch me with a pair of slippers in her hands. She eventually caught me, breathless, when I reached Omar. I was happy to be on this train, surrounded by the pristine vastness of Lake Baikal, with him. "Can I buy you coffee?" he joyfully asked. Irkutsk and its soulless hotels were years away from us, definitively vanishing from our consciousness.

In UU, Olga and her husband hosted us in their family apartment located in the old downtown area. Despite our generous smiles, their two teenage sons gently ignored us, which wasn't the case for the *babushka* living with them. On our second day, while Omar was conversing with Olga about the current economic and political state of this part of Russia, *babushka* approached me in her Buryat dialect. We were each talking in our respective mother tongues and savoring this unexpected conversation. We understood each other somehow, though what she shared with me has remained a complete mystery to this day. Olga was an exceptional host and mothered us as much as she could. She must have sensed our distress. On our fourth day she asked me if I would be willing to read her favorite French poem to her. Soon enough I was passionately reciting Rimbaud's "The Drunken Boat" in her kitchen, with Omar, Olga, and *babushka*'s enthusiastic encouragement.

I would realize later that this poem was premonitory for our adventures and a metaphor for my whole life. In the meantime, in addition to reading French poetry and chatting with our hosts, Omar and I spent quiet hours in a delightful summer garden down Lenina street. An elderly *literatura* professor, with whom we exchanged a few words every day in this bucolic place, surprised me with a bouquet of white and pink flowers. I was very moved by this kind gesture. It crossed my mind how little my ex-husband was familiar with such spontaneous gestures. I imagined that it wasn't my good doctor's strongest quality either. Addictions die hard, even in the heart of Siberia.

During those days we started to review our notes and made plans for the book that we had decided to write together and that had initiated this *voyage*. We were excited about it and began to introduce ourselves as aspiring authors. I also got into the habit of sharing bits and pieces of my own story – almost unnoticed by others, but my friend was clever enough to catch them each time they passed by. By the end of our first week in UU, I had lifted the veil on my calamitous divorce, my jumping out a window, and my time at Les Acacias. I was relieved to be sharing this with him, and he seemed relieved too. After all, we were both vulnerable and had had our share of dramas. I was learning to tell my story authentically, without the usual joking around. I was wondering what it was like for Omar to move through life as a recovering addict. I decided to keep this question to myself until the right moment to ask it showed up.

Another important objective for us was that of expanding our little knowledge of Siberian shamanism and getting introduced to the real shamans we had hoped to encounter during the Irkutsk workshop. With that intention, we invoked spirits every night when our hosts were asleep. We did not want to disturb or upset Olga and her family with our shamanic aspirations, and I was still meant to be suffering from the most serious illness, the only remedy of which was to be found in Irkutsk. I was almost starting to really believe this story. Thank goodness, we had traveled through Irkutsk and I was heading towards full recovery at the speed of sound. As a precaution, Omar suggested avoiding police cars and officers. It became a game for us to change direction each time one of them approached. This was a James Bond movie after all.

In our attempt to reach out to shamans, we stopped at the Hodegetria Cathedral, although this might seem contradictory at first. It certainly was for Omar, with his profound aversion to Catholicism and religions in general. Hence my surprise when he insisted we visit this place of worship and devotedly kneeled in front of the Virgin Hodegetria, a classic iconographic depiction of the Virgin Mary holding infant Jesus while pointing to him as the source of salvation for mankind. Omar began to mumble feverish incantations in an odd language that I assumed was a blend of his native Argentine Spanish, Russian, Latin, and possibly Sanskrit, along with various interjections. When he improvised an imitation of a gigantic bird and screamed "*Zdravstvuyte!*" I burst into gigantic laughter that strongly echoed around the building. My cosmic agent did not take notice of this thunder and remained focused on whatever ritual the Lady was imparting to him. This was first-rate entertainment.

After a couple of minutes of uncontrollable laughter, a young priest came out of the sanctuary and waved at me to be quiet, but I could not get myself together. When an older man, probably *nastoyatel* of the cathedral, threatened me with a silver crucifix and muttered incantations of his own, I deduced I'd better immediately take off. Omar eventually turned up radiant in the cathedral square, where I was waiting for him.

"That was quite a meditation, wasn't it?" he said.

"My dear, do you mean that you actually meditated? I'm not sure I would call it that," I replied, smirking.

"Well, you know… Let's have lunch! I'm starving."

"Would you rather have mullet, blackfish, heron, or crow?"

Omar smiled enigmatically, and we walked back to our summer garden. We hadn't collected any valuable information or befriended anyone during our Catholic expedition, but the gods had come up with divine laughter for my pleasure only, and with Omar's unconscious complicity.

Given that the Orthodox Church wasn't delivering satisfying results regarding our spiritual quest, we decided to divert our attention to Ivolginsk Datsan, a Buddhist monastery located twenty-three kilometers from UU and the only Buddhist spiritual center allowed in the former USSR. We soon discovered that the Datsan harbored many treasures, among which was a collection of old Tibetan Buddhist manuscripts written on fine silk. Buryatia's beauties kept unfolding under our intrigued eyes. Despite our almost non-existent command of local languages, we managed to initiate a conversation with an old monk who spoke a little English. Between Omar's sound knowledge of Buddhism and my skills at breaking the ice with strangers, we formed an excellent team. I encouraged Omar to show his sacred tattoos to the monk as a token of our sincerity, but he categorically refused. Was he hiding something? Maybe he had gotten his tattoos in Amsterdam on one of those wild naked nights, courtesy of a rival church. Maybe the sacred inked turtles and other serpents were bathing in secular fields of marijuana. I liked that idea. I was determined to investigate, even more so after what I had witnessed in the cathedral.

During our third visit to Ivolginsk Datsan, I had to lie down after lunch, which consisted of soup shared with the *sangha* at the monastery, because of sudden stomach cramps. Bolormaa, eldest daughter of the owners of the *letnii sad* where we spent most of our days, provided a translation of what was happening for the monks. I was installed in a comfortable corner of the temple for the next hour. A young monk brought me a cup of fresh water and sat beside me in lotus position, praying and meditating until I regained strength. I did not dare to confess that my sensitive body had occasional difficulties coping with local cuisine. By the end of the afternoon we were back in UU, inspired by this welcoming community.

Over the following days I experimented with another new level of emptiness. Not only did we hold long meditation sessions at home, but I also puked every morning. Omar offered me his full support so that I would feel better, but seemed to strangely rejoice at the prospect of those repeated waves of nausea. When I realized that he had been tracking with precision what I had ingested since our arrival in the city, my interest in his little machinations dramatically increased. Could he be testing his large range of therapeutic herbs on me? Was I sold as a guinea pig, the height of absurdity for a vegan, to the cause of his personal interpretation of experiential shamanism, potentially crossed with the unresolved karma of a drug dealer? Should I also expect to shapeshift into a bird and to scream *Zdravstvuyte!* next time we prayed at the Lady's feet? It was my turn to exult, for little did I know that Omar's company would be so amusing when we embarked on this journey together. I nonetheless double-checked what I ate and drank in his presence. I miraculously stopped vomiting.

Bolormaa had to leave for a few days in order to collect her sick *dedushka,* or grandfather, in Irkutsk – was he also suffering from the most peculiar and serious illness, the only remedy for which was to be found there? – and drive him back to his *dacha* in the woods. We opened up to Bolormaa's parents, with whom we had become familiar, about our burning wish to commune with nature. We were over the moon when they proposed organizing a visit to *dedushka*'s *dacha* with the help of Melscho, a distant cousin of the family.

On the day preceding her departure, Bolormaa disclosed that her grandfather, Bulagat Buchacheyev by his civil name, was nothing less than a shaman respected in all of Buryatia for his great power and wisdom and that we were about to meet this extraordinary man as part of the trip. What an immense blessing, topped with the opportunity to verify my level of intoxication by random therapeutic herbs. Synchronicities were accumulating, and our attempts to dive deeper into shamanism were paying off. We were thrilled with this, not to mention with the upcoming full moon. For a second I missed Carlito's arms and vigorous energy. I wanted to tell Omar what had happened that first night at Il Casolare, but he had drifted off in reverie and contemplation. Another time would do. My friend was so much more romantic than he was willing to admit. I was cut from the same cloth, in truth.

After dinner, Omar abruptly went out for a walk, leaving his laptop open, running a random program update that was taking forever. I hummed my way to the kitchen table and sat in front of it. I touched the keypad and an email popped up. With it came attached documents, photographs actually. They showed a younger Omar, stripped, bound, and gagged, and another man, fully dressed, engaged in sexual play, which did not surprise me. Besides, it was fun to pry into Omar's life. The email, written in English by a man named Andy, however, did surprise me. I assumed that Andy was the vampire lover who Omar had abundantly talked about, a guy who had brutally dumped him three years before. Omar had pictured Andy as a dull junkie who had abused his love and betrayed his trust. I knew that Omar had once wanted to marry Andy. Well, he had fantasized about it, at least. The story that Andy was telling in the email was rather different from the one I had heard so far.

A clean Andy was unilaterally breaking up with Omar because the latter had suggested that he use drugs again in order to regain the sexual vitality that he had lost in the withdrawal process. In giving up on drugs, Andy had become hooked on sertraline. He was obviously depressed and confessed that his libido and interest in his relationship with Omar had completely sunk, though he thanked him for having given him a comfortable shelter and paid for his therapy. Omar had never told me this side of the story. If Andy was telling the truth, the situation had degenerated into physical violence between them when Omar put ecstasy pills into Andy's hands in an attempt to reverse the situation. The next day, Andy was gone. I was feeling perplexed and angry. So Mr Perfect was not so perfect after all. His books and many references to spiritual masters had been of little use to him. In a bizarre way, I was feeling abused too.

It was 2:00 a.m., and Omar was still out. I started fearing that I would never see him again and that he hated me. He was gone for good, with his lovers, dramas, and secrets. I was feeling abandoned and hurt. I lay on the kitchen floor. Omar eventually appeared at dawn but did not notice my presence in the kitchen. When he emerged later in the morning, I was helping Olga cook breakfast. He looked so horrible and so terribly sad that my feelings from the night instantly vanished. I wanted to hug him, but he would not let anyone approach him. The truth was that he and Andy had probably abused each other equally. My truth was that I had abused people too. I knew how to manipulate, victimizing myself. Why had Omar not deleted the vampire's emails? Was he still living in the nostalgia of this relationship? It seemed to me that he kept punishing himself in the most painful ways for things that I did not even know or understand. Was I like that too, irreversibly condemning myself and others to atonement? I smiled at Omar, who ignored me. At that moment he did not seem to be capable of doing anything else but drinking coffee. He was absent and unreachable. Was he catatonic? Soon enough, I would be the one who would have to put pills in his mouth. I burned the toast, which provoked a motherly rebuke from Olga that brought me back to the present moment. A reality that would soon lead us to Bulagat's *dacha*. What stupidity of ours was this again?

Melscho was the proud owner of *Sputnik*, a motorized boat barely bigger than a canoe, which had been his faithful companion for decades. The Selenga River and its delta had no secrets for him and his beloved boat, and he was delighted to guide us into this blue wilderness toward Bulagat's *dacha*. I was reassured by Melscho's weather-beaten face and luminous eyes, witnesses of a life lived to the fullest and a real ability to overcome obstacles. His craggy hands proved to be strong and agile when he helped us on board, despite his advanced age – Melscho was a *dedushka* too. The vessel pitched a little too much for my taste, and we were not even down the Selenga yet. I decided to ignore my concerns and focused on the sublime surrounding landscape.

The closer we came to Lake Baikal, the grayer the sky became. When the drizzle transformed into rain, I had my heart in my mouth. The wind built up to the point that it was impossible to sail in the direction of the shore. Soon enough, Omar and I were frantically bailing out the water that Baikal was spitting into our vessel.

The situation went seriously out of control when the derelict motor broke down, leaving us at the complete mercy of the elements. And then *boom!* The vessel literally cracked and exploded under the pressure of the current. The Baikal water monster was wide awake and testing our resolve. We were projected into the lake's cold waters, where the temperature in the summer was no more than four or five degrees Celsius. I was hyperventilating, freezing, and running out of time. The risk of hypothermia was real.

All that time I had flirted with death, withdrawing at the last minute when faced with fatal endings. And now that I had finally decided to live, death was defying me in the most brutal way. I refused to die there and was desperate at the idea that Omar and Melscho, who I had so far failed to locate, might be dead. The moment I screamed a furious *nooooooo!* a wave of dark and freezing water submerged me. A piece of metal hit me in the forehead, throwing me into the silent depths of Lake Baikal.

> *But, in truth, I have wept too much! Dawns are heartbreaking.*
> *Every moon is atrocious and every sun bitter.*
> *Acrid love has swollen me with intoxicating torpor*
> *O let my keel burst! O let me go into the sea!* [17]

Sweet and bitter drunken boat, indeed.

. . . .

Lake Baikal, 17 July 2015

After what seemed like a full night, but was probably only seconds, I felt pierced by thousands of icicles, and I tried to howl. But I could not, because my nostrils were filled with water and my throat was

---

17 Arthur Rimbaud, "The Drunken Boat" from *Complete Works, Selected Letters*

choking with ice. I felt a spasm, as if I were about to vomit, and then recovered consciousness of my body. With tremendous effort I ignited a fireball that went from my guts, through my lungs, and out of my mouth. I cleared my lungs of water, but there was still more filling my nostrils. I opened my eyes with the awe of a newborn: I saw a splash of light, pure concrete photons, the quantum of light. This was no white light at the end of the tunnel. In spite of its unsuccessful attempt to gape for air, my reptilian brain made me swim madly toward the source of light. Alive. Here we go again.

A storm of unanticipated ferocity was upon us. The eerie silence that I had experienced underwater dissolved into roaring and howling wind, swirling waves, and rain that hit my face with the viciousness of bee stings.

I looked around and identified first the shore and later Benedetta, swimming not far from where I had emerged. She was making her way toward the shore with the determination of an icebreaker. I got hold of a large piece of wood that floated nearby, and, once I had secured it, yelled at her. She turned her head in my direction and she saw me. "I've got Melscho!" she yelled back and continued to swim. She had one arm around Melscho's neck. He looked unconscious and was bleeding profusely.

I was freezing, my arms were numb, and I could not feel my legs. Thinking that I was about to drown, I called all my helping spirits by name. *The loving and compassionate power of the spirits is the strongest force there is.* I started making for the shore, keeping Benedetta in my sight most of the time. In spite of the hardships, there seemed to be a current leading us toward the shore. I was not really doing much. I concentrated on floating and focused my mind on the pumping of my heart, aware that each pump was bringing warmth and life. I saw Benedetta on the shore, pushing Melscho out of the water with mighty force. My feet found ground, and soon I was on the shore as well. I made it a few paces out of the water, then collapsed.

I started feeling my body again, as if coming back from a shamanic journey. Benedetta was within view. I stood up and walked to her. Melscho was lying on the beach. I instantly knew that he was no longer alive. Benedetta sat next to his body, gently caressing his hair. I fell to my knees, started sobbing and then howling. My cries caught the attention of Benedetta, who stood up and walked to me. I felt like hugging her and crying out in pain and terror. When she was close to me, totally drenched, as she had been that first morning at Il Casolare, she picked the two nearest large pebbles and put them in my hands. "Drum for me!" she exclaimed, pinning me with her steely blue eyes.

I was paralyzed. I did not understand what she meant and did not know how to react. Putting the pebbles in my hands, Benedetta made me knock one pebble against the other, reproducing the monotonous beat of the shamanic drum we had lost in the wreck. I understood; she had tuned in to the emergency of the situation, and our first priority was to assist the recently dead Melscho. I collected myself, sat next to Melscho's head, and started knocking the pebbles rhythmically. I was cold and in shock, but the sense of urgent purpose had steadied me, and the thought of companionship for Benedetta overrode any other desperate fluctuations of my mind. I was fully aware, as never before, that at that exact moment we were going through a rite of passage maybe only second to reincarnation. I discarded all the feelings that my karmic imprint generally drew upon – sadness, desperation, self-pity, and terror – and instead chose to feel grateful.

Slowly my mind yielded to the monotonous sound, and I closed my eyes and breathed into a timeless space. It felt as if someone else was doing the drumming. I summoned my helping spirits, and, without realizing, I started journeying.

Finding myself on the crater of Popocatépetl under a heavy sky, I ask my bear spirit to take me to the presence of Melscho's soul. We swim through dark matter and find his soul under the form of a younger Melscho, fearful and disoriented. Benedetta, in a long white gown and with flowers in her hair, is caressing his hand and talking to him lovingly. Neither of them can see me, and I feel that Melscho is being taken good care of. I send rays of blue light to them and stand looking at my heart made of red crystal, throbbing universal love to all souls lost in the middle world.

I start hearing a muffled music, a deep throb that separates from the throb of my crystal heart and materializes in a long staircase taking me to deeper and darker recesses of the space where I have left Melscho and Benedetta. My red crystal heart comes out of my chest and precedes me by a few steps, lighting my way. I start following the almost imperceptible cry, what seems to be the voice of a child. This quest takes me to a maze of black cardboard walls with no other light than that of my glowing heart. My heart stops at a corner of the maze and starts projecting light over a child curled on the floor, who sobs with great sadness. "I miss my mom," he says to me with bright green eyes turned red with tears. It takes me a moment to recognize the soul of Leãozinho, the young man in the Brazilian club who is lost in an infinite night having not acknowledged his death, craving alcohol and love.

I curl next to him and ruffle his hair. I can smell the stench of urine, vodka, and sweat. He is barefoot, and his tattoos are softly floating around him.

"*Oi* Leãozinho. We meet again!"

He does not respond. Perhaps he cannot see me.

"*Oi* Leão. I came to look for you. Do you want to get out of this place?"

"Yes, take me to my mom, please."

"Where I can take you, you can find your mom, Leão. If you want to come, take my hand."

He stops sobbing, rubs his eyes like an infant, and takes my hand. He stands up in all his majesty, proud son of the sun and the beach. Stardust lights his hair. I grab his hand firmly. He startles as if awakening from a dream.

My bear spreads immense feather wings and takes us to the place where souls enter the lower world. Leãozinho jumps to the shore of a turquoise lake and starts washing his feet, hands, and face. His tattoos disappear during the flight. A spiritual entity radiating clean white light approaches Leãozinho with motherly love, which he recognizes and greets cheerfully. The entity embraces Leãozinho in its shining aura, comforts him, and helps him to lie on the shore next to the lake. This is the time for the souls of those like Leãozinho to take a moment to sleep. In that sleep all memories from the last incarnation will be forgotten. He is allowed to choose a few happy memories to take with his soul to the new life: the sun on his face, a victory at *futebol da praia*, the smell of *açaí*. Done. All the sadness, abuse, loneliness, pain, hollowness in the heart that was never filled, the craving for fleeting love, the sexual prowess in all the dirty alleys, it all turns to ashes. A life lived in the darkest corners is left behind. *It shall no longer flourish here.* So many times he could not choose where to go. Now he can: out of the cave.

I feel that our connection has terminated. I am moved and grateful. I sit down next to my bear and start singing a monotonous yet sweet spirit song that is building inside my head. I hide my face in the furry back of my bear and start to cry. So many times I could not choose where to go. Now I can. I can be vulnerable, and I will be loved. I have a new heart that I must learn to use. What happened in the past must be treated like a previous incarnation. It is a perfume of a past season. I am still in the same body but have a new soul. I will learn to listen to the new soul; there is no need to go back to old patterns, for they do not belong to me any more. I will learn not to want to be there any more. I have this opportunity to be the man I was before darkness. This time I will take a new route and do it right.

"You are on to a new journey," my friend Pak says to me, holding my gaze and wrapping me in his crimson robe. I am confused to see a spirit that comes in the form of Pak, a person who is alive, and for a second I fear that Pak has passed away. The next moment I get clear reassurance that the image of Pak represents the force of the purest love that comes to visit me as a promise of what the future may bring.

I then see Benedetta in her priestess gown, watching Melscho walking toward the same lake where I left Leãozinho seconds, hours, or days before. A large group of shamans has gathered around them. I can sense a magnetic connection among them. My red crystal heart signals that it needs to come back into my chest and that it is time for us to go back to the non-ordinary reality. I gently close my eyes as if caressing the landscape and souls with my eyelashes, feel the warmth of my heart expanding in my chest, and start knocking the callback rhythm.

We were rescued later that day. An elderly man first approached us. We could not speak to each other, but he gestured that we should go with him; but neither of us was ready to leave Melscho. Eventually the police arrived, together with Bolormaa's mother and some relatives. They covered us with blankets and gave us hot tea. After much debate among them, Bolormaa's mother drove us to the grandfather's *dacha* nearby. She cooked us a restoring meal and stayed with us that night. Neither Benedetta nor I understood very well why we were there or for how long. We gratefully accepted the fact that we were being taken care of.

The following day, Bulagat, Bolormaa's grandfather, arrived at the *dacha*. He did not pronounce a word, but he looked at us with genuine kindness. He made us follow him to the beach, where he had put together a small *ovoo* next to the place where Melscho had rested. An *ovoo* is a heap of stones used to perform certain Mongolian shamanic ceremonies. We had seen lots of them as we wandered around UU. I gathered that it was auspicious to start an *ovoo* before going on a journey. Other passing travelers might add stones to the original heap.

We spent quite some time collecting more pebbles to make our *ovoo* higher. We sat around the *ovoo,* and Bulagat started reciting and singing. We might have spent the whole day doing that. I am not sure – my memory of that first day after the wreck is blurred. In the end the three of us were reciting, singing, and dancing around the sacred heap of rocks.

During the following nine days, after a frugal breakfast, Bulagat shared with us simple shamanic rituals by the *ovoo.* Borscht soup followed in the early afternoon. After that, Bulagat left us on our own until dinner. Bulagat cooked on the first night, Benedetta and I cooked on the remaining days. We took our time washing and peeling vegetables, either in silence or humming the songs the spirits had given us in the morning. We did the dishes while Bulagat smoked his pipe. Benedetta slept in Bulagat's bed, I slept on the floor next to her over a folded carpet, and Bulagat sat on a chair; he was still there at dawn. We slept soundly and peacefully in the *dacha,* thanks to his protective vigil.

We spent most of the time on our own and in silence. This gave me a lot of space to think about some of our most obvious choices that I had taken for granted. English, for example. Benedetta and I had started talking in English between ourselves because that was the *lingua franca* of the workshop where we first met. Then the English language stuck. We could have spoken in French if we wanted, but then it would be Benedetta's mother tongue we would be using. The fact that we were both using a language that was not our mother tongue gave a certain neutrality to our communication and was also an interesting way of limiting how much we each showed of ourselves through the language. Neutral English is simply that: neutral. I put in a lot of effort in my teenage years trying to grasp an English accent in order to sit for exams. It was a hard task that never came to fruition. As I matured I made the conscious choice of speaking English with a heavy Spanish accent, casually leaving room for some words in Spanish to be mixed into the conversation.

Interjections like *Claro!* or swearing, in extreme cases. Unfortunately, there was a lot about Benedetta that I failed to understand, because we spoke to each other in this neutral language. Whether she had a classy accent in her mother tongue, or if she used politically correct words. Or the way she swore. I learned more about Benedetta in those ten days spent in silence at Bulagat's *dacha* than in any of the very long conversations we had had previously.

However, writing our book on experiential shamanism in English – well, actually only the few notes that had sunk in Lake Baikal – was a positive side of that neutrality. We had to concentrate on what lay beyond words, because as far as words were concerned, we would never be able to write proficiently. And we had learned that language was the child of separation. So the challenge for us was to write a book in a language that we had not mastered in order to provide a transcendental message. *What remains unsaid, what is purely of a vibratory nature, is of the utmost importance.* Perhaps we could not grasp what our book was going to be about until we were left with nothing but a dead body on a deserted shore.

Apart from the ceremonies that Bulagat was hosting and teaching us, Benedetta and I performed daily *Phowa* ceremonies for Melscho's spirit. We later came to know that in an attempt to mitigate the strong current against us, Melscho had miscalculated his trajectory and run into rocks in shallow water. We would have been able to see them had the water not been so high and the sky so cloudy that afternoon. Melscho's spirit had suffered a tragic event, for which he was probably not prepared. In the beginning I wondered whether Melscho's spirit could find its way to the other side without having had time to prepare for it. Observing Bulagat's serenity during the morning ceremonies made me less anxious about it each day.

Melscho belonged to a tribe, a close-knit community, that had looked after him since birth in so many different ways, which included his spiritual needs for the afterlife. Melscho counted on his good shaman friend Bulagat. At the time of his last breath he knew that Bulagat would perform those ceremonies and that his passage to the other side would be smooth, in spite of the tragic circumstances.

We came to understand that under the guise of sharing some of his shamanic knowledge with us, Bulagat was actually performing a long ritual to protect us. But it was too early to understand anything about this. Benedetta and I were pariahs. We had nothing, we belonged nowhere. In spite of our worldly possessions, which qualified us as rich compared with the average Buryatian, we were destitute community-wise. Our tribe had evaporated in the incinerating heat of modern life.

We had in fact lost everything. In a metaphor of cosmic magnitude, we had lost our money, credit cards, traveler's checks, laptop, iPads, and iPhones. My four thousand US dollars in cash, our homeopathic and Ayurvedic potions, together with any Valium that Benedetta could have stashed somewhere, it all went down with *Sputnik* to the bottom of the lake. I had a notion that we should be calling our credit card companies, our travel insurance companies, and respective embassies. However, doing the slow shamanic drill with Bulagat was at that moment the only thing that appeared real and that mattered.

A police car with two plainclothes cops arrived at the *dacha* on the third day. Bulagat greeted them outside, and, after a grave and lengthy conversation, the policemen left. They had orders to take us back to UU to interrogate us about the accident, but their revered shaman had told them that Benedetta and I needed additional time to integrate the experience. The shamanic prescription overrode the police department's summons.

They came back on the tenth day. Bulagat escorted us to the car and gave us two stones that I assumed were part of Melscho's *ovoo*. As we had lost everything, he gave us something that we would presume magical to appease our Western addiction to owning stuff.

Benedetta and I became more and more depressed as we drove back to UU. Miraculously, our passports were waiting for us at the police station. Our host Olga had kept them to register our presence upon our arrival. We had forgotten to get them back, and she had been asked to deliver them to the authorities. The police checked us in at the bleak Hotel Barguzin, in two narrow rooms each with a single bed, a small desk, a noisy fridge, and a TV that did not work. I felt that we were being spied on. We spent half the day at the police station telling our story. Our passports were withheld, and we were asked not to leave town until further notice. The terms of issuance of Benedetta's visa appeared to have become an issue that would involve federal muscle.

We were escorted back to our cells at the Barguzin. An indelible sadness started walking by my side and was gradually taking me over. I lay in bed and started trying to make sense of what was happening. *You know what you have to do,* my spirit guide had told me on that Antarctic pebble beach during the journey that I took at Il Casolare. I did not understand then, and when I asked for an explanation we disintegrated into the cosmos. Interpretation is not the best friend of shamanic journeying. However, I could not stop thinking that I had an inkling of what was going to happen. The Antarctic pebble beach of my journey was similar to the pebble beach of Lake Baikal, where we had landed after the wreck. "You know what you have to do" was the mysterious formula that appeared to unlock the events at Baikal. Maybe my spirit guide was telling me that something of the utmost importance was about to happen and that I needed to be prepared. Prepared how? Ready to disintegrate into the cosmos, which could be one loose way of explaining what shamanic activity is. We were approaching a portal, we were going to witness death, and we would have to know what to do. If we did, more would be revealed. Maybe this was the medicine that the book was supposed to deliver. *Progress can be achieved more rapidly during a single month amid terrifying conditions in rough terrain and in the proximity of harmful forces than by meditating for three years in towns and monasteries.*[18]

Why now? Why at this stage in life? What else had to die together with Melscho? *It will soon be over.* What did I need to leave behind, sunk at the bottom of Lake Baikal? *You are on to a new journey.* I regretted the religious education that I was given as a child. Anti-communism and anti-Semitism were two strongholds of the family dogma. My parents raised us as Roman Catholics, more out of concern for separating ourselves from communists and Jews than out of honest spiritual belief. And of course, this was in order to marry at church, celebrate Christmas, christen the children to have them accepted at Catholic school, which would also shelter the children from communists and Jewish children.

But like many families in my country, we were Roman Catholics à la carte. My mother's mother knew how to make incantations. We routinely asked her to do charms to help us pass exams, divination to find lost items, and other magical procedures to protect us from the evil eye. We were taught that Granny was "white magic," whereas my father's mother, according to my mother, was a witch. Of course, this matter could not be addressed in front of my father, which caused certain perplexity among my brothers and me. Many years after the "witch" and my mother had both passed away, I discovered that the "witch" was an avid reader of Krishnamurti and had published a sweet little book about spirituality that showed a sensible soul.

In turn, my father hung potatoes cut in half tied to a ribbon in a dark corner of his closet, allegedly a powerful remedy to cure skin warts. Any bad thing that happened to us was unquestionably bad luck brought by envious people, so pilgrimages to various *curanderos*

---

18   Tagpo Tashi Namgyal, *Mahamudra: The Quintessence of Mind and Meditation*, quoted in Ian Baker, The Heart of the World (New York: Penguin Press, 2004)

and fortune-tellers were frequent. We never went to mass, and we ate meat on Fridays in Lent.

I was taught that turtles and fishes bring bad luck. An arsenal of charms was available to protect us from envy: red ribbons and leaves of *ruda macho*, a pungent plant. Of course, the red ribbon was worn under the socks and the leaves of *ruda macho* wrapped in plastic and worn inside the shoes. This would prevent anyone at school from realizing the ambiguous syncretism under which my brothers and I were being brought up. Contradictory messages coming from my parents taught me that to survive in the family environment, I would have to refrain from questioning anything that I did not understand. *Reflection of fear makes shadows of nothing.* This is not Sogyal Rinpoche; this is actually *Naruto*. Also high in my recovery toolkit.

Benedetta, always resourceful and pragmatic, managed to make a collect call to her lawyer in Brussels, who had miraculous contacts in the Russian Federation. She was obviously more worried than I was about her immediate fate. She might be facing prison – again! – this time for violating Russian immigration rules. I had to be present and available for her at this bleak juncture.

In less than two days, the lawyer arranged for Benedetta to withdraw 20,000 *rubli* from a shady tour operator close to the Barguzin. New credit cards and traveler's checks were waiting for her in Irkutsk. In turn, I managed to make a collect call to my bank, who offered to replace my ATM and credit cards in Moscow. However, since Benedetta had received clear instructions from her spirits that we should go east, backtracking to Moscow was not a possibility. Astonished, my account manager offered to replace my cards at the next eastern capital city where the spirits would guide me. Would I mind giving the bank forty-eight to seventy-two hours' notice?

That evening, the police informed us that they would escort us to the airport to board a plane to Irkutsk, where we should make arrangements to leave Russia within the next few days. Olga and Bolormaa brought us second-hand clothes. We looked like orphans from a Dickens novel, but we could not care less. We spent ten hours at UU Airport, where we shared coffee and cheese sandwiches with our friendly yet unforgiving police escort. Shortly before dawn we boarded a turbo-prop Antonov with a few other passengers, which landed us in Irkutsk in less than an hour.

We checked in at the Irkutsk Hotel. Only three weeks earlier, freshly arrived in Siberia, we had found this hotel a mammoth concrete post-Soviet example of architectural brutalism. We now found it clean and efficiently run. We spent one day on logistics, getting Benedetta's money and credit cards and checking up with the police. Benedetta was firmly invited to depart the Russian Federation within the next seventy-two hours. I was to follow her and vouch for her compliance with this administrative decision. Benedetta's lawyer had emphatically recommended abiding with this dictum. Should we leave within that term, no record of Benedetta's immigration offense would be kept.

We were drained and decided to leave any decisions about our future for the morning. I skipped dinner, retired to my room, and sat to do my spiritual practice. I was counting on Benedetta spending the entire night juggling alternatives. I went to the business center of the Irkutsk to check my email and found that my twelve-step recovery program sponsor was worried because I had not been in contact for a long time. Whatever I was doing, I had to remember that maintaining my sobriety was the priority. He was expecting my call. *We sought through prayer and meditation to improve our conscious contact with God as we understood Him, praying only for knowledge of His will for us and the power to carry that out.* This is step eleven, and we say "we," not "I," because I cannot do it alone; I do it with the strength that my sponsor and my recovery group have granted me. Yet I was in Siberia, worlds away from my recovery *sangha*, following the most hermetic clues. I should have returned home and clung to the recovery program with every fiber.

Like a virus that rewrites itself to avoid detection, after some time of sobriety, addictions can crawl back under new codes. In hindsight I realized that I was in denial and subtly preparing for the most spectacular relapse, and yet I thought I was on the brink of witnessing the Second Advent. I had visions of Our Lady of the Way pointing with her finger to the Holy Child. I understood that my immediate spiritual path dealt with being supportive of whatever Benedetta wanted to do next and taking good care of her. I was filled with a positive sense of purpose that allowed me to fall asleep. I dreamed of Benedetta and me running like children around the terraces of the Borobudur temple.

We gathered for a buffet breakfast in the hotel restaurant, which was sterile, though the view of the Angara River was breathtaking. We were silent. I noticed that Benedetta was fidgeting with her spoon but was not eating anything. We had shared the depth and the sadness of the previous days, but neither of us had hinted whether we wanted to go home. Whatever home meant to each of us.

"My dear, have you any idea of what you want to do next?" I asked, filling the space with all my supportive energy.

"Bangkok," she replied with graceful firmness. My jaw dropped. This was decidedly the least expected answer.

"No. No, my dear. I cannot go back to Bangkok. How about Borobudur?"

"Bangkok!" she commanded, her fiery blue eyes ablaze.

. . . .

Lake Baikal, 17 July 2015

A violent storm was upon us, and I was sinking into the lake's troubled waters. Omar was nowhere to be seen. Death did not have to fight hard, for the boat propeller had gotten the better of me. So, in the end that would be it: no jumping out a window, no sharp blade, no anorexia, but a fatal blow from a rusty boat part that belonged to *Sputnik*. The spirits were cynical and destructive. I was surrendering to the fate of an unexpected yet imminent departure. So disappointing in earnest, and much ado about nothing. I had always hoped to kick the bucket with a little more panache, but this was no Greek tragedy. Just a stupid Siberian shipwreck.

Melscho's hands dragged me to the surface, bringing me out of my lethal torpor. I abruptly regained consciousness and started to spit water from my lungs and throat in a panic-stricken way. *Dedushka* was close to me. We both clung to the piece of wood that he had managed to grab after rescuing me, last gift from the sunken vessel. I caught my breath. I was alive but shivering, a sign that my body temperature was dropping dangerously low. We had been struggling against those freezing waters for far too long. I tried to move my legs in an attempt to warm my body. This could not be the end. I just had to stay focused.

It struck me that my entire life seemed to converge on this moment. Rage invaded my heart, and hopelessness too. With a hollow voice issuing from those depths, I implored all the helping spirits that I could think of to show me a way out of hell. *The loving and compassionate power of the spirits is the strongest force there is. Never forget that the spirits always answer positively when you ask for their help.* I begged Lusud-Khan, the Baikal water-dragon master, to let us live – the three of us.

The shore was at swimming distance, but the winds were implacable. Melscho was badly injured and bleeding, and Omar was still nowhere to be seen. I started to be able to swim, holding Melscho with one arm around his neck. A strong current pushed us toward the shore, with the piece of wood supporting our laborious progress. I then heard someone yelling at me. It was Omar. It took me a few seconds to locate him, though he was swimming close to us. He was making his way out of this nightmare too. "I've got Melscho," I yelled back at him.

I hauled Melscho out of the water up onto the deserted pebble beach, for he had drifted into unconsciousness. In addition to his head, other vital parts appeared severely wounded. He was still breathing, though almost inaudibly. I knelt beside him, enveloped his hands in mine, and gently kissed him on the forehead. At my touch, the brave *dedushka* opened his eyes and died in a last breath on the land of his beloved ancestors. His face was strangely peaceful as his soul was leaving his body. I closed his eyelids and caressed his hair. And then time stopped.

Omar's howls and cries brought me back to our disastrous condition. I stood up, trembling, and walked to him. We hugged each other, acknowledging that we had both survived the shipwreck but that Melscho was gone. We refused to let go of each other. My legs gave way under me. It was not the first time that someone had died in my arms, but Melscho's intervention had saved me from a premature and meaningless death. I would be forever linked to him and his lineage. We had met only this morning. Morning sounded like an eternity ago. Omar and I had died a thousand times since we embarked on *Sputnik*. We had to assist Melscho in his transition to other and hopefully more serene realms.

I picked up two large pebbles, put them in Omar's hands, and asked him to drum. The rocks fell to the ground. I picked them up and placed them back in his hands, which I enclosed in mine. I made him knock one pebble against the other until he became aware of the ongoing movement. "Drum for me!" I said. Omar rose from numbness and started to drum with all the force that he could muster. We had very little experience of actual death rituals. I had witnessed Gail performing her own *Phowa*, and I recalled our conversation in *la piccola piscina*. Maybe she had known about the shipwreck at that time and was now expecting me to complete some sort of initiation. As a matter of fact, Omar and I had been hurled without notice into a powerful yet merciless rite of passage.

Omar closed his eyes. I called him, but he did not respond. He was already gone in his own shamanic journeying. He continued to knock the pebbles with presence and regularity, which was impressive. I went to kneel beside *dedushka* again. I told him how much I loved him and thanked him for having saved my life. With my heart torn apart, I whispered that the time had come for him to leave this reality and say goodbye to his loved ones. I wanted to help him in transitioning, though I was lost as to how to proceed. *You know what you have to do.* I placed Melscho's hands on my heart. *Show me how to help you, dedushka,* I thought and prayed. *Please, show me, Melscho.*

Melscho and I are thrown back into squally Baikal waters, fighting for survival. This whole experience is getting worse and worse. "How many times will I have to die before you spirits are satisfied?" I scream at the top of my lungs. The least one can say is that their response is quick. An immense face, smirking, appears above the yellow horizon. Melscho drowns in the lake before I can endeavor to rescue him. The face then vanishes in a click of a finger, and so does the storm. I swim to the shore.

I walk on the beach, which consists of white sand, pebbles, and herbs. I take solace in a summer sun shining at the zenith. I wear an old white linen dress, sleeveless and torn at the neck. I call my spirit guide. This journey begins in such turmoil that he takes me to walk on the beach to take notice of his absence and realize how much I need him. After a certain time, the duration of which I cannot sense, I stumble over a large pebble and fall to the ground. I sob, each of my tears coloring the rocks a little more. "I'm sorry, Melscho. I'm a failure. I just cannot lead you over there," I say between sharp breaths. Melscho materializes, radiant, in front of me. It is his turn to place my hands on his heart.

"That's all right, Benedetta," Melscho compassionately says, like the wise elder that he is. He remains silent until I stand still and am able to look at him. "I don't expect you to lead me over there.

I am well taken care of by my ancestors," he adds, smiling, gently caressing my cheeks. He then sings in a language unknown to me that echoes like the deepest voice of the earth. Various birds and other animals approach us ceremoniously. They all want to listen to this peculiar voice. My hands are still resting on his chest. Melscho is summoning the animals, in fact. Pronouncing magic words and formulas, he invites me to join his sacred chanting, which I do. And for one precious moment we melt into a single energy, chanting a sweet spirit song that I seem to know by heart.

When silence resumes, the animals depart. *Dedushka* looks profoundly into my eyes. "Drop the masks, Benedetta," he says repetitively until the message pierces my skull and is imprinted on my brain. It looks like multicolored shamanic surgery. I then ask the most powerful shamans of Siberia, though I do not know who they are, to come and take care of him. They are twelve in total and each enters the frame by a different gate in the horizon, forming a perfect medicine wheel. Melscho releases my hands, stands up, and joins them. He is waving at me above the lake-turned-into-ocean when I hear Omar's energetic callback drumming to ordinary reality.

When I opened my eyes, Melscho's cold body was still resting in the same position in which he had died, but his soul was traveling to non-ordinary shores.

I was disoriented. To secure Melscho a safe journey beyond the veil, Omar suggested that we put together an *ovoo*, which was usual in Mongolian shamanic traditions. Later that day, when we were rescued, the storm had departed and the lake waters were deathly quiet. People gathered around the dead body, prayed for a while, and added small pebbles to the sacred cairn. Bolormaa's mother drove us to Bulagat's *dacha*. We assumed that relatives and local police officers would take care of the deceased. We were too exhausted to enquire about the situation.

Despite the comforting presence of Bolormaa's mother and Omar, I was obsessed with Melscho. By bedtime I was convinced

I could feel his breath on my neck. What were those masks that I was supposed to drop? One thought leading to the other, I naturally came to the conclusion that Melscho would still be alive had he not rescued me after the shipwreck and that he must have realized by now that my life was too insignificant to be saved. The situation was delicate and my breasts painful. Not wanting to wake anyone, I remained motionless and decided to concentrate on uncovering any sign of Melscho's presence. When the day broke, I was staring at the wooden ceiling, in a posture unchanged for hours. My bladder was on the verge of explosion. Looking motionless at one single and preferably luminous point had always provided quiet and focus to my restless brain.

Omar and Bolormaa's mother were still asleep. I listened to their synchronized breathing, which had a soothing effect. During the night, I had considered the possibility of drinking a little something that would have knocked me out, but accessing the shelf on which the alcohol bottles were stored would have meant waking up Bolormaa's mother, which I wanted to avoid. This was how I spent my first night at the *dacha*, not sleeping a wink all night. Guilt was eating me alive, and I preferred to stay alone with my self-generated dramas. Not exactly true. There were some spiders on the ceiling and a couple of bats in the belfry. Was that a sign that I was turning into a shaman? When Omar woke up and greeted me with an enthusiastic *priviet!* I welcomed him like the one and only messiah. I had survived the night and I rushed to the toilet, which was down in the woods.

Bulagat arrived later in the morning. Amid loss and sadness, he was peaceful. On the beach we recited, chanted, and danced to exhaustion. Omar and I had little memory of those first ceremonies. When we returned to the *dacha* it was twilight. No David Copperfield around, though. The sky was clear and magnificent with the promise of a memorable glowing moon. Bizarrely, the full moon had taken place the day before. Was there something to understand in these violent lunar energies? Undoubtedly, I preferred the comfort of Il Casolare and Italian lovers to tricky Siberian waters and awful shipwrecks. I did not have the nerve to imagine what the next full moon would serve us. Could anything be worse than what we had just experienced? And where would we even be?

Interrupting my prolific stream of thoughts, a generous red eight-sided plate of food landed in front of me. It was marked with a small heart-shaped "I am in love with a mathematician." Oh no. Not again. *Please don't tell me that Bulagat and Cylindro Anarchia share the same karma*, I thought to myself. We were supposed to spend a few days at the *dacha*, and my knowledge of Shakespearean sonnets was in fact very limited. *I believe that everybody should live according to his true nature,* Indro had said during our first conversation. There was great wisdom in those words. I hoped Indro was doing fine.

Bedtime was approaching. I was still obsessed with Melscho and ruminating on the idea that he had wrongly sacrificed his life for the benefit of mine. I kept this to myself. During our second night at the *dacha*, I was awake and another storm broke. Omar and Bulagat were snoring. I have always loved storms. I remembered how I once forced a friend, who actually needed little encouragement, to walk with me all the way to the end of a North Sea dock in raging stormy weather. I was about twelve. The wind was so strong that we had to hold on to each other tightly simply to be able to move forward. Engaging fully in the battle, we made it soaking wet all the way to the end. When we told our adventures to my friends' parents, they were livid. Mine would not have cared. We were told the true story of a child who had recently fallen from that dock and died. I did not really listen, the adrenaline still high.

During our days with Bulagat, we performed simple shamanic rituals with him, as well as *Phowa* ceremonies for Melscho. Omar insisted on doing these *à la lettre*, whatever that meant for him. Sogyal Rinpoche is at the top of his recovery toolkit. As much as I was willing to support my friend in this sensitive enterprise and eager to learn more about Tibetan Buddhism, I doubted that our ceremonies achieved their goal. I confided my doubts to Bulagat and how I was sure I was responsible for Melscho's death, a belief that was causing me anxiety and sleepless nights. "*Vnuchka*, Melscho wrong direction boat. He mistake and you not," he immediately said. The *Sputnik* captain had provoked his own fall by miscalculating the direction, and the winds had ruined any chance to avoid the rocks that tore our vessel apart. Bulagat added that Melscho had rescued me out of free will and that I was in no way responsible for his death. Everybody was relieved that Omar and I had withstood the storm and that Melscho's body was not lost to the waters. I breathed for the first time since the shipwreck and cried my eyes out in Bulagat's arms. Omar seemed puzzled by my sudden flood of tears. He came to sit beside me and held my hand until I calmed down. I was exhausted, in truth. That night, and all the other nights in the cottage, I slept like the dead. No pun intended.

The ten days we spent at the *dacha*, especially the last few, had their own magic. There was something utterly sweet and invigorating about them. We learned so much from Bulagat, merely by observing him and living the simple and authentic way of his truth. From the moment of my confession, Bulagat regularly plunged his eyes into mine as if he were massaging my brain, which was pleasant. I relaxed and started to enjoy our daily tasks, which included cleaning, fetching water, and cooking. I was delighted to tend to Bulagat's vegetable patch in his company and to prepare food for the animals. Omar and I got to know each other better, deeper, from this special place that only those who have shared drama know. We also laughed, when we were not silent. Or contemplating the stars. Or meditating. Or chasing ghosts – oh, just kidding.

Omar enjoyed meditating on the beach close to the small *ovoo* on his own. A private rendezvous with Melscho or with Buddha? Most likely with Ganbaatar and *la motocicleta*. The steel Mongol hero was attractive, and no one could ignore the seductive poetry of a romance lived in *la Mongolie profonde*. My friend had casually dropped his name into our conversations too many times for it not to be suspect. Despite this token of romanticism, my poor stomach remained shaky, and I continued to vomit here and there. *Part of me suspects that I'm a loser, and the other part of me thinks that I'm God Almighty,* said strawberry John. And between those extremes, shamans would be born and raised.

I spent a lot of my time at the *dacha* reflecting on how at times I could be grounded – yes, you can smile – yet so often lose myself in irrational fears. This seemed paradoxical to me. For three consecutive days and nights, I had been obsessed by my role in Melscho's end, to the point of losing sleep, without sharing it with anyone. I smiled. After all this time, after Les Acacias, after years of therapy. What was wrong with me? I struggled to understand the logic of my behavior. The good news was that my silence only lasted three days. Years ago, it would have taken on much bigger and destructive proportions. I was starting to see that the mental illnesses I had suffered were all symptoms of one same disease: loneliness. A very specific type of loneliness, though – the suffering endured by a soul that has isolated itself from its true nature and from the world. I was intrigued by the way one mental illness or obsession transformed into another. There must be a pattern there.

As an example, at some point my fear of spiders decreased and I was eating again, but I became obsessive about gas leaks. Going into the full story of my obsessive-compulsive disorders would be too long and too boring. By the age of twenty-one I was, however, spending up to five hours a night checking that the gas cooker was turned off in one endlessly repeated movement. I believe that this repeated movement was putting me in a state of trance that catalyzed my fears. I would usually lose track of space and time, hours feeling like minutes, and get my spirits back at dawn. I would then go to bed, exhausted and appalled, sleep no more than a couple of hours, if I remember right, and wake up tired. I always had difficulty recalling anything that happened during these night hours in the kitchen apart from the repeated movement. How normal was this?

It was strange, really strange. So were my days. I was still at college. My only way to avoid these horrible nightly operations was to go out and party. Preferably with alcohol. I never really did drugs; just a bit of cocaine, but I loved it too much to allow it to last. The last thing that I needed was to become a cocaine addict. Anyway, I am not the drug expert here. Like a virus that rewrites itself to avoid detection, one supposedly solved disorder would crawl back under a new form, under a new disorder. Spiders and anorexia into gas obsession and massive insomnia, in a rapid cliché. But the codes always remained the same, until I could track the roots of my virus. Loneliness and a terrible lack of love. And many other things. And Tony. And Frank. This was the pattern.

On the shores of Lake Baikal, it also became obvious to me that I had to learn to ask for help and to communicate what was happening to me. Only when I opened up to Bulagat and found support in our group of three did my fears and feelings of guilt start to dissolve. I had to learn to enjoy what life had to offer and stop wandering into imaginary worlds. I was, however, gradually getting bored by my realms of fantasy. After all, it was just a game, life was just a game, and I liked shamanic journeys better because they were real. "Drop the masks," Melscho had said. His message was clear. If my life belonged to me, I could stop hiding behind my masks. They had only offered a false sense of protection, yet perhaps a necessary one. And perhaps Omar had some masks of his own to drop. I loved him for that and for his determination to get over his addictions and to be of service. *Out of suffering have emerged the strongest souls, the most massive characters are seared with scars.*[19] One day, maybe. I suddenly felt proud of myself. Yes, I had survived, and I could perhaps start

---

19   Khalil Gibran

living now. Were Gail and Melscho plotting together? I felt proud of Omar too.

Ten days had passed – *tick-tock* – and the police officers were standing in front of Bulagat's door. He had commanded them, prerogative of a respected shaman, to leave us an airlock before any official interrogation on the accident in UU. He gave us two stones as a goodbye gift and accompanied us to the old *policeyskaya mashina*. "*Udachi*! *Udachi*! Omar and *vnushka* okay." I understood that he wished us well and trusted in the good outcomes of whatever awaited us next. In the city, they checked us in at Hotel Barguzin and took us right away to their offices. Thanks to Olga, we still had our passports, though Omar would have preferred that mine had sunk in the Baikal waters.

We spent an endless afternoon at the police station, telling our Siberian stories over and over again. The police officers were convinced that Melscho's death was accidental but were concerned about the issuance of my travel documents. They requested I prove that I was suffering from the most serious and peculiar illness, the only remedy for which was to be found in Irkutsk, since this was the story that I had served to just about everyone in Russia. I was naively counting on the officers' sense of compassion, which never came to fruition. I failed to produce any medical certificate of my precarious condition, but the shipwreck was a decent alibi for the missing documents. I did, however, offer free coffee readings *à vie* for all UU police officers. Strangely, they thought I was trying to bribe them with an unreliable European currency. What an appalling lack of imagination! I confessed that I was fortunate to have been cured during the shamanic workshop in Irkutsk, to which they reacted with loud *ochen' nadoyedlivyy* or something like that. When their in-house doctor declared that I was in excellent health – of course! shamans had cured me – they declared that it was frankly *podozritel'nyy*. I did not speak Russian, not my business. They wanted to know who I had bribed to get the visa waiver. I went silent.

We regained the Barguzin a few hours later, without our passports and with the inviolable restriction of staying in town. Cosmic Agent Omar 007 advised me to be careful, as we had probably been spied on since our arrival. In the middle of the night I managed to make a collect call to Mr Volchebnik, but the connection unexpectedly broke after two minutes – *kakoy syurpriz*! Once again, my salvation relied on my lawyer's creative solutions. I had to remember to send him a postcard. As night went on, I became increasingly worried about the menace of facing prison charges. Worst of all, Omar might be in trouble because of my behavior, as he had predicted at Sheremetyevo Airport. My friend was definitely a visionary.

Even in remote Siberia, Mr Volchebnik's contacts were efficient. From then on the police could only interrogate us in the presence of a certain Russian lawyer who presented himself the next day as an associate of Mr Volchebnik. This was going to cost me dearly. I would have to part with another fake Kandinsky that was hidden in a Swiss vault. LouLou's departure gift. Tony never saw through the trick, and it was excluded from the divorce settlement. A smart girl needs to keep a little something aside for emergency cases, and this was an emergency case. I decided not to mention the fake Kandinsky to Omar until we were out of Russia. The less he knew about Volchebnik, the better.

Like an angel fallen from the sky, the Russian lawyer settled an arrangement for us. What coffee blend did he use? Maybe not a Kandinsky. A Chinese mask? Melscho had advised me to drop the masks. No charges would be brought against me anyway, or Omar by extension, on the condition that we left Rossiyskaya Federatsiya within the next five days. Omar was vouching for me. Should I not exit Russia within the given term, he would be prosecuted as well. He was surprisingly supportive in this situation. If he harbored a little resentment for my immigration peccadillo, he gracefully swallowed it. By courtesy of our Siberian connection, a pink-dotted envelope containing 20,000 rubles had been deposited at a local tour operator, and my new credit cards were already waiting in Irkutsk. Omar's bank nevertheless complained when he refused to collect his credit cards in Moscow because he would only travel toward the east, following clear directives offered to us by the spirits during our stay at Il Casolare. How shockingly insensitive to the spirituality of their clients banks sometimes are.

Mr Volchebnik was tracking our moves and imposed daily morning check-in conversations with him to confirm that we were still out of jail. Should we have missed one of those calls, who knows what aggressive tactics he would have deployed to extract us from behind enemy lines. My lawyer was adamant that we had to take off within the terms of the ultimatum, meaning we had a maximum of three days in Irkutsk to make travel arrangements. Speaking about our next moves, Omar wanted to leave me the space to decide. I did not quite understand his deep motivations but did not enquire further. Too many questions killed the questions at the police station. We both skipped dinner and went back to our respective rooms. Despite our initial experience with its windowless ballroom, I was warming up to the Irkutsk Hotel, where we were staying. I immersed myself in a hot bath.

The meaning of the whole Russian experience confused me. Obviously I had to drop the masks, but there was more to it. I was continuously forced to make life-or-death choices, as if the same story was repeated over and over again. This had been going on since childhood. What was the crucial lesson I kept missing? Just in Siberia, I had survived a shipwreck, fought for survival with Melscho, and lost my possessions to the Baikal monster. At Il Casolare, there had also been the shamanic journey where I had chosen to live. When I was fifteen years old, I had prayed to God and his beloved son out of despair. I was then skin and bone and short on survival strategies. They were my last resort, and I asked them, crying from the bottom of my heart, to show me a way out of hell. That was a crucial night for two reasons: because I reached out to the spirits and because I asked for help for the first time ever. They answered positively. The spirits are the force greater than myself that kept me alive. I sincerely believe that. But for what reason? And why were Omar and I being challenged so harshly? Once again, I was asked to trust the spiritual path.

The kind of emptiness or nothingness that Omar and I were looking for in our Siberian days was of a new nature to us. It was born out of love and light. It consisted of a spiritual experience rooted in the reawakening of our indigenous souls and connection to ancestral lineages. Yes, the road was often challenging, but it was the price to pay for a better and more meaningful future. We had karma-cleansing duties to perform. Somewhere, somehow, I had always known that the adventure of writing our book was my way of growth. That writing the book was the medicine, our medicine. The spirits had only confirmed, actually preceded, this intuition. And it was a powerful medicine. Could it be that its power resided as much, even more, perhaps, in living and surrendering to the moves and turns of our journey than in the act of writing itself?

The spirits had instructed us to keep moving toward the east. I was prepared to continue following their instructions, despite the fact that it was an overwhelming perspective, considering what we had been through in Siberia. Where to go? To do what? Outside Russia, there would be no Mr Volchebnik to save us. I then realized that what we decided to do did not really matter. This journey was much more about learning to be than about doing anything specific. The entire experience revolved around birthing our new selves. And obviously, this included a devastating shipwreck, which we had survived, and the death of a man. I had no idea where to go next, but I was convinced that despite the hardships, we had to rise to the challenges that the spirits had laid down for us. The real test always comes when times get rough, and so does the gift.

Despite appearances, I was recovering well enough from the shipwreck and from my week in Brussels. Bulagat and Omar had taken good care of me, and I had loved staying at the *dacha*. I had come to consider what had happened with Carlito in Italy as anecdotic and of little consequence. Well, I felt a bit disgusted, in truth. *Learning to find the seedlings of our joy in what looks like sorrows and pain.* This is how we would be tested over and over again until we learned. There are two kinds of suffering: the kind that leads to more suffering and the kind that brings an end to suffering. Fearing what awaited us was useless, but this was hard. A matter of disciplining the mind and healing the broken heart, whatever that meant. This realization came to me as one of the gifts of our Siberian experience.

The water was getting cold; it gave me a welcome kick. I wondered whether Omar was doing all right. He had been a good friend to me since the start of our journey, which was a blessing, but he seemed absent at times. Some of his actions were intriguing, such as when he prayed at the Lady's feet in the cathedral in UU, and he was still tracking what I ate and drank. Omar easily talked about many things, but he remained shy and discreet about the true depths of his recovery process. I started to worry that the consequences of the shipwreck were falling harder on him than he was willing to admit to himself or to anyone else.

I understood fully for the first time that one of the reasons the spirits had created this journey of two was that one could sustain and bring light to the other when the other lingered in darkness. That was what Omar had done for me in Siberia and what I wanted to do for him now. I was determined to uncover what was going on with him as soon as we were out of here. I jumped out of the cold bath, wrapped myself in a towel, asked the spirits to give me guidance, and collapsed in bed.

The following morning, Omar was waiting for me in the breakfast room, the walls of which had been painted a loud orange. More proof that the interior designer had a knack for chakra-unbalancing options or was color-blind. Whatever. Omar seemed rested and welcomed me with a warm smile. I tried to eat a little something, unsuccessfully. Despite our troubles with the Russian police, my friend was willing to entrust me with the final word on our next destination. His faith in me was touching – or was he confused? I was carried away by the implications of the decision. I remembered that our destination did not matter so much, as long as we continued journeying toward the east and carefully listened to the spirits. Besides, they had commissioned a book from us, a challenge we had accepted.

"My dear, have you any idea of what you want to do next?" Omar asked with a lot of enthusiasm.

"Bangkok," I burst out unexpectedly. Omar's jaw dropped, and the apple that he was holding rolled to the floor. I read shock and disbelief in his eyes.

"No. No, my dear, I cannot go back to Bangkok. How about Borobudur?" A child went by behind Omar. He was laughing out loud and wearing a colorful *Welcome to Bangkok* T-shirt. Omar did not see him. The spirits had spoken their truth. *To search for God with logical proof is like searching for the sun with a lamp.* We had the T-shirt.

"Bangkok!" I repeated with an encouraging smile.

I was aware that Frank had established his practice in Bangkok, but my suggestion had nothing to do with him. This was, anyway, what I wanted to believe. The gods had never been short on jokes with me. Frank was a total snake charmer, in truth, of a more dangerous composition than Tony or Carlito could ever dream of being. I kept this to myself, considering how pale Omar had gotten. There was fear in his eyes. What had happened in Bangkok that he was not telling me? Could it be shame and guilt for a life that he had once led there and in other places of darkness? A life that he was committed to renouncing. Omar's past simply meant to me that he was human and that he had suffered. But I was perhaps missing something important. There were parts of my own story that I still struggled with and remained silent about. This would have to change.

Bangkok suddenly felt like one big mistake. Never mind the T-shirt or the lamp. When I suggested considering another destination, Omar categorically refused, to my surprise. It was too late – Bangkok had already exerted its merciless magnetism on us. My extravagant suggestion had become a common decision. From project manager to pariah, I was again flying too close to the sun. A lively *Ra-Ra-Rasputin* flooded the room. I started to wriggle on my chair. Our mood needed some lifting up. Omar smiled gently and mirrored my moves. In a minute, we were disco dancing by the buffet table, jeopardizing our fragile relationship with the local authorities. The time had come to leave Russia. *Za lyubov!* To love. I gulped a glass of Putinka Vodka for the road while Omar went to the kitchen to enquire about organic chamomile. We were both shaking.

AWAKE

PART 3

"Many wear the robe, but few keep the way."

KIM, RUDYARD KIPLING

Bangkok, 2 August 2015

"Awake!"

What the fuck! Did I just say that?

"What are you, brother?" Pak's voice reverberates inside my skull like a Tibetan bowl. No, my head is actually inside a Tibetan bowl. Not really; my head is inside a helmet. I am on the back seat of a motorcycle, racing like mad. The driver is yelling and dodging Bangkok's traffic down Silom Road at suicidal speed. "What are you, brother?"

"Awake!" I reply.

"Good. Now jump!" So I jump. I let go of the driver and open my arms. I feel my soles against the footrests and spring upward. I can fly.

Being in the air gave me clarity about the previous days. Benedetta and I flew from Irkutsk to Hong Kong, where we connected to Bangkok. We flew first class. Sogyal Rinpoche explains that *samsara* is the uncontrolled cycle of birth and death in which sentient beings, driven by unskillful actions and destructive emotions, repeatedly perpetuate their own suffering.[20] Yet we flew first class. We needed comfort, silence, and attention. We did what our Western education had taught us to do and what years of psychotherapy and spiritual workshops could not prevent. We hid the recent traumatic events in a sensual cloud of consumerism. Unskillful action. All it took to renounce our sacred postulates was a bit of a rough time in Siberia. *You know what you have to do. Writing the book is the medicine.* Destructive emotions. Indulging was our first mistake.

Landing at Hong Kong International Airport on Chek Lap Kok depressed me. What had life become? On my first trip to Hong Kong I had arrived in Kai Tak, one of the most dangerous airports in the world. Huge 747s landed on its only runway, ensconced between skyscrapers and mountains. One could peek during landing at everyday life through apartment windows. It was the most dramatic entrance to a fascinating city. The new Chek Lap Kok Airport felt like any other international-style piece of shit. The craving for the adrenaline rush was a serious indicator that a relapse storm was looming.

We had a few hours to spare at Chek Lap Kok before continuing to Bangkok; we spent them getting rid of our Siberian orphanage outfits. One may have the karma to find a teacher, but then one must create the karma to follow the teacher. We had found Bulagat, only to let bureaucracy snatch him away. Why not protest the police orders to leave Russia? Why not return to Russia with proper visas and sit with Bulagat in his *dacha* until something of the essential manifested in us? Sri Ramakrishna Paramahamsa said that tolerance, endurance, humbleness, love, harmony, faith, surrender, and devotion to God or to a fully realized guru should be present in ourselves at all times. One must always desire to be one with God or with a fully realized guru. Find God. That is the only purpose in life.

---

20   Sogyal Rinpoche, *The Tibetan Book of Living and Dying*

We strode into the Cathay Pacific lounge laden with glossy bags. *Enjoy it while you are still here. It will soon be over.* I emerged from the lounge's shower suite in Diesel shoes, 2(x)ist Gold Range underwear, an Egyptian organic cotton T-shirt and trousers, and an Ermenegildo Zegna light jacket. I kept the stone that Bulagat had given me in one of the pockets. I found Benedetta at the lounge's gleaming Long Bar, back to her colorful self in a silk Valentino gown, Prada sunglasses, and stilettos. She was sipping a Singapore Sling, lost in contemplation of the tarmac. I sat next to her and devoured the hors d'oeuvres. Our traveling budget had sunk in Baikal, and yet we were spending like there was no tomorrow. We laughed heartily.

Soon after we began taxiing toward the runway, the captain announced that we were running a few minutes late. Our plane was number eight in the take-off queue. He apologized, though he made it clear that the airline declined any responsibility for this calamity.

Elmer Magallanes was his name. The suffused buzz of the aircraft engines on hold brought to my mind Elmer Magallanes, the CEO of the Argentina subsidiary of a large American oil and gas company that had been my client. I had concocted a financing scheme for them that represented a tax saving of millions of dollars. Chuck Chowk, CFO and big fish in the world of oil and gas financing, flew to Buenos Aires to meet Elmer and my team because the structure was too good to be true. Chuck flew in the corporate jet. There has to be something beyond first class for executives who have earned millions but still cling to the money-making hamster wheel of ordinary reality.

I had arranged to take Elmer and Chuck to dinner at a fashionable grill where they could eat half a cow and keep the knife as a souvenir. Chuck and I were a bit late. When Elmer arrived at the restaurant, there was no reservation in either my name or his. A table was not ready for us. There must have been some confusion with the reservation. Elmer crashed. Ten minutes later, when Chuck and I arrived, Elmer was having a ferocious argument with the maître d'. I used to take clients to that place regularly, and, being a strong believer in redistribution of wealth, I had always tipped generously. In less than fifteen minutes, the maître d' organized a table for the three of us, in spite of it being one of their busiest nights.

Elmer was purple with rage. After doing the math, he realized that he had to wait the apocalyptic stretch of twenty-five minutes before he could sit at a table. "I've never had to wait that long in my life," he exclaimed. What was it with time and money? I felt a pang of resentment because our aircraft had to queue to take off, and yet I had paid for a full-fare first-class ticket. I was entitled not to queue at check-in or at the boarding gate – how on earth was I obliged to queue at the tarmac? I felt Elmer's rage boiling up my blood and fully realized the suffering that comes with power and money.

I had taken the wrong turn many years before, and finding the way back entailed a season in purgatory. I tried to dispel my pessimistic thoughts by reading the *Tintin in Tibet* that I had bought at the airport. I bought one each time I saw one; I probably owned twenty copies in spite of the fact that I kept giving them away. I offered it to Benedetta, because the author was Belgian, but she declined. Instead, she encouraged me to share my ruminations with her. Women are unfathomable.

"This was my last shopping spree. I'm done. I'm depressed. These unskillful actions can cost us our entire future. I will ask Pak to find me a *sangha* and check in to a Buddhist temple for the rest of my life." The thought of spending my life in the tropics wearing the robe was appealing.

"Temple? But, my dear, you're not even a Buddhist!" I was pissed. Benedetta's pragmatism was demolishing the romance.

"I don't care. I shall ordain as a monk." I could certainly do that. I had thought about it. Benedetta had even shown me an online tutorial about how to become a Buddhist monk.

"Monk? But, my dear, you travel business class!" That was fresh.

"This is no good time to bring up my contradictions, Benedetta. You are being cruel."

"Cruel? It is a pure observation of reality, your luggage tags show—"

"And the Dalai Lama?" I snapped.

"What about the Dalai Lama?" she asked cautiously. I had finally gotten her interested.

"Do you think the Dalai Lama flies economy class? Do you really think that? I've been to the Potala, my dear. He had a loo, a full-fledged Western bathroom with tiles and everything. The Potala Palace. In Lhasa." That was a hard fact.

"Can I offer you Benadryl? I bought them prescription-free at Watson's in Hong Kong Airport. Three 25mg tablets will knock out anyone." She was the ultimate pharmaceutical-junkie connoisseur.

"No. Let's have a drink." Did I really say that?

"The Shangri-La is sending a limo to pick you up." She knew how to handle me. I was still halfway between heartbroken and envious because she had arranged to go on a short honeymoon with Stein, a Belgian psychiatrist who she had never mentioned before our days at the *dacha*. The fact that the guy had set up shop in Bangkok made me wonder whether he was a refugee who fell from grace in the West and fled for a second life in the antipode.

Also, I was furious at the prospect that the lineage of the shaman-messiah could be questioned because of intercourse between the Mother of God and the runaway doctor. Maybe I had been called to take the place of Saint Joseph, the magnanimous guy who stepped into the shoes of the fleeting progenitor of that other powerful shaman. I might have been chosen to look after the ultimate Shambhala Warrior with fatherly love. However, I had checked my Facebook at Hong Kong Airport and learned that Carlito had taken a position as an analyst with an investment-bank in London. Maybe the eagle spirit made himself one with Carlito for breeding purposes only.

An impeccable flight attendant woke me up, helped me out of my duvet, and put my seat back into the upright position. To undertake the training to abstain from using luxurious beds is a rule adopted by members of the *sangha* and is followed by the layperson on special occasions, as an addition to the basic Five Precepts of Buddhism. Would I like to have an espresso, guava juice, or an aperitif before landing?

Stein was waiting for Benedetta at Suvarnabhumi Airport. We took an immediate dislike to each other. He looked as if he had come straight to the airport from a night of hard partying. I had an eye for that. We exchanged courtesies, and then they vanished. So there I was, freshly arrived in Bangkok, mentally and morally confused, freezing inside the hotel sedan in the most torrid heat man can conceive, missing Benedetta already and thinking about the reasons for which I had initially objected to coming to Krung Thep, the city of angels, as locals call Bangkok. My love affair with Bangkok had started long before and was the only one that I had been able to sustain.

After graduating best in my class, I received a job offer from a prominent law firm in Buenos Aires. Those were difficult economic times in Argentina, and getting a job offer bordered on the miraculous. My parents were ravenous. I said yes. I had a three-month window before starting my new job, so I took off to India. My contract entitled me to a miserable fifteen-day vacation for the first five years of employment. I did not fully grasp the grim prospect and the brutal grinding that my soul was about to undergo in embracing the corporate life.

Although I had done my fair share of backpacking in Latin America, nothing prepared me for India. I landed in New Delhi in late March to scorching heat and a shared YMCA bedroom with fan. My health deteriorated rapidly. I managed to crawl through Agra and Varanasi to Kolkata. I was feverish and had uncontrollable bouts of diarrhea. I was also determined not to go home. I read Forster's *A Passage to India* at Varanasi's burning *ghats*, where I wrote a poem about unrequited love. I arrived in squalid Kolkata in desperate shape and collapsed in a ten-rupee bed in a Salvation Army dormitory. An Irish guy sleeping next to me, who must have been the embodiment of my spirit guide, gave me Lomotil mixed with a purifying tablet in a glass of tap water, and said, "You look like you are going to die. Either you go to Bangkok or you go home. Make up your mind, and I'll take you to the airport in the morning."

Bangkok it was. It changed my life forever. A few nights later I was half drunk at an infamous Patpong bar watching Thai boxing and sharing beers with a flamboyant *katoey* – they don't like to be called ladyboys. She introduced me to Khao San Road, the Valhalla of the backpacking world, where I learned about the best routes for sneaking into Myanmar without a visa and how to trek in the Karakoram without being shot by the rebels. I read London's *The Call of the Wild* and started wondering whether by accepting that job I had mortgaged my life at a cheap premium.

There was no debauchery on that memorable first stay in Bangkok, with the exception of a little ganja and a puff of opium. Most importantly, I sat at temples. I made long distances on the overcrowded motorboats that run the Chao Phraya River in Bangkok, only to sit at temples. And I sat, in awe first and in precarious meditation later. The heat, the noise, the promise of nocturnal hedonism, all melted down when I sat. But I still came back to Buenos Aires and took that poison pill of a job. I had to get seriously sick before finding the antidote.

I returned to Bangkok several times. Each sojourn reflected the state of my decaying morals. More bars, more clubs, the occasional massage, a permanent relationship with a dealer, purchasing expensive furniture that I shipped home, returning to Khao San to sit at a bar and wonder when I had taken the wrong turn. I never stopped sitting at Wat Chana Songkhram, a minor temple near Khao San. Wat Chana saw me in different robes over the years. I had a residue of hope that within those walls my desire to be one with

God or with a fully realized guru could manifest itself, if I could just sit long enough.

This time I was booked for a week at the Shangri-La, courtesy of Benedetta's credit card. Luxury accommodation was another mistake, but I did not want to disappoint her by declining the generous offer. *There is no need to go back to old patterns.* The massage was the trigger. I booked an Ayurvedic oil and herb compress massage at a celebrated spa. As I entered a dimly lit room, I was welcomed by a masseur who invited me to take a shower while he prepared the oils. I came out of that shower with a fierce desire to demolish everything that my recovery had painstakingly put together over the last two years, ten months, and fourteen days.

One thing led to another. Had we come to Bangkok to confront our darkest fears and illusions? A few hours later I was dressed as a hippie ready to be eaten alive by the incessant human tide that is Khao San Road on Saturday nights. I mingled with the young and hallucinating backpackers, discovering the cool side of the world, feeling invincible, immortal, with enough energy to spin the universe. Coming back from full moon parties, having handed their passports to shady tour operators who would get them visas to Myanmar, knowing that they might not get their passports back, toying with the idea of never, ever going back home. I can get a gig as a DJ in Koh Phangan for the season and travel for the rest of the year. I can buy gems in Sri Lanka, sell them in Singapore, and travel for the rest of the decade. I can bring a suitcase of *bhul bhuliya* pills to Mumbai and travel for the rest of my life. I can write a novel about my life in a Thai prison. Anything is better than coming back to Leeds, Birmingham, Lubbock, Bethesda, Canberra. My brain exploded with possibilities. There was a six-year-old black B-boy dancing on breakbeats and performing stabbed windmills into a backspin, and I wondered: How could his dance reproduce my thoughts so accurately?

One thing led to another. *What was your most recent episode of acting-out behavior? What precipitated it? Identify your feelings and thought patterns before, during, and after the incident. What attempts did you make to try to stop the behavior?* Question twelve of "The First Step to Recovery" guide was ablaze like a billboard the length of Khao San. I said the serenity prayer again and again. The loudspeakers were madly sending waves of reggae, rock, and house. I fell deeper into the throbbing heart of Khao San. A grilled scorpion, a soup that smelled of cinnamon and star anise, Cinderella-snorting-coke T-shirts, fake driver's licenses, a hill-tribe woman in traditional clothes selling handicrafts, a foot massage in a bowl with fish, a tattoo parlor that reeked of incense.

What precipitated it? Was it surviving a shipwreck in Siberia? Or was it risking death, prison, and being summarily ordered to leave a country? Perhaps the lavish duty-free shops at Hong Kong Airport? *Identify your feelings and thought patterns before, during, and after the incident.* I was feeling empty but trying to be content. I was trusting. However, a relapse is the result of a chain of minor decisions. I was not paying attention to them: not writing to my sponsor, not going back home after the shipwreck, believing that Benedetta was the Mother of God, indulging in luxury, vanity, and an empty lifestyle. Not facing my fear of being abandoned and my feelings of inadequacy, anger, and loneliness. Denying my feelings and sinking into isolation. The growing feeling of failure, guilt, and frustration. It was a one-way road to relapse.

What attempts did you make to try to stop the behavior? I was out in Khao San. I did not know how it happened. I bumped into a guy near the tattoo parlor, we smiled, and he said something in Khmer. I knew this routine. I kept walking, and five pills of *yaa baa* landed in my right hand. A few baht banknotes slipped out of my pocket, and then we were gone. It was the eternal flux of energy down Khao San, the ethics of the trade, trusting the accuracy of bad karma. The pills in my palm burned like a stigma. I feared that my sweating palm would dissolve the meth and the caffeine. Holding the potentiality of the gift that *yaa baa* brings was so powerful. What if I swallowed the five of them – would I become Christ? Pol Pot? Buddha? Was I the new shaman-messiah?

"You okay my friend?" said a *motorsai*, a motorcycle-taxi driver. He touched my elbow and smiled at me. "Need water? Can I take you somewhere?"

Could it really be that Irkutsk was only two days ago? "Yes please, my friend. Silom. DJ Station. How much?" Oh no. Not again. Not after all this time. Was DJ Station what I was craving? To be suffocatingly packed into this legendary club, to feel "Alive" inside my skull, to have all the energy that *yaa baa* could give me, to dance and sweat like mad until I disintegrated into the fleeting, hot, humid night among the young, the invincible, the immortal?

The *motorsai* gave me a knowing wink. We raced like thunder, dodging traffic. I hoped that the adrenaline of the ride would make me feel alive, but it was not happening. Suddenly, the infernal traffic noise started to melt down into a long and serene *om* mantra. What the fuck? Was it a bug inside my ear? I was tightly holding on to the driver with my left arm and clutching the *yaa baa* in my right hand.

"Remember Baba?" What the fuck? Is Pak talking inside my head, or is it a flashback? Baba? Yes, Baba Ram Dass. We drove at light speed by the Hindu temple on Silom Road, the multicolored pyramid clad with sculptures that looked like Disneyland on acid. And then time and space disassociated. We were still racing like a thunderbolt, but the temple stayed with us, and it became alive. The carved lions, monkeys, cows, the gods, the Hindus chanting and lighting candles: I could see it all in slow motion. Baba Ram Dass. *In these few years we had gotten over the feeling that one experience was going to make you enlightened forever. We saw that it wasn't going to be that simple.*[21]

Pak was reciting from Ram Dass's *Be Here Now* inside my head while the whole world around me was coming to a standstill, with

---

21   Ram Dass, *Be Here Now* (New Mexico: Hanuman Foundation, 1978)

the exception of us on the motorcycle, still racing like a *vajra*, a thunderbolt. What the fuck? *And for five years I dealt with the matter of "coming down." The coming down matter is what led me to the next chapter of this drama.* The *yaa baa* was glowing like embers in the palm of my hand. I breathed in. My nostrils widened to their maximum width. I breathed in the whole Mariamman temple, the entire Hindu cosmogony, thousands of years of *pujas*, the burning *ghats*, and my fever as a lonely kid in Kolkata. *I have a new heart that I must learn to use.* As I breathed out, I stretched my fingers and let the five pills fall from my hand into a turmoil of street vendors, heat, rain, and a flash of lightning from heaven.

Where had I left this? Oh yes, I said that I was Awake, before jumping from the motorcycle. Pak and I used to ask each other, "What are you?" and the other would reply "Awake!" in reference to *The Dhammapada.*[22] "Good. Now jump!" said Pak. So I jumped. I let go of the driver and extended my arms. I felt my soles against the footrests and sprang upward. I could fly.

I fell on the sidewalk, rolled against the hard surface, and landed against a tree at the entrance of a restaurant. Unscathed. I took off my helmet and saw that the motorcycle I had just jumped from had skidded sideways in the wet street and had hit a car. The driver was lying on the ground. Traffic came to a total standstill. Other *motorsai* gathered to help him. I threw the helmet away and scurried for cover at the first *soi* that crossed Silom Road, all the way to Surawong, where a taxi was quietly waiting. I could not deal with another wreck.

"Do you know who I am?" Pak's voice still reverberated inside my skull; with less urgency, though.

"I'm not sure who I am. Shit, my *motorsai* guy is dead, man."

---

22 One of his students asked Buddha, "Are you the messiah?" "No," answered Buddha. "Then are you a healer?" "No," Buddha replied. "Then are you a teacher?" the student persisted. "No, I am not a teacher." "Then what are you?" asked the student, exasperated. "I am awake," Buddha replied. *Dona Sutta*, n.d.

"His name is Prasong. He passed out, too much *yaa baa*. He will be all right in the morning. I will tell the guys to wake him up after we leave for the temple."

"Do you know him?"

"I remember him."

I stopped asking myself what was real and what belonged to non-ordinary reality. Maybe it was a flashback. I had been attributing every strange thought to the withdrawal effect. I had also stopped asking myself if I was going to die. After that night, I knew that I was not. This was not a flashback. *You are on to a new journey.* I got into the taxi and checked and rechecked myself for injuries: no blood, no bruises, just short of breath. My money and Chinese counterfeit iPhone were still in my pocket. The clock on the driver's panel read 4:45 a.m. I called Pak and started crying the moment he picked up. *I am still in the same body, but I have a new soul.*

"Where are you, brother?" he asked kindly.

"Silom. Taxi. Accident."

"I know. You need doctor, brother?"

"No." I checked and rechecked again.

"Are you a mess?" This was the safe word we used back in our clubbing days whenever we needed to be extricated from a situation that had become too intense.

"Yes, brother." I started sobbing silently.

"*Learn to listen to the new soul. There is no need to go back to old patterns, they do not belong to you any more.* Pass me the driver." I passed the phone to the driver and they had a brief conversation in Thai. The driver then passed the phone back to me, smiling amicably. "You can sleep now," Pak said.

I hung up and followed his instructions.

I woke up to a hazy sunrise. The heat was starting to build up. We were somewhere in an ugly industrial area. We drove into a small temple-like structure with soaring Garudas made of concrete perching on the roof. An elderly lady greeted us and escorted me to a crowded waiting room. The driver indicated that he would be outside. I sat on the floor like everybody else and took a moment to absorb the environment. Two plastic fans swirling in opposite directions created the illusion of a breeze. There was no breeze. Maybe I was ready to cross to the other shore and find God, if I could just sit long enough.

A catchy tune was intermittently coming from a flat-screen TV that hung from a wall. A family ranging from a minute gray-haired matron to a couple of infants and their pet monkey were smiling as one of their offspring, a beautiful Thai girl, received a double-tiger magic tattoo on her back from the expert hand of the *ajarn* in the adjacent room. An *ajarn* is a monk who has learned the art of tattoo magic. We could hear the *ajarn* chanting the ritual *kata* in the ancient Khmer language in order to instill the protective magic in the tattoo.

Next in line to get a tattoo was a wiry guy, most likely a Muay Thai fighter, who had already a *Gao Yord* magic tattoo on his back. *Gao Yord* represents the nine spires of mythical Mount Meru, extending the highest level of protection to the bearer of this tattoo. I had gotten my own *Gao Yord* several years earlier in the temple where my friend Pak had ordained as a monk. By taking these vows he was committing to service, poverty, and celibacy, leaving behind the lifestyle that we had shared since we met. For the protective magic of the tattoo to have effect, the receiver must observe certain moral principles that typically include not drinking alcohol, not using intoxicating substances, and not having sex with someone else's partner. It is also advised to observe a celibacy period from the day of getting the tattoo. I was not becoming a monk, but I would be getting a taste of Pak's new life by abiding by some of these moral principles.

The young girl came out and was cheered by her family. She kissed the monkey on the cheeks, and they left. The Muay Thai fighter and I smiled at each other with sympathy; we had both come alone. A young assistant approached me with a plastic basket containing cigarettes, orchids, incense, and a few baht banknotes. Could I offer a few more baht? I emptied my pockets and produced my remaining Thai currency plus a couple of wrinkled US dollar notes. I looked the assistant in the eyes for a second, took my cellphone in my hand, took out the Thai chip that I was using, and left the device in the basket as well. It is a millenary tradition that an offering including incense and flowers is made to the *ajarn* in exchange for the magical tattoo. In modern times this offering is complemented with cigarettes, cash, and the occasional electronic device.

I was naked: no money, no cellphone, no Benedetta, no *sangha*. There I was again, detached from it all. I had no lover in bed, no children to send to school, my kitchen was empty of any perishables while being on the road, no work to go to, no plants to water. I had a fat, smiling monk ready to pierce my flesh a hundred thousand times with a sharp steel needle that had not been sterilized, with an ink of his own making that included serpent's poison together with a mix of herbs. A tattoo that he would pick on the part of my body that he deemed appropriate. I had no say in the affair. Not quite what my mother expected. Would I ever be able to find my way back into the legion that was at that moment sleeping in Buenos Aires? Maybe I had been cut out forever. Maybe I was awake for a reason larger than a lover in bed and morning coffee. Maybe it was just the flashback. Two years, ten months, and fifteen days.

The wiry guy indicated with polite gestures that I should go next. I was, as always in Buddhist temples, in awe of the presence of the monk, a big, fat one, smiling lovingly, all visible skin covered in magical tattoos. The wiry guy would stand by me during the tattoo ceremony and provide the needed help. Everybody was happy. In this very surreal chapter of my life, a figment of self-preservation made me notice that nobody had washed their hands. I yielded to the experience and decided to neglect the bacterial concern.

"*Ajarn*," I said, kneeling respectfully in front of the monk but talking to his assistant, who knew a little English. "Can I ask which *sak yant*? And where?" I was not totally out of control. Before the fat monk started inking my body, I wanted to know what type of tattoo he was about to give me and on which part of my body. *Sak yant* tattoos are truly beautiful, but I wanted to have a modicum of information before he tattooed, for example, a soaring Garuda across my forehead.

"*Rishi*. Chest," the *ajarn* said gravely, without need for translation. The monk knew that I would not dare contradict him. Besides, I had no money left, no cellphone to call Pak, and the driver waiting outside the temple would not make a strong ally if I decided to flee. I knew the *Rishi* tattoo: the hermit, the sage, the shaman. This was the holy *sak yant* tattoo that granted the protection of the wisest teachers and entailed the highest moral commitments from the tattoo bearer. I could not have *Rishi*. I was not ready to sustain such moral commitments. I was going to fuck up on one of the most sacred spiritual vows I could ever take. I had wondered whether there would be a time in my life when I would feel ready for *Rishi*, but it was not that day. No matter how honest a part of me was about living a life in recovery, another part of me was freaking out. Had the previous night been the last crazy night in my life?

"No *Rishi*, *ajarn*, I'm not ready yet." I placed my palms together, touched my forehead with my thumbs, and prostrated even deeper. "No *Rishi*, *ajarn*. Please," I mumbled again, my lips brushing the fake Persian carpet. The monk chuckled, grabbed me by an arm, and looked into my eyes.

"Now relax," was all he said.

The *ajarn's* assistant and the Muay Thai fighter helped me out of my T-shirt and stretched me on a futon on the floor. They placed the palms of their hands over the sides of my chest, creating a canvas where the monk would start his work. Their humid hands gave me a warm sensation of love and a faint cellular memory of tribal life. From the floor perspective I could see towering Buddhas, golden Garudas, plastic flowers, and a rotating fan that reminded me of a pizza joint in the neighborhood where I grew up. The monk then stabbed me in the chest, and he stabbed me again and again with the merciless inked needle at the speed of a sewing machine.

. . . .

Bangkok, 5 August 2015

"What do you mean? Frank is real."

"No, Frank isn't real. The story you have with him isn't real. And you won't jump out the window. You can use the door now. You just have to get up and walk out the door."

"I cannot."

"Yes, you can. You aren't imprisoned any more. The prison of your own thoughts is collapsing. Jump out windows if you want, but only in shamanic journeys."

"I'm terrified."

"We know you are, but you have to confront your darkest fears and illusions. There is no other way around it." I woke up. The alarm clock indicated 4:45 a.m. Frank was God-knows-where but not in the bedroom. *We live as a dream, alone,*[23] as Omar used to say. Who was he quoting? I was feeling sick and nauseous again. My head was banging. The air conditioner was panting and rattling. The heat had become unbearable.

Omar and I had left Irkutsk a couple of days before, escorted by the police. We had decided to travel first class, in compensation for the difficult days behind us. At least, that was how we had justified the extravagant expense. We were anxious about what might happen in Bangkok. We bought expensive clothes at the airport's duty-free during our stopover in Hong Kong. Omar mumbled for hours about how years of subliminal consumerist propaganda had instilled dormant codes that had led us to mistake safety for comfort.

---

23   Joseph Conrad, *Heart of Darkness* (London: Penguin Classics, 2007)

"Too much Marx killed Marx," I said. We nevertheless got rid of the clothes that Bolormaa's mother had donated to us with gratitude and relief. *Adieu*, destitute orphan fashion.

Shortly after take-off from Hong Kong, I observed Omar interacting with this upper-crust environment. He was at ease. For a second I had a glimpse of the lawyer he had been, a charming *conquistador* of modern times sealing deals the world over, dressed in Prince of Wales checks and herringbone, flying from one nightclub to the next. Yet bored and absent, despite the kindness and the smiles. Out of curiosity I wondered whether his activities had been legal. Not that I really cared. I reckoned that they must have been, for my friend had little in common with Mr Volchebnik. That being said, laws are shaped by man, and legality has never sheltered against immorality or unethical behavior. This thought made me yawn. I had ruled on the matter years before. As far as I was concerned, Omar could have the past he wanted.

I went to the toilet and looked at myself in the mirror with satisfaction. My new Valentino dress was risqué, if a bit tight at the hips. I was not the same woman as the one who had looked at herself with tears in her eyes in the Venetian mirror in the toilet of Pisa Airport only a few weeks earlier. Something was changing in me. *Learning to find the seedlings of our joy in what looks like sorrow and pain.* I had a vision of myself meditating at one of the temples Omar had mentioned. Frank might even take a liking to that. I sincerely hoped that Frank would allow me space in Bangkok to integrate what we had learned in Siberia.

I went back to my seat and found Omar pretending to read the *Asian Financial Times.* He raised his head, smiled at me, and went happily back to a *Tintin au Tibet* hidden behind the newspaper. I giggled. I loved it when he did things like that. I thought that he was reading it for pure juvenile fun, but soon he tried to start a conversation about Hergé, the Belgian author of *The Adventures of Tintin.* In a Marxist-anti-colonialist tirade, which I found rather amusing, he stated that Hergé was racist and that this was especially visible in *Tintin au Congo*. Though I agreed with the latter, I did not pursue this conversation, out of boredom. Belgian privilege. I would also not mention my father's business in Congo, remembering how Omar had lectured a poor French backpacker who had joined us for breakfast one morning in Ulan-Ude on *Le livre noir du colonialisme* and Frantz Fanon. I nevertheless asked Omar why he was reading *Tintin au Tibet*. "Because I like it," he answered enigmatically. I smiled and asked a flight attendant to bring us two espressos.

Omar was still reading. How had a glorious businessman and partygoer become a Vipassana coach with a passion for Ayurvedic mixtures? Not the why but the how. This must have been a gradual process. Maybe the work of a lifetime. I was not certain whether he fully acknowledged his new identity, but this thought might have been a projection of my discomfort with my own identity shift. Because this was what my life had been about since I had jumped out the window and what this journey revolved around for me: opening the cage and birthing a new identity, being reunited with the ancestral mysteries of my soul. I shared these views with Omar, and he replied that I was being vague and repetitive. Temporary sequel to his previous self, for sure. Fair enough.

The sensation of safety that we had enjoyed during the flight vanished the moment we landed in Bangkok. The heat was suffocating. I was under the impression that the Siberian shipwreck was only a foretaste of what awaited us in this city. *Welcome to Bangkok*, said the T-shirt. A double-sided message with an irony that was breaking open on the tarmac. *The fool doth think he is wise, but the wise man knows himself to be a fool.*[24] Had we come here to confront our darkest fears and illusions?

"We need to talk. Please join me in Bangkok." I had received this text message from Frank while Omar and I were still in Irkutsk

---

24   William Shakespeare, "As You Like It" from *The Complete Works of William Shakespeare*

finalizing our travel arrangements. It took me by surprise. To what degree was Frank being sincere? I chose to believe that he was completely. A fantasy junkie always looking for love from a place of fragility that excluded discernment, this is what I was. Frank knew this very well, for I had been his patient on the olive sofa. Omar looked disappointed when I brought up Frank's invitation. "What sort of a psychiatrist has sex with a patient? Moreover, for a financial consideration! Open your eyes. Stein is a bitch." I was not willing to open my eyes to Omar's remarks. I retreated into a childish and exasperated silence. The good doctor was my pagan idol and crooked love my religion.

Frank suggested that we spend a week at his place in Bangkok. Obviously, his invitation excluded Omar, who started building an argument about how we had come to the Orient to learn about shamanism and not to indulge in the sensual life, of which the West could provide plenty. It had not provided plenty to me, so I presented my absolute need of a short break to recover from the recent events and be able to continue in our spiritual quest. "What you do today can cost you your entire future," he warned me. Patronizing. I nevertheless loathed leaving Omar on his own, and I booked him in at the Shangri-La Hotel, anticipating that he would enjoy a spell of five-star treatment. This was my way to show how sorry I was to leave him stranded and that I cared about him. Each time I had tried to enquire about his recovery from addictions, I had been served a laconic "I'm fine." I was not sure my friend was fine at all. The Shangri-La would provide a fine shelter during my absence. But the more we tried to have plans, the more we were thrown off track.

Frank was waiting for me at the airport. Bangkok had given him an exotic aura. His eyes radiated ambitiousness, selfishness – everything that I mistook for lust. He was more attractive than ever in a casual linen outfit that represented for me the fantastical promise of tropical love. He smelled of tobacco, cheap cologne, and sweat. He placed his arm around my waist as if to mark his possession and curtly greeted Omar, who responded with glacial enthusiasm. I hugged Omar briefly, and then Frank and I headed for the exit. We had to wait for more than an hour in the taxi line. Didn't Frank have a car? *Hell is empty and all the devils are here,*[25] obviously standing in taxi lines.

The moment we crossed the tollbooth to the highway, Frank grabbed my knee and slowly pushed up my dress, caressing my thigh to the crotch. Once again I would live with my good doctor's terms. The driver caught us in the rearview mirror and tuned the radio to strident Korean pop. I was embarrassed but could not prevent myself from moaning. It was working magically well, but I suddenly had this image of a sovereign inspecting his troops in a far-off colony. "The oppressed will always believe the worst about themselves,"[26] Omar often said. Who was he quoting again?

Frank had a tiny, uninspiring apartment down an alley in the heart of Chinatown, with a narrow entrance amid multicolor neon signs and smoky food stalls. An IKEA chair had replaced the olive sofa of yesteryear. I sighed. The gloominess of the room was only the preface to the jumble inside. "I don't have a maid," Frank said by way of an apology. Chinese music from the alley could be heard all day and night. There was no flower bouquet, no champagne bottle, nothing welcoming whatsoever. I could not make the connection between this apartment and the Frank I knew, or thought I knew – someone clean, controlling, and organized to the point of obsession. I followed him to his bedroom, and we had sex: regular, mechanical, ordinary sex. It seemed the only possibility available to us. When he was done, he went into the bathroom. I heard him fumble in the cabinet, and then he smashed the mirror. I was surprised but not scared.

---

25 William Shakespeare, "The Tempest" from *The Complete Works of William Shakespeare*

26 Frantz Fanon

A couple of days went by. Frank said that it was too hot to be roaming around. He brought takeaway food or we sat at nearby food stalls. We had regular, mechanical, ordinary sex in the mornings and in the evenings. His mind seemed to be anywhere but in the bedroom. He would be absent a couple of hours a day to run undetermined errands. I had better not come with him, he insisted. The traffic was preposterous, and he was riding motorcycle taxis; I would be scared to death. He promised to take me to the temples, palaces, and parks. He never did.

I started venturing out of our hovel when he was away. I could spend up to two full hours inside the nearest 7-Eleven. I enjoyed their air conditioner. I found a cyber-café next door that served tepid filter coffee. This was definitely not the Orient that Omar raved about. Or was it? Only joking. I made a bold move and called the Shangri-La. I wanted to catch up with my friend. And I wanted to ask him how bad it was to use heroin. But I hung up. What would I say if Omar asked me how I was doing? We had agreed to meet by the end of the week. I felt terribly alone, and it was entirely my fault. *The oppressed will always believe the worst about themselves.*

It was past midday, and we were lying in bed. Frank was sound asleep. He was using drugs. Not pharmaceutical drugs, the other kind, the ones sold by shady men in alleys or by gangsters in limousines. My mental hospital episode had given me a good knowledge of pharmaceutical junk, but I had remained hopelessly illiterate on the other side of the drug universe. How bad was it anyway to use heroin? I recalled the film *Trainspotting,* which looked pretty grimy. It could not possibly be good in any way. Besides, Frank had started borrowing money from me to buy food, cigarettes, and beer. My fairy tale was letting me down.

I turned over in bed. A syringe dropped on the floor. "Diamorphine hydrochloride," Frank had said. Who was this man? He must have started to take heroin after settling in Bangkok. Perhaps he had fled Brussels to take a final plunge in his own darkness, away from everything he knew. If so, why had he reached out to me? Did he hope to be rescued? But what did I really know of him? Not much, and his past was a well-guarded mystery. Besides, my mind was so blurred at times that I could very well have missed the most obvious, that Frank had been a drug addict for years. And if that was true, what to do? I started to cry.

I had hardly slept since Irkutsk. It was my turn to fumble in the bathroom cabinet. The shattered glass was still there after two days. Frank had promised to buy a broom, but he had not done it yet. I could probably find a broom myself at the 7-Eleven or at the nearby Tesco-Lotus supermarket. I found painkillers, antacids, and laxatives in the bathroom. I held the pills in my hand and smelled them. Would they still taste the same as before? I put the pills in my mouth. Would I still enjoy the ride? Before I could swallow them, I spat the pills on the floor and slammed the cabinet door. I grabbed a can of Singha beer, then a second one and a third one. I eventually landed on a bottle of gin. I wanted not to feel anything for a few hours. I wanted to forget everything. "Ambien, floor," I thought. And I indeed fell asleep. Knocked out.

There is a trail of blood on the stone floor. It is past midnight, but the lights are on. I am cold. The windows have been left open. As silent as a mouse, I follow the trail until I reach the white marble hall. I know this place. I know it well. I have been here before. I look up. His body is hanging from a rope tied to a chandelier. He is spinning like a top. The movement suggests that he might be alive, but this is an illusion. He does not react when I touch him, and I cannot find a pulse. I hear voices. They are still in the house. I rush under a marble table, which is covered by a large cloth that shelters me from their sight. My breathing is extremely loud, too loud. I try to stop breathing.

I woke up disoriented and thirsty, with the image of a faceless body hanging from a rope above my head. Frank was by my side. I went to the bathroom, looked at the smashed glass on the floor, and drank warm beer from a can I had left by the toilet seat. Disgusting. I opened the refrigerator and grabbed another beer. I closed my eyes and rolled the can on my face. I enjoyed its coolness. The air conditioner worked only intermittently, but Frank did not seem to care. He was still asleep. Maybe he was dead too. I opened the can and gulped its contents in almost one go, which refreshed me. I sat on the bed beside Frank and kissed him gently on the lips. My pagan idol was still breathing. His chest was moving up and down. Not dead. I drifted off again.

LouLou pours himself a glass of brandy and lights a fire in a monumental fireplace. The night is chilly. Unexpected voices make him jump. His glass glides from his hand and falls to the floor, shattering in a million tiny crystals. "My love, where art thou?" It is Frank. Too bad LouLou is not in the mood for love. "In the drawing room," he answers. While Frank is mixing a drink, my uncle replays the scene of their meeting. He likes doing so. LouLou runs into Frank at the Baden-Baden Casino. "Monsieur, follow me please," Frank says to him, expressing the anguish of lovers who meet for the very last time. He follows Frank into the gentlemen's toilet. Frank gives a crisp 5,000 Russian-ruble note to the young and uniformed toilet attendant. "Five minutes," he commands. The attendant obediently stands at the door, diverting clients to other toilets.

Frank grabs LouLou by the wrist and shoves him into a cubicle. LouLou is ready to surrender. He curls his lips as if to say something. "I need to pee," he begs in the lowest possible voice, hoping that Frank will rescue him from distress. Frank kneels in front of LouLou. He takes his hands inside LouLou's pants, grabs him by the testicles and slashes them with a pocket knife. LouLou screams with divine delight. He wants more. "One minute," announces the nervous toilet attendant. LouLou's high-pitched sounds are compromising him. Frank emerges transfixed. He washes the blood from his hands and face and wipes it with toilet paper. *Will all great Neptune's ocean wash this blood.*[27] Back in the drawing room, Frank hangs LouLou from a chandelier and leaves him to spin.

I woke up howling. I was hyperventilating and my heart beating too fast. What was this? A dream? It was as if I had been part of the scene watching my uncle dying from a concealed back door. This was horrible, and Frank was there too. How could that be? My mind must have made up a false story. Not the first time. I was taken by a strong wave of nausea and rushed to the bathroom. I vomited and vomited again on the toilet seat, in the corners where we had piled the broken glass, and on the bathmat. Violent stomach cramps had gotten the better of me. I fell asleep on the floor, prostrated on my right side, amid pills, empty beer cans, and a bottle. Frank eventually woke up. He gave me a glass of water and spooned me until I recovered from the spasms.

"Are you awake?" he asked me in a distant tone. He did not seem happy about the situation. What to say?

"I don't know," I answered, shaking. He mumbled that I would have to clean the bathroom later. Bloody maniac. He swallowed some pills and helped me to stand up. He brought me back to bed, and, touching my forehead, declared that I had a fever. After a short silence, he added that he needed to pay gambling debts. Was I willing to lend him money? I was finally beginning to see my good doctor's true colors. I was indeed burning. Frank looked at me sternly, as if my fever was some bland excuse not to talk about his problems. He went back to the bathroom and brought two 400mg ibuprofen tablets and a can of Singha. "Here, take two. You'll be all right in no time," he said. I gulped the tablets and choked on the beer. He then slowly prepared to shoot heroin. My teeth were chattering. I wrapped myself in our only towel and fell asleep.

I am standing on a large window frame. I recognize this place. I have slept in this bedroom. The frame is my exact size, and the

---

27   William Shakespeare, "Macbeth" from *The Complete Works of William Shakespeare*

window is wide open. I am seventeen years old, and I want to jump off this window frame, like the soaring Garuda. But things do not go according to plan. Before I can make my move, the window frame breaks and starts flying, with me as a passenger. Followed and pushed by a group of eagles, the frame quickly goes up into the sky until I reach a galaxy, and then another one. My window frame suddenly tips up horizontally, opening a black hole in the galaxy. I almost topple over the edge, but I manage to keep my balance. A voice tells me to jump into the void.

"Are you scared?"

"Yes!" I yell.

"Good. Now jump!" I let go of the window frame and extend my arms, and I jump. I feel my soles against the frame and spring upward. As I am falling, a large white dragon with crystal mauve eyes catches me on his back. I hold him tightly as he makes loops and flies extremely fast. I like him. He is gentle. We both giggle like the children that we are, although he seems ageless to me. A creature from another time, another space, another era.

The wind starts blowing to the point that I fall from the back of the dragon. We are both sucked into an enormous spiral of green and silver light mixed with rocks and stardust. I scream, but there is nothing I can do to stop it. Strangely, the dragon seems to be having the time of his life. Colored bubbles burst from his mouth when he tries to speak, as if he has eaten intergalactic soap. I close my eyes and surrender to the brutal winds of the spiral. In a curious way, I enjoy it too. After an endless time, the spiral spits me back into the galaxy, where friendly animals have been waiting for me. I am dirty, and my clothes are torn apart, but I do not care. The horizontal window frame is there to hold me again, but I do not need this vessel any more. I can fly and walk among stars. An eagle comes to rest on my shoulder.

I enter a white tunnel with the eagle, a wolf, and a panther. They are protecting me. Or am I protecting them? As I am walking, each of my steps projects colored shapes on the white walls. I am inside a magical instrument with a vibration I cannot hear yet. A muffled song plays inside my heart. I walk to the point of exhaustion and exit the tunnel. Out there the sky is blue and the sun shines high. It reminds me of the desert plains of the shamanic journey I made at Il Casolare. *Writing the book is the medicine.* I walk toward the east, and Apollo appears in front of me. My god of light, of sun, of life. The eagle is with me. I have turned back to being thirty-four years old.

"I'm scared to jump out a window if I wake up from this dream," I burst out.

"This isn't a dream, Benedetta. This is a journey," Apollo quietly replies.

"I'm still scared," I say shyly.

"Why would you be?"

"I don't know."

Apollo takes me back to 13 March 2013. Perched on a cloud, I observe myself jumping out the window at Damocles. The scene is verging on the ridiculous. What was I thinking, that day and all the other days that led me to this desperate breakout? "Your suffering isn't ridiculous," says Apollo. "Suffering never is." I see myself lying unconscious on the pavement surrounded by paramedics dressed in red. They are busy checking my vitals. Shortly after regaining consciousness, I ask to be driven to Les Acacias because "I believe they have been waiting for me." The next minute I sign the admission form at the madhouse. The full let's-get-better package. Amen.

"Is this how it looked from above?" I ask Apollo, taken aback.

"It depends on the observation angle. I show you what you need to see," he answers. "You see, Benedetta, you cannot die. This is impossible."

"But this body, my body... it can die."

"Of course it can, and it will for sure. Your soul, however, is on a different journey. You have things to accomplish in this life." My spirit guide shows up at Apollo's side. He approaches me and chants a long and deep *yes* into my heart. I cannot take it any more. "Stop!" I yell at them.

I land alone in a field of wild grass and red flowers. I run from a man who is chasing me. Is this a punishment? Short of breath, I collapse by a great oak tree. The man sits by my side. We laugh. This is a game. This man is nothing like Tony or Frank, neither in character nor in looks. Maybe no punishment after all, who knows. I am brought back to the cloud from which I have observed my suicide attempt. Apollo and my spirit guide are watching the horizon.

"I think I'm mad," I sternly declare.

"What did they tell you at Les Acacias?" Apollo enquires.

"Nothing. They just gave me prescription drugs."

"There we go. There is nothing wrong with you. You have survived. Not mad, whatever you think or others want you to believe." I am not convinced by his perspective on the matter, though I have grown used to him and his ways. Gaining wisdom works in layers for me, and my skull is thick.

The year 1857. I am the fifteen-year-old daughter of an aristocratic family. A carriage is waiting for me. It is just before dawn. It is imperative that I leave. My mother obliges me to dress while my father is looking at me, only too pleased to see me go. I will spend the next year in a secluded convent, where I will learn to accept the beatings and find a good husband. I do not agree with this. I did not agree either when my mother's lover forced me to sleep with him. I may be pregnant. I have to be hidden somewhere. I am an embarrassment to the family. The devoted Sisters will take care of my virtue.

The year 1967. The Hollywood Hills. I am seventeen years old. In a couple of hours I will be dead. I married a film producer after I graduated from school. My parents are psychoanalysts with questionable methods when it comes to their children. I am one of those kids invited to parties where kids should not be allowed. I started to take cocaine when I was ten and lost my virginity at the age of twelve. I am in our bedroom, searching for a fix of heroin. I know it is hidden somewhere. My husband has decided that I should stop using drugs, but I do not want to. He thinks I have lost control. Maybe he is right. Maybe he is wrong, who cares. I am so bored and do not know how to escape from this golden, rotten cage. My wings have been damaged a long time ago. A few hours later I overdose and die. I try to reincarnate several times, but all my attempts fail. Until this day in December 1980, when I land on earth again under the name of Benedetta. Protected, blessed by the gods. Strange name.

"Take me out of here," I scream at the top of my lungs. Back on the desert plains, I lie on the ground, facing the sun that burns my skin. When I wake up I realize that thousands of animals are sitting around me in circles as if expecting something to happen. An eagle lands on my shoulder. "Writing the book is the medicine," the eagle says before flying away.

"What if I jump out the window when I wake up from this dream, when I wake up in Bangkok with Frank beside me?" I ask Apollo.

"Your story with Frank is a fantasy."

"What do you mean? Frank is real."

"No, Frank isn't real. The story you have with him is not real. And you won't jump out the window. You can use the door now. You just have to get up and walk out the door."

"I cannot."

"Yes, you can. You aren't imprisoned any more. The prison of your thoughts is collapsing. Jump out windows if you want, but only in shamanic journeys."

"I'm terrified."

"We know you are, but you have to confront your darkest fears and illusions. There is no other way around it. And you are not alone in this journey. I am with you, your spirit guide is with you, and the animals... we are all with you. We love you. Wake up!"

I opened my eyes. The clock alarm indicated 4:45 a.m. Frank was god-knows-where, but not in the bedroom. I was feeling sick and nauseous again. Nothing to fear but the coming of that morning light.

The heat had become unbearable. Bloody broken air conditioner, panting and rattling. My head was banging. I opened the window and gasped for fresh air. An infernal loop of Chinese music came up the alley. It made me feel that I was not alone, though. That was reassuring. A putrid smell came from the bathroom. I grabbed the soiled bathmat on which I had vomited and threw it out the window. Dogs were barking in the street. I went into the shower and sat on the floor, which required a certain level of audacity, because of the bits and pieces of broken glass all around me. My feet started to bleed, and I remembered Frank's hands covered in blood. I had a splitting headache. I needed water, cold water. I turned on the tap and sat on the floor under the shower. I took long and deep breaths. Sitting in meditation might have helped for sure, but I was exhausted, and I hated headaches. I swallowed two more 400mg tablets of ibuprofen.

After an hour I began to feel the coolness of the water, meaning that my fever was dropping. I got out of the shower and rolled myself in our only towel, which was drenched with sweat. The sun had risen above the alley, and women were hanging clothes to dry on the terraces surrounding us. Apollo was again bringing light and his reassuring presence. There is comfort and power to be found in the rhythm of stars and planets, in this dance of night and day. Could I be tripping on ibuprofen? Likely not. Frank was not back yet. Maybe he *wasn't* real. Maybe my love story with him only existed in my mind. Maybe he was just expecting me to lend him money. Had it always been about money? A fantasy junkie, that was what I was. That was what I had always been. I wanted Ambien. That was real. My bladder was exploding, and I was feeling weak, so I sat on the shower floor and started to pee. Familiar maneuver. In the hope of cleaning my piss, I started to lick the shower floor. What the hell was I doing? I stopped and vomited again.

So there I was, in a sordid room in Bangkok at the core of the matter. Before the obsessive-compulsive disorders, before the anorexia, and, later, overweight issues, before the gas leaks and the spiders, before everything else, there had been the stories, or rather the fantasies that I was living in. I could trace them back – some of them at least, because there were many – to the age of six or seven. The mechanism was always the same: building a whole world in which I was feeling safe and enjoying myself, usually based on one real element of my life. By some mystery I had always managed to keep one foot in reality. However, the intensity, duration, and frequency of my delusions made them pathological. So there I was in a sordid room in Bangkok demolishing my strong belief that Frank and I were about to start a good life together. I was finally about to be reconnected with my true identity. Amid piss, vomit, alcohol, and drugs, my life was starting to make sense, to my biggest surprise.

....

Bangkok, 6 August 2015

I spent the following days at the temple where I had received my Rishi tattoo. It was not properly a temple but rather an ornamented house where the monk performed his tattoo magic. An adjoining open pavilion provided shade and a place to rest. The living quarters of the monk and his entourage lay within an old crenelated wall surrounding the whole compound. A Thai family looked after the place, cleaned, cooked, and assisted the monk. There were dogs dozing in the open pavilion and cats sleeping on the roofs. A few chickens roamed freely, and two roosters announced sunrise, invariably out of sync. I was tacitly adopted by the family and given small chores to keep me busy. I was thankful to them for providing me with a purpose, even a temporary one, and seized the opportunity to bask in the present moment. I refused to speculate about the future, because I instinctively knew that those days in the temple were going to be the only truce in a final combat of sorts.

The tattoo was healing nicely. I had finally taken the vows to bear the *Rishi*. Under duress, I had to admit. The *Rishi*, who leaves all worldly goods behind. He has no house, no car, and no money. A farewell to family, lovers, and alcohol. He does not cut his hair any more, eats fruit, and fasts. Perhaps I had already left worldly goods behind without realizing it. The *Rishi* sits in meditation. If I could just sit long enough.

I tried to spend most of my free time in meditation and connecting with the force of the *Rishi* magic in my chest. Maybe I had forgotten the rules of a game that had once been my life, and as in video games, I had to reach the next level to accomplish a certain objective. Video games are a construction that results from experience in ordinary reality. They promote no significant differences between the real and the virtual world. This is no Rinpoche wisdom but something I learned from Kirito in *Sword Art Online*, also high in my recovery toolkit. I felt I was at a gap between two levels, which in games is a useful time to save what one has earned, decipher the data encrypted in the background, and rest. The next stage had to be the feared mortal combat. Though maybe games are designed to make us believe that the next level is always the last, I was starting to suspect that there were no levels at all, just a long continuum.

In spite of these musings, I had managed to enter a quiet inner space. It felt so good that I convinced myself I might stay meditating and doing easy chores with the monk in his little temple for ever. A form of sweet *samsara*, this time not distracted by addictions to substances or unsuitable bedfellows but rather fueled by the candid belief that I was on a road to the Truth. A belief that can be addictive too.

The family and I watched Thai soap operas in the evening under the faltering plastic fan. I imagined that this was what I would want to do when dead. Float around the compound, observe the family cooking, follow the dexterous hand of the monk inscribing magical tattoos. Enter the mind of the savvy businesswoman who asks for a tattoo that will bring her good fortune, of the Muay Thai fighter who comes for a magical tiger that will make him fearless, or of the *motorsai* driver who wants a turtle tattoo for longevity. Witness them falling in and out of love, their grief and happiness. Observe the slow flow of their existence, as I was doing then, but exempted from the tyranny of linear time. Being lost in an overlapping loop of Thai soap operas was one approach to enlightenment that I could relate to. Being dead was going to be awesome.

The fact that I could not understand a word of the soap operas did not bother me. I was thrilled by this kind of meditation, where I had to make sense of bizarre images projected in front of me. Or make no sense at all, as was the case most of the time. One evening we watched a rerun of *Khun Chang Khun Phaen*, based on the Thai epic poem of the same name. Chang and Phaen are the leading male characters in a tragic love triangle where Phaen, handsome but poor, and Chang, ugly but rich, fight for the love of beautiful Wanthong. Eventually, the king condemns Wanthong to death for failing to choose between the two men. I realized that, similar to the poem, two sides of me had been fighting for my soul. If I failed to choose a side, like silly Wanthong, I would be condemned to repeatedly perpetuate my suffering in lifetimes to come.

A couple of days went by. One morning the family got up earlier than usual and prepared a meal different from our daily breakfast of sticky rice, steamed vegetables, and eggs. I offered to lend a hand, but I was sent to dust the monk's quarters. I wrapped myself in a sarong and went out to the courtyard, where I caught a glimpse of a wiry, dark man, most likely Khmer, smoking cheroots with the monk. He pointed at me and they both laughed. I recognized the word *farang*, which loosely translates to "foreigner" across Southeast Asia. There was something powerful about our visitor that contrasted with his friendly gaze and simple clothes. The monk showed a camaraderie toward him. I went back to the pavilion, rolled my mattress, and put on my best clothes for the occasion: threadbare black Thai pants and a gray cotton shirt that had been left behind by a *farang* like me who came for a tattoo on his shoulder and left the temple too dazed to remember to put his shirt on again.

Our visitor was a Khmer shaman from Battambang who had come overland from Cambodia to visit the monk. I remembered an ecumenical council of ecclesiastical dignitaries that I had watched on TV. In comparison, our holy get-together seemed more real; the men did not feel the urge to impress either their peers or the congregation. The lack of papal tiaras, ruffs, and cassocks gave an air of honesty to our small conclave. I relaxed and felt proud as I beat the fake Persian carpet and dusted the plastic ashtrays of our modest Sistine Chapel. A jaded poster of a Garuda Indonesia Douglas DC-8 was peeling off the flimsy glass partition.

Our monk and the visiting shaman had a lengthy conversation while burning thick incense sticks. Eventually, they gestured that they were ready for breakfast. A feast of *congee* and grilled pork with rice and beef noodle soup, with sweetened iced coffee, was served on a makeshift tablecloth of freshly cut banana leaves on the floor. I was given the minor task of bringing a garnish of fried garlic to the table. Well, rather, to the floor. The shaman took the saucer from my hands with a polite *or kun*, thank you in Khmer, and gave me an approving nod, as a music teacher would do to a six-year-old kid who has just played "Für Elise" before an audience for the first time. I was exhilarated. I washed the dishes with a sense of pride and dozed under the scorching heat. I woke up alarmed, sensing a shift in the energy of the house and with a revolting emptiness in my stomach.

Our monk and the shaman had killed two chickens. There was blood on the floor, a stained stone, and a few feathers still floating around. The cats and dogs were alert. This was a ceremonial sacrifice, not our usual kitchen slaughter for the household meal. The two men were dismembering the chickens while repetitively murmuring words of respect and gratitude for the lives that had been taken. I vomited into a bucket. I washed my face by the water tank and retreated to the back of the house to lie down in the shade. I was scared and sad. I was not fond of spirits that demanded the sacrifice of a life to produce their magic, but who was I to judge? I had sacrificed my own life for far less valuable goods.

The next thing I know, an orange mushroom explodes in my sternum, tearing my ribcage apart. Bone fragments, cartilage, mucous matter, and connective tissue erupt from my ripped ribcage with volcanic violence. My spirit guide floats in front of me, holding a blunt obsidian knife in one hand. "It is going to hurt," I say calmly, a statement rather than a question. My spirit guide smiles lovingly. It has to hurt if we are to defeat and survive the present foes. Pain is inherent to passing from one level to another in this new game that I am invited to play.

My spirit guide opens my skull with the obsidian knife that cuts into bone as if it is butter. He pops out my eyeballs and gashes the optic nerve with his dirty nails. I feel his greasy fingers in my mouth as he rips out my tongue and throws it away. Now comes the turn of my knee joints, wrists, and shoulders. He grabs my penis at the root, cuts open the shaft, and tosses the internal spongy matter away. He slashes my scrotum and uses his teeth to remove the vessels that attach my testicles to the rest of my body.

Members of his spiritual family join him. They pull apart my bones and burn them on a pyre. Dark birds flock out of the smoke, fly in circles, and turn into clouds of dust. I am no longer there. I am not my body parts. I am some form of conscious presence, feasting alongside my spiritual family. They tear out my teeth one by one. A child plays with my toothless jaw and throws it away like a boomerang. It does not come back.

"How am I ever going to be in human shape again?" I wonder, with curiosity rather than desperation. I indulge in the exhilarating sensation of being free from the heavy pull of a physical body. *Being dead is going to be awesome.* A thick stream of lava is poured down a trachea that happens to be mine. It feels so real that it hurts. It *is* real, and it does hurt. I choke.

The burning liquid down my throat ignited my adrenal glands. Being back in human shape felt sharp. The Khmer shaman was feeding me chicken broth with fatherly love, a kind of love that I had never experienced before. My esophagus was in flames. I felt the thick broth crawling down toward my stomach, the leftover bones and skin from the chicken carcass making an imprint in my guts. Fuck! It really hurt.

In my explorations of the margins of ordinary reality, I had engaged in sexual role playing involving dominance and submission. Leather bars, porn, dildos, chaps, handcuffs, rubber briefs, canes, paddles. *Fuck!* It hurt. But I had learned to endure the pain in anticipation of the endorphin-induced analgesia. I had learned to crave the unskillful actions and destructive emotions that perpetuated my own suffering. I would rather face the pain derived from sexual role play than my fear of being abandoned and my feelings of inadequacy, anger, and loneliness.

The Khmer shaman was feeding me the sacrificed chicken, holding me as if I was a newborn. Its scorching steam and pungent smell filled my nose. I sniffed the hot broth's vapor and then started tripping on it as if it were poppers. I actually had this vision of the shaman teasing me and feeding me poppers. He likes to force me to take more huffs. He feels excited to make me very horny and beg for more. Sniffing poppers together makes me feel connected to him. No matter how casual or anonymous the encounter, all that I care for is connectedness, the bonding of two soulmates. In the absence of love, feeling at one with poppers is the next best thing. I get more poppered-up and more stupid as I get deeper into a trance that I want to believe is love.

For some people sex is just sex, and that is not a problem, just as for some people a drink is just a drink and they seldom have one too many. For some of us, sexual behavior turns into a metaphor for what the self is trying to express. Perhaps I had too much sex, or too little, or in ways that isolated me and threw me into a cycle of suffering. Thousands of hours of therapy had helped me to become fully functional in an alien society. I had studied, gotten a job, paid my mortgage, and contributed to a pension plan. All this came at a hefty price, and did not last for ever. The self was not getting what it needed. The self continued to cry its metaphors, spilling from sex to substances and vampires. It would go on until I paid attention or died. It had to hurt so much that at a certain time I would start paying attention. I did not want to die.

I suffocated. The old shaman held me with all the tenderness in the world, as I had been held before by strangers in dominant sex play, because I had surrendered to a painful ordeal with blind acceptance. A sexual partner well versed in the art of domination would reward me with this kind of aftercare, being held and nurtured as I chilled under the continued release of oxytocin in full-blown endorphin bliss. Holding on to the last trace of dopamine before eventually sliding toward a dark spiral of moodiness and depression. There is always a trade-off in ordinary reality. Feeling grateful for the ride and the care. Feeling loved for yielding to someone else's power. Feeling the illusion of love disintegrate as I realized that there was no such thing as love in these places of artificial bliss.

Of course, it had to do with my father. It had to do with past life karma also, but it was my father who put all that pain in front of me and helped me to deal with that karma. He used to whip me with a belt. It was not just a belt. He had fabricated a whip that consisted of a section of a broomstick that acted as a handle and a leather belt attached to it that served as the thong. It hung from a nail in his bedroom door as a constant reminder of his power over the household. But the whip only gave him a false sense of self. He was always sad.

He was not meant to be a father. He was a karmic agent in the guise of a father, with the mission to put all that pain in front of me and help me deal with that karma. It was a tough job for him as well, a mission that he had to endure for his own karmic reasons that he most likely did not understand. He had conceived and brought up a son, yet he was not allowed to enjoy fatherhood. I became an adult without ever solving the equation of fatherly love. The only constant in the equation was that I had to endure pain to earn the promise of love. All the time I had been looking for love in the wrong places, losing parts of my soul in each casual encounter. The pain-induced sexual experiences tagged along with a spiritual dismemberment that still hurt. Two years, ten months, and eighteen days, and it still hurt.

More molten lava is drained down my throat; the pain is excruciating. I am eleven years old. I have this vivid memory of my father sobbing. His mother has just passed away, and he is sobbing like a child. I see him cry for the first time in my life. I am intrigued but also sad because I cannot comfort him. He does not love me, and I do not know how to express my sympathy for him. I learn the meaning of loneliness.

I was left with only two options: craving the unskillful actions and destructive emotions that perpetuated my own suffering, or desiring to be one with God or with a fully realized guru. It was my father who had programmed me to seek desperately for love until I solved the puzzle or sank in a frozen lake. He was my teacher, yet I harbored bitter resentment against him.

My bear spirit draws a large circle of urine around my father, and I set fire to it with a torch. This is not a vengeful action. This is a restoration of fatherly love. "Make direct amends to such people wherever possible": step nine of the twelve-step recovery program, referring to all the people one has harmed. I approach my father and extend my arms toward him in a gesture of reconciliation. My arms catch fire, and my father burns to the bone. The fire blinds me. My body is made entirely of boiling water. I evaporate into a thin mist that clings to the crater of a volcano.

I woke up feverish and drenched in my own sweat.

The monk and the shaman were smoking cheroots again. They smiled approvingly at me: I had survived. The monk wiped my forehead and my mouth with a wet sponge. "A little extra help," the monk said to me in English, with a paternal gesture of appreciation. I understood. All the sadness, abuse, loneliness, pain, hollowness in the heart that was never filled, the craving for fleeting love, the sexual prowess in the dirty alleys, it all turned to ashes. I had walked this path before. *We came to believe that a Power greater than ourselves could restore us to sanity.* Help can only come when one is ready to admit his addictions and to ask for help.

"I need help," I murmured to myself that night as I was peeling a mango. It came as a revelation. My shoulders loosened, and I felt that I had just woken up from a lucid dream. Pak was standing in front of me, in flesh and bones, frowning but lovingly absorbed in the situation. He recited the magical chanting associated with the Hanuman tattoo: "Nobleness is to refrain from desire, to abstain from the world defiled until no enemy exists in body and mind."

"Pak, brother, are you my spirit guide?" I asked. He rolled his eyes.

"First you fall in love with me, now you think that I am your spirit guide. Can't you just be content with what you have?"

"I'm trying, brother."

"Try harder."

I took a long, deep breath. The presence of Pak brought me joy, but I also knew that it meant the end of the truce. I was being called to fight the final combat. I had wondered whether there would ever be a time in my life when I would feel ready. That day had arrived.

"Here, take this, ten thousand dollars and two Japan Airlines economy-class tickets to Lima via Tokyo, leaving tomorrow morning. You are off the grid, untraceable until tonight. The tickets are counterfeit. No checked baggage, only a small carry-on. If you get busted, say that you purchased the tickets from a street stall at Khao San Road. The hacker will check whether you actually boarded; if not, a brother from the *sangha* will come and help you. Throw your cellphone into the river, throw your laptop, whatever has email or messages on it that can be traced to Stein or to me. Dress inconspicuously. You should be fine. Understood?"

Pak was being gentle and efficient, yet the message was cold and brutal.

"How am I ever going to explain all this to Benedetta?"

"She will meet you at the JAL counter. We are looking after her. She has taken something from Stein that belongs to us. In doing so she has done a valuable service. She gained merit. Great merit."

"What the fucking fuck?"

There was no time for metaphysical disquisitions. "Now listen, brother." He grabbed me by the shoulders and commanded my full attention. "I am going to disrobe. You may not hear from me for some time. It is safer that you do not try to contact me." My eyes filled with tears. This meant that he was about to engage in activities against human trafficking that he could not pursue as a monk.

"If it is the abbot, maybe you could explain…"

"It's the Dalai," he replied shortly. I gaped.

"The Dalai probably doesn't have a sister who was kidnapped," I ventured after a long pause.

"The Dalai never worked as a prostitute," he retorted with determination, staring at me with his deep black eyes and long eyelashes. I felt all the grief that had been slowly building inside him from the first time we met. "One way or another I will contact you," he finally said while holding my hands.

"One way or another?" I asked, fearing that I was abandoning Western linear time and entering the juxtaposing layers of shamanic reality.

"I'm on to a new journey. If you do not hear from me in a couple of months, assume that I will come back as your child." My jaw dropped.

"I'm on to a new journey..." I repeated to myself. "Pak, brother, chances that I have a child are—"

"Be creative. Don't give up on me. This fight will take many lifetimes. I need to do what I need to do now, and I also need to look after you. And you will look after me. There is no other way."

He wrapped himself in the crimson robe and kissed me on the forehead.

This was the last I saw of Pak in this incarnation.

I arrived at the airport early. I was terrified. How could things have taken such a horrible turn? Only a few weeks earlier, Benedetta and I were at an innocent retreat in Italy. Reality as I had known it had disintegrated. Lima? Pak said that he needed to send us far away and that Lima was an easy destination to hack. No alternatives. I was somehow relieved to be going back to South America, but I did not know how to deal with Benedetta. The best thing would be to spend a couple of days in Lima to recover from the experience and see her off to Brussels. Maybe that was just what I needed: to go home, water the plants, fill the fridge, go to work in the morning. Hopefully that would lead to a lover in bed. *Rishi?* What was I thinking when I embarked on this quest?

My train of thought was interrupted as Benedetta entered the terminal. I perceived her before I saw her. There was a vibration, a shift in the energy around me. Then I saw her, making probably the grandest of all of her entrances, Monte Carlo included. She had shaved her spectacular hair and was loosely wrapped in a white cloth like a Buddhist nun, wearing plastic sandals and expensive sunglasses. People made way for her and bowed respectfully. I was speechless. What the fuck was this woman doing dressed as a nun in Suvarnabhumi's departure hall? Reality was again dissolving in front of me, and my brain threatened to enter shutdown mode. I had time to take three deep breaths before she approached me and indicated with a regal nod that I should follow her to the check-in line. The passengers in the line made way for her as if Queen Sirikit herself had shown up unexpectedly. After a brief exchange with the JAL clerks, she turned around and flashed me a smile, passport and boarding pass in her hand.

I saw her walking ahead of me with the radiance of a martyr going to the cross, nonchalantly living in the moment while a many-headed dragon was vomiting fire only a few steps ahead. And a many-headed dragon there was. Stein and a couple of robust friends were scanning the passengers who crossed the gate into the boarding area. We were about to enter a portal to our new beginning. I was livid. Benedetta stopped and waited for me to catch up. I held my breath, because I instinctively knew that she was about to do something that would change our lives for ever.

"My dear, do you have Bulagat's stone?" she asked me quietly. I gaped. "The stone he gave us..." she insisted without losing her temper.

"Oh yes. The stone... No, my dear, I threw it to the river together with all my stuff."

"That is not a problem. Can you imagine the stone in your palm?" I could imagine the stone very well. Actually, it felt soothing to imagine the stone, beautifully shaped into a thin oval smoothed by the passing of glaciers for billions of years.

"Yes, I can, my dear. I am holding the stone in my hand."

"Good.' She nodded appreciatively. Then she sighed and said, "And this is the moment when we become invisible and cross this portal."

So this was the new journey that the spirits had told me about. Pak, Benedetta, Stein, and I, we were all about to enter a new life.

It was not about dying. Attachment was so strong that I would rather think about dying than losing Pak and Benedetta. This was a new beginning. And also a moment of mourning for what we were leaving behind. I assumed that Benedetta was totally out of her medication, whatever it was she was taking, and that Stein had probably supplied her with other drugs. Her confusing stories, the too-many adjectives and abundant examples buried somewhere in a deep crevasse of Lake Baikal. Her fiery eyes, the exalted tone, the high pitch, it all gave way to the quiet flow of the Chao Phraya River.

As Stein caught sight of Benedetta, he called her name and elbowed his way through the crowd toward us. At the same time, a swirling group of monks, nuns, and children surrounded us in a kind of flash mob. The children appeared to know Benedetta. Some of the young monks made a human barrier and stared defiantly at Stein. One of the novices had a Hanuman *yant* tattooed across his chest. Hanuman, the courageous and faithful hero. The novice had one fist clenched against his robe, behind which one Hanuman eye fiercely secured his position from the novice's naked skin.

Although a part of my brain alerted me that there was no time for reverie, another part of it acknowledged the many spiritual layers of the moment. A combat of sorts that meant the end of the world as I had known it. I closed my eyes. *Nobleness is to refrain from desire, to abstain from the world defiled until no enemy exists in body and mind.* When I opened my eyes, Stein had disappeared. There is no combat if no enemy exists.

Benedetta and I made it to the departures gate and crossed this portal unscathed. We went past airport security guards as if we were in fact invisible. We could still hear the voices of the children sending blessings to Benedetta. A senior monk led us through immigration as if we were Buddhist VIPs.

We boarded the flight to Tokyo, and the connecting flights to Los Angeles and Lima with our counterfeit tickets, without any incidents. I was impressed by the skill of Pak's hacker. The flight was eternally long. Benedetta slept most of the time and drank enormous quantities of orange juice that a devoted flight attendant poured for her at regular intervals. After a brief layover at Tokyo's Narita Airport, we changed planes again at Los Angeles International Airport. We had a few hours to spare, and, despite being exhausted, we took a long stroll, arm in arm. We were walking from the Burberry boutique to the Gucci store when Benedetta started laughing. "So many things! So shiny and new! I'm so relieved that we don't have credit cards any more." I realized that she was trying to cheer me up. We laughed and hugged. This was all she said for the rest of the journey. I could sense that her days in Bangkok had not been at all pleasant. Whatever happened to her had left a mark deeper than a tattoo.

As we began our descent to Lima Jorge Chávez Airport, the flight attendant brought her Nescafé in a styrofoam cup. "Hello, my dear. Are you all right? You have slept the entire flight!" I whispered. She peeped out of the window to see the sunrise over the bright white Pacific Ocean and the strip of beach that runs along the border of the continent.

"My dear, we have crossed to the other shore!" she rejoiced.

The rippled water of the Pacific Ocean reflected the rising sun like shattered glass. A solitary eagle was flying unusually low ahead of us, as if showing the way. Or maybe it was someone flying a paraglider. Did life still have something good in store for me? The unexpected had been revealed with tremendous force. The bad times were over, and the great adventure of my life had begun. I had been given directions, and it was time to start walking.

In spite of all the learning and the love that the spirits had granted us in this expedition around the world, I would still doubt them and myself at times. On such occasions, all the sadness, abuse, loneliness, pain, hollowness in the heart that was never filled, the craving for fleeting love, the sexual prowess in the dirty alleys, it all came back to life from its ashes and burned me alive. But most of the time I walked close to the spirits. If I kept doing it, maybe one day there would be no more demons. One day at a time.

Walk close to the spirits. I found shelter in Benedetta's blue eyes, her shaven head, and the wrinkles and stains of the white robe in which she was still wrapped. The joy and freshness of the children who had surrounded us remained with her. So many times I could not choose where to go. In preparation for landing, I fastened my seat belt and took her hand.

. . . .

Bangkok, 6 August 2015

It all had to do with Frank and the cascade of disastrous events that led me to him. Loneliness and a terrible lack of love. This was the pattern. The source of this cascade could be traced back to this lifetime and my previous incarnations, though it seemed to me that I was living many lives at the same time. As elusive as the source of the Nile once was. The Pale Abyssinian. Omar had told this story about the quest for the source of the Nile a dozen times in the many dead hours of our trip around the world. His mind was cluttered with literary anecdotes – how did that work for him at the leather bars in Amsterdam? Bruce, his name was Bruce Something. The Pale Abyssinian. The guy at the source of the Nile. Something Bruce. Omar could be quite a chatterbox at times. Bruce Chatwin? Likely not. Bruce Almighty? I was feeling illiterate.

Of course it had to do with Frank and my belief that we were about to start a happy life together. My good doctor was standing in the doorway. He had the bathmat that I had thrown out of the window in his hands and started vociferating. What the hell was wrong with him? He smashed the IKEA chair in the living room. I started sobbing like a little girl. I was nothing but a fantasy junkie buried deep in her illusions. He came back to bed with a small lacquered box and looked me in the eyes. His breath was stale with alcohol. Pungent, he reeked of sweat, cigarettes, and cheap male cologne.

"You smell like piss," he whispered. I did not know what to reply. "Now be a good baby girl for Daddy." The cheap line, the abstruse incantation, the trigger. The source of the Nile. I felt sucked into his vortex of destruction.

"I started to take cocaine when I was ten and lost my virginity at the age of twelve," I recited as if it was poetry. Did I really say that?

"Good girl, you are a good girl." He was drunk. "You can tell Daddy," he mumbled soothingly as if talking to an infant. He put his thumb in my mouth.

"I am in our bedroom searching for a fix of heroin. I know it's hidden somewhere," I went on enticing him. I started to suck his thumb, reciting by heart.

Even at the time of writing this, I still do not know the words to describe what happened. It was all so alien to me and yet so familiar. How could I do things that I would not know how to explain or write about? But it was not the first time. *I was walking on down Churchill Avenue trying to find somebody to tell my troubles to.* I had been down that avenue before. I had buried my troubles somewhere deep, somewhere remote. Frank was the excavator, the spade, the exorcist. He took a glass pipe from the lacquered box and a thin vial with something like tiny sugar loaves inside. He filled the bowl of the pipe with it, lit it up, and put it in my mouth. He was going to bring ashes to life again.

"There, be a good girl. Have a little toke," Frank said. My first thought was *I don't know what the word toke means.* I had heard Omar tell stories over and over again about substances. I had picked up a thesaurus that I was familiar with: he *did*, he sometimes had *snorted*, he did not *tweak*, he had never *candy-flipped*, that kind of thing. Enough to make the other party feel that I was following the conversation, even when I did not. Everybody was impressed.

Or so I thought. I was always too shy to ask and too embarrassed about not knowing.

My father spent most of his time in Congo. Being away in a remote land was the perfect alibi to escape my alcoholic mother and their deranged children. What was he doing there? Papa was allegedly supporting the development of Congo through governmental agencies that only served as a front to loot the richest concentration of precious metals and minerals on earth. Sucking blood is some kind of a family tradition.

My younger sister drowned in Belgium. Maman and Papa had had one of their awful rows. My mother packed her incredibly large suitcases and left for Ostend with my younger sister, a nanny, and me. My mother obliged me to dress while my father was looking at me, only too pleased to see us go. I later knew that Ostend was one of Maman's favorite places to meet her vampire lovers on the rare occasions when my father visited us in Brussels. The daughters and the nanny provided the cover for her extramarital pursuits. We stayed at the George V, which was not so rundown then as it is today. My sister, the nanny, and I shared a suite of rooms. We did not share rooms with Maman on account of my sleepwalking, the nanny had told us, and my mother's long nights at the casino. The latter I learned from observation.

It happened in the early hours of a gray morning. I was walking along the shore to collect shells, and the nanny ran after me. The water was cool, and my little sister started to swim, which created ripples. *Glory is like a circle in the water, which never ceaseth to enlarge itself, till by broad spreading it disperse to nought.*[28] She went into the water, singing, and then we lost sight of her. "*Un, deux, trois, allons dans les bois. Quatre, cinq, six, cueillir des cerises,*" she was singing: "*Sept, huit, neuf, dans mon panier neuf. Dix, onze, douze, elles seront toutes rouges.*" I knew this voice and this French children's song, which

---

28   William Shakespeare, "Henry VI" from *The Complete Works of William Shakespeare*

gave me a twinge of sorrow. A light drizzle started falling on the beach. Water has cleansing properties, and my tears were melting with the rain.

That morning Maman had not yet returned to her room after having left for the casino the previous evening. It was only after lunch that she made her grand entrance at the George V. She was not in good shape but knew how to camouflage the inevitable effects of alcohol on her face. She had slipped into a suggestive black dress and made the most of her hair. She had fantastic hair. She had topped her dress with spectacular diamond jewelry, courtesy of her only-too-absent husband. She had lost a hefty quantity of Belgian francs at the English roulette and then decided to spend the night with one of her lovers. It was all that mattered to her.

"Come on babe, have a little toke," Frank insisted encouragingly. I felt embarrassed and hesitant about the right course of action. Omar said that I was resourceful. He had seen something of value in me that I could not grasp. He meant it as a compliment. I did not feel resourceful at all. Most of the time I was lonely. I never really knew what to do. The suffering of a soul that has isolated itself from its true nature and from the world. That was why I started to drink. And why I booked appointments at celebrated hairdressers, bought expensive shoes and lipstick, ate too many *bonbons,* and watched vampire B-movies. It distracted me from the feeling of loneliness and the terrible lack of love. That and many other things. And Tony. And Frank. That was the pattern.

Omar stated that I paid too much attention to details and that I strived to make everybody comfortable and happy. He compared me to Mrs Dalloway. "Mrs who?" He smiled at my blank face. I assumed it had to be a book. I laughed because I did not want to disappoint him. Definitively illiterate. Actually, I did not want to disappoint anybody. That was such an excruciating task.

I had gotten the best marks at school. I was going through chemistry and philosophy without it making the slightest notch on me. I was dead. Rather than dead, I was an intellectual zombie. I could recite hundreds of stanzas of *The Song of Roland* that did not mean anything to me. It did not move me. I had recoiled into a space where I could be a child who was loved. There was nothing in chemistry or philosophy or *The Song of Roland* that could be of use for that child. I went through the whole syllabus of secondary education perplexed, as if crossing a scorching desert without a compass.

Enter sex. Terrifying, intrusive, and unhygienic. I needed to pee all the time. It hurt, or in the best case, bored me. A feeling of inadequacy filled the void. And the stories, or rather the fantasies that I was living in. That and the obsessive-compulsive disorders, the anorexia before the too many *bonbons*, the depression, the jumping out the window. A horrifying pattern. Not only was I not engaging in intellectual conversation with the highbrows, but I also was not engaging in sexual relationships with the promiscuous. Similar categories. I thought that Tony would understand that side of me. He was shallow in his own sweet way. I supposed that because of his métier there had to be something in him beyond sex. Omar said that on occasion sex is a metaphor for something else. Tony and I had our good moments. Orally he was very gifted. That is the closest he got to satisfying me. Satisfying myself was something that I could do proficiently and was what I liked the most about sex. It was also what I was most at ease with. In public toilets, in particular. Not that it ever made me happy. The best part, nonetheless, remained that it excluded the presence of a sweaty, smelly someone panting on my face, a wet, hot iron rod entering my flesh and dissolving into the darkest night.

"Come on babe, a toke," Frank said playfully. He was fumbling with iTunes on his cellphone, shifting between playlists that sounded hostile and metallic.

"*I knew it was hidden somewhere,*" I replied, as if I were reciting *The Song of Roland.* I smiled at him knowingly, projecting the complete opposite of my true self. *You are not imprisoned any more* burned to ashes in the pipe as Frank flickered the cigarette lighter. "What is this?" I asked, hoping that my broad question would encompass not only the meaning of "toke" but also the exact nature of the sugar-like crumbles burning in the pipe. At that moment an electronic version of Chopin's Funeral March enveloped us, and I sank deeper in the density of the grimy room.

"DJ Shadow, I guess," he replied nonchalantly. "Come on, naughty girl. Here, be easy. Have a toke and come to Daddy."

Are you ready to die? I took a huge puff of crack. Time and space disengaged. I was lost, contemplating a missing photogram that dissolved into sound. I could not tell the difference between the pipe and Frank's thumb in my mouth. I started licking, nibbling, sucking, flicking my tongue at his thumb that was the pipe. I heard Frank laughing at my confusion and encouraging me to take yet another "toke." I started hallucinating, but the images were disconnected from sound. *I have fed my eyes with too many illusions and have remained blind as a consequence.* I could still hear Frank laughing and saying dirty things to me. I had his undivided attention; that was all that mattered. All it took was a few tokes of crack.

I am barefoot inside an igloo somewhere over permafrost. The snow falling over me feels like ermine fur that keeps me warm and chills me at the same time. Frank's voice becomes more suffused until it dissolves in the snow. I cannot decide whether I am tripping on crack or journeying with the help of crack. My hesitation provokes my fall through a crack in the ice.

As I am falling, the gigantic white dragon with crystal mauve eyes catches me on his back. I have to hold him tightly as he makes loops and flies extremely fast. I am alone with him. I like him. He is gentle. "Hello again!" I tell the dragon. "You are chasing the dragon, baby girl. Easy on the dragon," Frank replies from far away. How can he know? My bond with the white dragon is so pure that I do not want Frank around to mess things up. I choose to disconnect from Frank and embrace the white dragon. As my dragon and I fly to the far-off corners of the universe, I start losing track of Frank's abusive words, his panting in my face, a wet, hot iron rod entering my flesh and dissolving into the darkest night.

So there I was in this sordid room in Bangkok, at the core of the matter. Before the obsessive-compulsive disorders, before the anorexia, and later overweight issues, before the gas leaks and the spiders, before everything else, there had been the stories, or rather the fantasies that I was living in. I can trace them back, some of them at least, because there were so many, to the age of six or seven. I have an urge to pee. I am six or seven years old. I wear a knee-length red dress with short sleeves and a matching hair ribbon. I hold my beloved teddy bear in my arms and suck my thumb. I so need to pee that I cannot sleep. Maman has ordered me not to leave my room under any circumstances. Strict orders for my own good. I have sleeping disorders, she says. I might sleepwalk stark naked. That would be an embarrassment for the whole family. I fall asleep again.

Shortly after midnight I wake up to the sound of steps in the corridor. I stay alert in bed and confirm that some movement is taking place outside. I try to go back to sleep, but the sound of the steps in the corridor makes me feel curious, so I go out along the corridor to the terrace, from where I will have a good view of any nocturnal activities. Maybe Maman is there, and I can ask her permission to go to the toilet.

On the way back to my room I notice that the door of Maman's bedroom is slightly open, allowing the moon to filter its light into the corridor all the way to my bare feet. I look inside the bedroom and catch a glimpse of Maman in bed dressed in a prudish nightgown. Her eyes are half open, with the strange serenity of those who see spirits or of the epileptic after a seizure. I am about to whisper her name when a shadow moves across her. At first sight it looks like a large bird, but it turns into human form under the moonlight. I am presented with the naked butt of a man. The light gives it an eerie appearance, as if it were a marble statue or a ghost. It is, however, a young man, who is now relentlessly humping Maman. My mother jerks her head back. After the initial surprise, I wonder whether she is conscious of what is going on. A bat flies over them. Or maybe it is a dream. Maybe I sense the archetype of a bat. Perhaps a young vampire is feeding on my mother's blood, just as I have fed on her milk. A bat clings upside down and therefore has a reverse image and perception of the world, just as I have most of the time.

I hear a brief, hushed exchange of words, and the naked vampire comes to the corridor. I stand frozen, holding my beloved teddy bear in my arms and sucking my thumb. He shuts the door of the bedroom behind him and starts making his way toward the bathroom. The moment he sees me, he puts his hands to his mouth to repress an exclamation of surprise. "*Putain de bordel de merde!*" he hushes. I giggle because we are not allowed to say bad words at home. He comes close to me. The vampire is tall, muscular, and naked. He has a prominent kind of trunk dangling from a thick, black tuft of hair in his crotch. I had never seen a naked man before. Only glimpses of Papa coming out of the shower. But Papa's anatomy bore no relation to that of the naked vampire. Papa had wide, feminine hips, soggy arms, and fat legs. His crotch was peppered with sparse gray hair. He had no trunk, only a kind of greyish worm that wiggled between his fat legs.

By contrast, the trunk of the naked vampire is heavy, veiny, and purple. It is pungent. I make an ugly face as he approaches me. He puts a finger to his mouth to indicate that we should remain silent. We tacitly agree to keep secret our impromptu rendezvous, the naked vampire and I. The vampire with the dangling, pungent kind of trunk. "I need to pee," I beg in the lowest possible voice. He kneels in front of me and starts caressing my cheeks with one hand. He takes the other hand to his trunk that strongly springs from the thick, black tuft of crotch hair. He puts his thumb in my mouth. It is a fat, sandy, salty thumb that reeks of cigarettes. I start licking, nibbling, sucking, flicking my tongue at his thumb as I am bursting with pee. I start losing track of his abusive words, his panting on my face, a wet, hot iron rod entering my flesh and dissolving into the darkest night. I burn.

I cannot hold it any more, and I pee myself. I let go of my beloved teddy bear. I cannot repress a short and shrill cry. As I pee myself, the naked vampire withdraws his pungent, veiny trunk from inside me and clumsily tries to hold my pee with both his hands. He is agitated and wet. I produce a piercing shriek. I am shivering. "*Connard!*" My mother is at the bedroom door, crying her lungs out. I panic. This is my fault. The vampire springs to his feet and approaches Maman, fumbling with words. She does not stop yelling. "*C'est en taule que je vais t'envoyer. Dégage de là! Laisse-la tranquille! (...) Tu croyais que j'allais te laisser filer? (...) J'en ai vraiment rien à foutre.*"

I feel very sorry for what has just happened. I should not have disobeyed my mother. "He would have left, should you have asked for it," she told me later that night as she tucked me into bed without even giving me a bath. Or a kiss. We shall never address the subject again. Maybe Maman wanted me to die, like my sister in the sea. From that day I would have so few peaceful nights.

The dragon comes to my rescue. I embrace him and tell him that I have fed my eyes with too many illusions and have remained blind as a consequence. I must now learn to discern what really matters and to open to reality as it is and not as I want it to be. "The time has come to remove the blindfold," the dragon replies as more colored bubbles burst from his mouth. I touch the bubbles with the tip of my fingers, and as they burst I stop tripping.

I started shaking as the memory of the little girl bit deep into my flesh. What she could not understand then surfaced violently, up my spinal cord into my limbic system. The long-buried memory of childhood abuse came down on me like a ton of bricks.

I woke up in Frank's bedroom with a splitting headache, as if a buffalo herd had run over me. A tropical storm was raging outside, and the windows were shaking. How long had I been gone? I wiped my tears away. The clock indicated 1:12, meaning that I had been sleeping for about seventeen hours. Or twenty-nine hours, I could not quite figure it out. The sheets were wet with cold sweat. Frank must have gone on some crusade, like the desperate warrior that he was. I preferred being alone to Frank mainlining dope next to me. What I needed was to take care of me. I noticed a bottle of water, a mug filled with noodle soup, and an apple on the night table. I sat on the bed and stretched out one arm in an effort to catch the bottle. The soup was cold. I hate cold noodles. They are either too spongy or too sticky. I tried to eat the apple, but it tasted like sandpaper. The bottle of water miraculously turned out to be vodka.

I sat on the toilet and started to cry. I was sore. I checked my body and realized that Frank and I had had sex while I was riding the white dragon. I was dirty and sore. Unprotected sex. I started sobbing at the realization that he had abused me after I had passed out. *I have fed my eyes with too many illusions.* I cried my eyes out until I eventually calmed down. I took a long shower, the longest possible one, until the tepid water ran cold. So there I was, meeting the truth. A part of me would have preferred to continue denying it, while another part of me was relieved. Gazing at the ceiling like the little girl that I had been, I contemplated the revelation: the true roots and nature of my pain and shortcomings. It had actually happened. This one was no fantasy of mine. My behavior made now perfect sense to me. I was feeling bizarrely emotionless and overwhelmed at the same time.

What was I supposed to do next? I did not want to stay in that sordid bedroom in Bangkok. I needed to hear a friendly voice. I wanted to call Omar, but my phone was dead. I searched in all drawers, shelves, and closets for a charger, but I could not find one. There were five burner phones in the apartment. Why so many? They all required a password.

Gail, please help me, I thought. *Never forget that the spirits always answer positively when you ask for their help.* Nothing happened. "I cannot stay here. Gail, please help me," I tried out load.

"Just get out of this place."

"What do you mean?"

"Walk out the door. Just. Walk. Out. The. Door. Simple," Gail said as if it were the most obvious thing to do. Not for me; but I trusted her. I put on my dress and grabbed my passport and all of Frank's phones. For some mysterious reason I thought that they might be useful. And I walked out the door, feeling like a circus tiger jumping through a ring of fire.

The building door slammed behind me, which awoke me to the grimy alley. The strong smell of noodles being fried in a sticky gray matter that reeked of soy sauce slapped my face. I dug one finger into the burning wok, to the amazement of an elderly Chinese lady. It burned like hell, yet my finger did not catch fire. "I am the fallen Benedetta," I whispered. This made her smile. Did I really say that?

It was pouring with rain. I came out to the main road of Chinatown. I was amazed by the pulse of commerce that had not stopped for a bit during my many hours of excavation in the deepest recesses of my brain. I walked toward the nearby Tesco. A couple of minutes later, which could also have been hours, I stood in front of it. I could not remember why I wanted to go to a supermarket, considering that I had brought no money with me. I kept walking, hoping that, as in a shamanic dance around a circle, the spirits would take care of me. I was starting to feel paranoid. Was everybody looking at me? *Where is my Valium, please? Oh, really joking. Xanax will do too. Perhaps perhaps perhaps! And Lexomil. If I would like some tea?*

"Yes. Ice tea, madam?" said the girl at the Starbucks counter, who appeared to have asked that same question a few times already. She was still being friendly.

"Give me the macchiato," I recited as if it were a line in a play.

"All right. Espresso macchiato. Sixty baht, please. What is your name, madam?"

Of course they wanted money in exchange for coffee. I realized that I was standing at the counter of Starbucks at the corner of Ratchawong Road without a penny. I took stock of the situation. It was pouring with rain, and I was barefoot.

"Her name is Benedetta. Here, let me pay for her," said a friendly voice from behind me. The woman to whom the voice belonged grabbed me by the arm and guided me to the end of the counter, where we waited for my coffee.

"What are you doing here?" she asked in a maternal tone. She had fine light hair, beautiful blue eyes, and a necklace made of conchs and tassels.

"I don't know," I said hesitatingly.

"Not true. You just don't want to look into your heart and be honest with me," she rebuked me in a tender manner. I decided to change the subject.

"Thank you for my coffee. I needed it." The caffeine boost had started to ground me. Everything around me started acquiring gravity and making sense.

"I'm glad to hear that, Benedetta," she replied in her calm voice.

"How do you know my name?"

"Do you know who I am?"

"I'm not sure who I am. *Merde*, Frank!" I was slowly becoming aware of my recent actions.

"Oh, Frank. Don't worry... He isn't real."

"What do you mean? Frank is real."

"No, Frank isn't real. The story you have with him isn't real. And you won't jump out the window. You can use the door now. You just have to get up and walk out the door."

"I'm terrified." I felt that I had rehearsed that line. Was I really terrified?

"We know you are, but you have to confront your darkest fears and illusions. There is no other way around it."

"This is too much information." I covered my eyes with my hands. "Who are you?" After a moment I burped. This woman seemed so familiar to me, yet she escaped my memory. She stayed silent. "Are you Gail?" I eventually asked.

"There is no Gail," she replied. "There is only you, Benedetta. And the spirits that guide you. This is why I saved you, why we saved you, on that day of March 2013 and many times before. Now listen very carefully, for this is the last time: you are now able to navigate your life on your own. You are free to go wherever you want and to do what you like. We told you that like a tree, growing branches would be useless if roots did not reach deep enough and were not strongly anchored in the ground. You have excavated the roots. You have found all the answers. *You know what you have to do.*" She gave me a reassuring smile. She stood up, gave me a light kiss on my cheek, and walked out the door. It had stopped raining. She disappeared in the glaring sun.

I sat for a moment longer, absorbing the melodious accent of the Thai people chatting at the tables around me. I gulped what remained of the macchiato and played with my empty paper coffee cup. It felt solid, and it had my name inscribed on it with a black marker. That was real. There was a ticket printed on thermal paper that described a hot beverage, the time of the purchase, and the amount paid. It had *PAID* stamped across it. That was also real. It suddenly occurred to me that the best thing I could do was a coffee reading. I focused on the shapes of the grounds at the bottom of my cup. The message appeared with clarity: *She was a treasure hunter, treasures of the soul, and an inspiring peace-warrior who acknowledged her right to be saved and her power to save others.* I laughed out loud. Pretty vague yet true.

I realized that I had just met the woman I was going to be for the rest of my life. My mind was sharp and clear. That might have been the first time in my life that I knew what I had to do. I walked out of Starbucks with the radiance of a Miss Universe about to be crowned. Traffic was maddening. There was a constant flow of cars, *tuk-tuks, motorsais,* bicycles, and taxis of all colors. I loved the bright pink ones. Everything had changed. I had replaced a vampire with an eagle.

As I prepared to dodge the swirling traffic of Yaowarat Road, I noticed a Thai man wrapped in a crimson robe standing in front of Starbucks. What I could see of his body was covered with tattoos. I had met this man before, but I could not remember the circumstances, once again. He looked calm and patient, as if he had been waiting there all day. We made eye contact. *You know what you have to do.* The man introduced himself as Pak. Yes, he was a monk. Yes, he had lived in Amsterdam, and yes, he knew Omar. I could hardly believe it. The only thing that had ever been needed was walking out the door. Pak had been sent by the spirits to save me. Why had I kept myself in prison for so long? *You are not imprisoned any more. The prison of your own thoughts is collapsing.* Pak and I made our gateway.

I was out of breath and balance. Pak walked in front of me and forced me to slow down. We walked in the direction of the night bazaar. When we reached the Chao Phraya River, I regained my stance. A large bird flying unusually low caught my attention. The sun was setting by the time we arrived at a tiny compound in an area called Khlong Toei that had turned itself from a drug den into an attractive canal-side community. The compound was a safe place for children in need of temporary shelter. We did not talk any further that evening. Before taking me to a dormitory, Pak explained that Omar was well but out of reach, staying with monks. Why had he left the Shangri-La?

Pak welcomed me the next morning with a cup of jasmine tea. My body was desperately crying out for crack. The tea did nothing to distract from the yearning for dope. I was terribly embarrassed at not being able to concentrate, though his calm and firm talk somehow soothed me. I reminded myself that I had the confidence of a Miss Universe about to be crowned. He summarily explained that he belonged to a group of radical monks devoted to fighting child prostitution. He would soon renounce being a monk to have more leeway to pursue this fight. I sensed fatality in his determination. He was in the process of shifting identities. Pak had been following Frank for the past months. They suspected that Frank could lead them to information essential for their quest. Frank acted as small-time dealer for wealthy Westerners residing in Bangkok who organized occasional sex parties for a select group where minors had been spotted, and he might have turned a blind eye to it for the sake of keeping his business running. *I have fed my eyes with too many illusions and have remained blind as a consequence.*

Without hesitation, I opened my bag and handed all of Frank's phones to Pak.

"What are these?" Pak enquired.

"They belong to Frank. I took them from his place." He started studying them with the utmost attention.

"Passwords?"

"I don't know. I have tried a couple of them... Shakespeare's birth date maybe?"

"No worries, these are easy to crack. Benedetta, do you know what this is? You are giving us a list of Frank's clients." I startled as I heard the word *crack*. He was adamant that Frank would try to get his phones back at all costs. Frank would be in mortal danger the minute his clients realized that his database had landed in Pak's hands. He made it clear that Omar and I had to leave Bangkok without delay. *As long as I don't get back to the madhouse,* I thought. I was exhausted.

I needed to focus. Pak repeated that we needed to leave town in a matter of hours. I vaguely explained that I had left my money and belongings at Frank's. My naivety was borderline. How was I supposed to get out of the country? I was the most stupid person on the planet. *The oppressed will always believe the worst about themselves.* Not me, not any more. If I was strong enough.

"Do you have your passport with you?"

I nodded. Pak reassured me that my passport was all I needed. He would find a way for Omar and I to leave Thailand safely. My stone, the one that Bulagat had given me, would however not be of any use in that operation. He advised me to rest until then and not to leave the Khlong Toei house. An old monk was living in the shelter, looking after a few children. I stayed there for two days.

The old monk and I did not speak a common language. I knew a few words of Tibetan, but that did not really count. There was this Mahayana–Theravada gap in Buddhism that Omar explained to me a couple of times but which I still struggled to grasp. I tried to participate as much as I could in the daily tasks, mainly cooking and cleaning. Doing nothing was also enjoyable; it offered me a distraction from my uncontrollable train of thoughts. I was obsessed with Frank and my memories. I was obsessed with smoking crack too. I went cold turkey, whatever that expression meant in English. I had always associated it with a dead turkey. I felt cold and dead.

During my last night at the shelter, I sat alone by the kitchen window admiring the sky, which was magnificent, and listening to the incessant street life. I reflected on the idea that there had always been a way out. Only my thoughts had been my prison. That and the traumas, the fear, the abuse, the loneliness. But most of all, my thoughts. This was so simple yet so complicated. I grabbed a pair of scissors from the table. Without hesitation I gave myself a new rite of passage. My hair, like my old self, had to fall to grow new and healthy again.

Pak found me in the kitchen at dawn. He smiled approvingly and provided me with a sharp razor to finish the ceremony. He blessed me and then swept the floor. Avoiding any sentimentality, he sent me to the airport in a car driven by a novice and escorted by two nuns. Omar and I were booked to fly to Tokyo and Lima on that day. We kept going toward the east. I was delighted to be reunited with my friend. Something of the darkness of the previous days started making sense and therefore dissipated.

Pak was convinced that Frank and his thugs would be at the airport on the lookout for us. We later knew that the information contained in the phone proved to be too important. My shaved head had been of inspiration to Pak to implement an escape plan. I crossed Suvarnabhumi Airport dressed as a confident nun in a white robe. Passengers and staff greeted me respectfully and gave me priority access. As I approached the check-in counter, I noticed that Omar was following me at a short distance. The clerks at the counter checked my ticket and passport. I offered them a bright smile, which they mirrored, wishing me an excellent flight. I gave a triumphal glance to Omar. I was through. On my way to being crowned. A very different scenario from the one used to enter Russia.

I waited for Omar to check in. We locked eyes. The energy suddenly shifted. There was some agitation around us, too much for it to be normal. I saw Frank and his men scanning the passengers on their way to the boarding area. I took Omar's hand in mine.

"Do you have Bulagat's stone?" I asked him. He looked at me quizzically and shrugged. "The stone he gave us…" I repeated.

"Oh yes. The stone… No, my dear, I threw it to the river together with all my stuff." He was quite nervous, but it was good to hear his voice again. I had missed him.

"That is not a problem. Can you imagine the stone in your palm?" I was carrying mine in my hand. He pondered for a second or two.

"Yes, I can, my dear. I am holding the stone in my hand."

"Good." I nodded. "And this is the moment when we become invisible and cross this portal."

Frank caught sight of us. I heard him call my name. Suddenly, a group of young monks and children of the shelter ran in our direction. They were exulting and wanted to say goodbye. Their happiness was contagious. I wanted to say goodbye too. Goodbye to Tony, to Frank, to my mother, to my dead sister, to Brussels. Even to the naked vampire. The time had come to free them all. They were characters in the puppet theater that my life had been up to that day. They had all guided me to revelations of the utmost importance. Loneliness and a terrible lack of love. And many other things. And Tony and

Frank and the cascade of disastrous events. I had understood the deepest layers of the pattern. I took the stone that Bulagat had given me to my chest and started singing, with utmost gratitude, a song of forgiveness and farewell.

I sank deep into the sacredness of that moment of closure. I must have lost track of time, because the next thing that I remember is Omar holding my arm, guiding me through the airplane to our seats. I saw the little boy that he had once been. This touched me immensely. We were sitting together in the economy-class cabin flying toward the east. I slept soundly. During our stopover in Los Angeles I noticed that Omar had a new tattoo on his chest. A kind of saint. It was still reddish but healing nicely. Omar told me that it was a *Rishi*, a hermit. I could not tell whether he was in seventh heaven or petrified. In a funny synchronicity, he had a monk's tattoo and I had a nun's dress. I laughed. There had to be a message there. I would bring oranges and Xanax to my Argentine monk. Was he aware that Pak was in the process of renouncing? Personally, I had no intention of becoming a nun. Omar's eyes were tired, as if he had fought the most daunting dragons. Had he excavated the peaceful warrior within him? He was unusually silent. He could not hide his fatigue, though he was smiling warmly.

I slept for almost the entire flight to Lima. Yes, I would still compare myself to other girls who were prettier, cleverer, and more interesting than I would ever be. Yes, I might be depressed again. This was impossible to know. That and the shadows and the destructive behavior. But for the moment I was fine and feeling alive. For the first time ever, I started to have faith in the world and the people who surrounded me. I was not an accident. My life was not an accident. I started to have faith in myself too, just a little. I was feeling immensely grateful for that and for the love that I had received.

"My dear, are you awake?" Omar asked in a hushed voice that overlapped with the voice of the captain informing us that we had begun our descent to Lima Airport. Everything was new. I was feeling like a newborn, fragile yet resilient. Omar was watching me curiously. He smiled. We had not exchanged more than a couple of words since we left Bangkok. I did not know what to answer. Awake. Really?

"Awake and more alive than ever," I replied. One day at a time can lead to a glimpse of eternity.

Disclaimer

This book is by no means a guide to shamanism.
Shamanic healing experiences and journeying should
only be undertaken under the explicit guidance of an experienced
shaman or shamanic practitioner. The authors cannot be held
responsible for any injury, accident, illness, or other misfortune
that may occur for anyone involved in shamanic experiences.